Fight for Me

Fight for Me

ERIN CHESNUT

The Cypress Valley Sweethearts Series

Fight for Me

Copyright © 2024 by Erin Chesnut

ISBN 979-8-9902820-0-1

Editing: Mild Mannered Editors
Cover and interior design by Alt 19 Creative

*When my oldest child was born, I promised her
I would publish something before she graduated
from high school and prove to her (and myself) that
all dreams are possible. So, this one's for you, baby
girl—may you find out what your heart is made of.*

1

T HEY SAY SOME people never quite grow into their ears, and Dr. Marchenko—bless his heart—was a prime example.

Jake hid a smile behind his Canon and focused through the viewfinder, snapping the old professor's headshot with as much professionalism as he could muster. It was never a good idea to laugh at your clients, even if they did look like they might fly away at any moment.

"There you are, sir," he said. "Quick and painless."

Dr. Marchenko rose shakily from the metal stool, taking an extra step to stabilize his stooped frame.

"Thank you, young man," he wheezed. "I don't know why they need a new photo every year. It's not like I can get any better looking."

Jake chuckled, setting his heavy camera on a side table as the old man shuffled away. The room emptied for the first time all morning, and he heaved a sigh of relief before ducking into his cubicle. Julie Carter's voice rang out from the hallway seconds later.

"Andy, are you here?"

"That depends on what you need," Jake's boss answered, emerging from his office.

Jake kicked his well-worn boots up onto his desk as their voices buzzed in his mind like white noise. He caught the words "intern" and "first day" in the hum of conversation, followed by the name "Lexie Preston." He froze, his blood pressure automatically rising. Surely they hadn't said—

"It's nice to meet you, Lexie. Just have a seat, and we'll get your staff photo," Andy replied.

"Thank you, sir. I'm excited to be here," said a young woman, and Jake's heart hammered in his chest at the familiar sound. He pressed his feet against the edge of his desk and stretched back in his chair, trying to peek around the partition. He could see Andy's back and shoulders. Then, leaning a little farther, the side of Julie's head came into view, her dark hair twisted into a sleek bun. But Jake still couldn't see who was on the stool—the new intern, the girl who *couldn't* be . . .

Distracted by his own curiosity, Jake forgot to account for the laws of physics—namely, the fact that objects fall downward—and he crashed to the ground in a thunderous avalanche of limbs and equipment as his chair whipped out from under him. Several photography books and his computer keyboard joined him on the floor.

"As I was saying, I have an intern as well," Andy said as Jake rolled into view. "This is Jake Tanner. It's his second year working with me, and he takes better pictures when he's right side up."

Jake swallowed a groan and managed a weak wave in the general direction of his new audience—his internal body temperature hovering somewhere around eight million degrees. As he opened his eyes a fraction, he registered a head of blonde hair and a dark blue dress on Andy's left. A pair of green eyes swam into focus a second later, and Jake noticed they were full of laughter, undoubtedly at his expense. He did his best not to spontaneously combust as he slowly disentangled himself from the chair.

"Well, that was quite an entrance," Andy said dryly after the women had gone. "Can I get you anything? Tylenol? A defibrillator, maybe? I think we've got one in the hall."

"I hate you," Jake muttered, drawing a laugh from his supervisor who, at only six years Jake's senior, often felt more like a friend than a coworker.

"You know her?" Andy asked.

"Not exactly," Jake admitted, righting his chair.

"Oh, well, don't worry about it, Tanner. You've got a whole year to prove you've got a brain."

A year. A *whole year* with Lexie Preston.

Maybe the universe had taken pity on him after all.

⁂

"HONEY, I'M HOME!" Lexie called as she pushed open the door of her new off-campus apartment. She stopped in the doorway, caught off guard by the enormous bouquet of red roses that took up a large portion of the small dining room table.

"What's this?" she asked, raising her voice to be heard above the staccato of exploding popcorn kernels coming from the kitchen. She dropped her laptop bag onto a chair and plucked a small card with her name on it from among the blooms.

For my best girl. I can't wait to see you! —C

"Some delivery guy dropped those off a little while ago."

Lexie looked up to find her roommate, Olivia, leaning across the small bar that separated the kitchen from the dining area and open living room. She set the card down on the tabletop and bent to inhale the thick scent of the flowers, which were all perfectly shaped and identically vibrant. The whole arrangement must have cost a fortune. But then again, Colton Derricks had never been one for small gestures.

"How's all that going?" Olivia asked, her voice tentative.

Lexie glanced up to find her best friend watching her carefully, searching for cracks.

"It's good," Lexie said. "He's at a conference today, or he would have come by."

Olivia continued to stare in a way that made Lexie feel like she was being scanned by airport security. "So, there's been no more . . ." Olivia trailed off, her question unasked. But unfortunately, Lexie knew exactly what she meant.

"Of course not. I told you that was an accident, and he felt really bad about it," Lexie said, waving her hand dismissively. It wasn't totally a lie; Colt *had* felt bad about the bruises. But mostly because they'd shown past the edges of her sleeves. She drifted over to the couch and plopped down onto it just as Olivia emerged from the kitchen with a bowl of fresh popcorn.

"I honestly think I'm going to love this new job," Lexie went on, trying to change the subject. "My boss, Julie, is amazing, and I already have assignments lined up for next week. It's a lot of writing, but there's also some advertising and social media marketing, too."

Olivia cocked her head and folded herself onto the cushion, tossing a handful of popped kernels into her mouth.

"Isn't there a guy who works up there? Josh or Jase or something like that? He was taking pictures at the mixer for social work students—very official looking. And very cute."

A boyish face filled Lexie's mind, and her thoughts stuttered.

"Yeah, Jake. He's the photography intern."

Olivia tossed back another handful of popcorn, one eyebrow raised as she waited for more information. "Do you know him already?"

"Not really," Lexie answered. "I'm pretty sure we had a class together last semester, but we've never actually talked."

"What has Colt said about it?" Olivia asked, a neutral expression on her face. While her voice was casual, the darting glance she gave her friend was not.

Lexie took a long, slow breath and tried not to dwell on the way Jake's dark eyes had locked onto hers earlier or the way her stomach fluttered when they did.

"What he doesn't know won't hurt him," she said, reaching for the television remote. She found her gaze drawn back to the towering floral display on the kitchen table and tried to quiet the foreboding feeling growing in her mind.

Sometimes it was better not to poke the bear.

JAKE GOT HOME, still trying to organize his thoughts, and found World War III in progress.

"Knock it off, man! I need to get to my room!" Conner bellowed, his bare back covered in orange paint splotches. The bath towel around his waist was soaked and leaving puddles on the fading linoleum, suggesting something had gone horribly wrong.

Jake ducked back into the garage as a small orange ball exploded against the kitchen cabinets to his left, temporarily scattering all thoughts of Lexie Preston. It was a good thing Conner's father planned to tear the old house down and build over it once they moved out. Otherwise, they'd end up owing a landlord a small fortune in property damages after graduation.

"You can get in. You just have to break through the duct tape first," Noah shouted from his hidey-hole between the couch and the wall. The shiny barrel of a paintball gun was just visible around the edge of the furniture, which was as tattered and stained as the rest of their ramshackle bachelor pad.

Jake peeked around the doorframe as a drawer clattered open. Conner yanked a large carving knife from the assortment of mismatched silverware and headed for the hall, presumably to cut his way through whatever barrier Noah had erected between him and his closet.

Another shot found its mark, and Conner howled in rage.

"I'm going to kill you as soon as I put on pants!" he roared, the sound accompanied by the frantic ripping of what could only be the aforementioned duct tape.

Jake stepped tentatively into the kitchen, leaving the door open in case he needed a quick escape, and surveyed the scene. Orange paint dotted the walls, and an overturned bucket sat in a large puddle of something immediately outside the bathroom door.

"You know you're going to have to clean this up, right?" Jake said, addressing the head of black hair that popped up from behind the couch.

"Totally worth it," Noah replied, clearly pleased with himself.

A mighty crash indicated Conner had gained access to his room, and Noah collapsed to the floor, his head and shoulders appearing from behind his barricade.

"He lost the towel," he wheezed, clutching his sides as laughter overpowered him.

"Dude, you better not be here when he gets dressed. You're a dead man," Jake said, genuinely concerned for his friend's personal safety. He'd seen Conner on a warpath, and it wasn't pretty. But Noah made no move to flee.

"Oh, don't worry, unless he wants to tie a jacket around the family jewels, it'll be a while. I nailed all his drawers shut."

Jake's eyebrows disappeared into his dark hair. "Wow, leave something for the rest of the semester, would you?" he said, moving quickly toward the staircase along the far wall. A horrible splintering noise rang out just as Jake reached the relative safety of his upstairs bedroom, suggesting Conner had given up on conventional means of freeing his clothing.

"Go big or go home, right?" Noah called, but Jake only shook his head.

Dropping his bags on the bed and heading for the bathroom, Jake heard the door to the garage slam shut and the wheezy whine of an ancient car engine trying to turn over.

Noah had apparently decided to run for his life.

❧

CYPRESS VALLEY STATE University wasn't located in a valley, nor did it boast any cypress trees on the grounds, but it was the crown jewel of West Tennessee, regardless. The academic buildings, with their Gothic arches and winding trails of ivy, circled an open quad dotted by centuries-old trees that predated both the college and the little town for which it was named.

In the middle of it all was a soaring bell tower, and the circular area at its base was Lexie's favorite thinking spot. Normally, she would lean her head back against one of the wrought iron benches and watch the clouds wander overhead, but on the first Friday of her senior year, she found herself standing on one of those benches like it was a life raft, a sea of chaos swirling past her feet.

There were students everywhere—lying on the grass, hanging from the lower limbs of trees, waiting in snaking lines that led to striped tents serving dressed-up cafeteria food on paper plates. The student council had even dug up a balloon artist from who-knows-where, and multicolored tubes now formed dogs, monkeys, flowers and several kinds of hats that bobbed here and there among the crowd.

Go help Jake. The assignment hadn't seemed that complicated, until Lexie had realized she had very little chance of ever *finding* Jake in this mess, much less helping him with anything. She glanced down at her phone, wishing for the hundredth time that she'd thought to find his number on the staff roster before she'd left the office.

She swept her gaze over the shifting crowd until she found a group of students posing with their arms around each other like a cancan line. Sure enough, a young man with a large camera crouched a few yards in front of them. The back of his crimson T-shirt read "University Photographer."

Jumping from the bench as if it were on fire, Lexie shouldered her way through the crowd, hoping to get to Jake before he moved again. She dipped through openings wherever she could find them, dodging and weaving until she burst into the pocket of space where the group had been. But when she got there, they were already dispersing, and Jake had disappeared. She raked her hand through her hair in frustration, lifting onto her tiptoes in an effort to see over the crowd.

Finally, she caught another glimpse of Jake's shirt as he moved away from her. She darted through a line of people waiting for popcorn, apologizing over her shoulder as she went, and finally latched onto his forearm with both hands.

"There you are!" she blurted, relief flooding her chest.

Jake blinked a few times in confusion, a crease forming between his eyebrows as he looked down at her.

"Sorry, that was really random," Lexie backtracked, still trying to catch her breath. She gave a small wave with one hand while the other stayed clamped around his wrist. "Hi, I'm Lexie. We work together. We met Monday, sort of."

Jake continued to stare without comment, and Lexie felt unease begin to buzz inside her chest. Was it possible she had the wrong person?

"I'm sorry . . . you're Jake Tanner, right? Julie sent me to help you," she said, scrambling to understand why his blank expression hadn't changed in the full minute she'd been standing beside him.

Another few seconds passed before his eyes finally moved, jumping from her face to the place where her hand gripped his arm as if he might float away. Lexie instantly released him and stepped back to give him space to breathe. Something in his expression changed, and he took a sudden breath before pulling a narrow notepad and a ballpoint pen from the back pocket of his jeans.

"Names and hometowns from left to right," he said. "If you can get their majors, too, that would be great."

Lexie took the pad he thrust into her hands, surprised by his abrupt tone.

"Okay, I can do that," she said, but when she looked up, he was already walking away. She sidestepped a girl with a fluffy white dog and hurried to keep up. Jake moved like a hunter on safari, as if looking for specific details within the crowd. Every few minutes, he would stop and ask a group of students to pose for a photo, and Lexie would rush to collect their details like she'd been told—doing her best to create an awkward sort of team.

"Thanks," he said at last, turning to her as the final group wandered away. "It's a lot faster when I don't have to do that myself."

"Of course, yeah, no problem," Lexie stammered, still trying to figure out what she'd done wrong. "Listen," she said as he turned to leave, "I really like this job, and I'd like us to work well together—to be friends, or whatever." She offered a small smile, but instead of accepting her olive branch, such as it was, Jake simply gave a quick nod.

"See you Monday," he said, his voice strangely tight, before melting back into the crowd.

Lexie stood with her mouth slightly open, watching him go.

"Well, alright then," she said to nobody in particular. "Nice meeting you, too."

❧

"SO, LET ME get this straight," Conner said, pacing around the small kitchen table where Jake sat with his head in his hands. "You're working with this girl—*the* girl—that you've been hung up on since freshman year. Then today, she stumbles out of a crowd, grabs your arm and says, 'There you are!' and you said . . . nothing."

Jake groaned, rubbing the heels of his hands over his closed eyes. Every second of the horrible encounter was tattooed on his brain in neon ink.

"I froze," he muttered darkly. He wished he could wipe out the whole day and start over. Introduce himself, shake her hand, smile . . . say anything except—

"Names and hometowns from left to right," Conner said, his voice full of disbelief. "Three years pining for this girl, and all you come up with in your big moment is 'names and hometowns from left to right'?"

Jake dropped his head to the tabletop, letting his forehead smack against it for good measure.

"Did you at least talk to her after that? Maybe ask how her first week went?"

Jake groaned again, squeezing his eyes shut tighter. Every gear in his brain had ground to a halt when Lexie had magically appeared beside him, her warm hands on his arm. He'd forgotten how to put words together in the English language, how to move the muscles in his limbs, even why he was standing outside to begin with. And then, afterward, he hadn't known how to fix what he'd already broken.

He turned his head toward Conner, who was eyeing him with his eyebrows raised.

"I'm going to take that as a no," Conner said, gripping the back of the nearest kitchen chair and leaning over it. "Dude, what is wrong with you?"

"Give the guy a break," Noah cut in from his place on the couch. "It's a lot to suddenly be face-to-face with your daydream.

What would you do if Natalie Portman walked out of Pennington Hall and grabbed your arm?"

"I'd ask her to homecoming," Conner shot back, a cocky smirk on his face.

"Maybe. If she was still there when you finished wetting yourself," Noah said.

Jake couldn't help but laugh dryly, feeling the sound vibrate across the cheap Formica tabletop. "Guys," he groaned. "What am I going to do? It's not usually this hard."

"You're making too much of this," Conner said. He cleared his throat and resumed his pacing. "She's a girl, not an alien life-form. You've got to take her off her pedestal and treat her like anybody else."

Jake lifted his head cautiously.

"Look, girls seem to like this farm boy thing you've got going on," Conner continued, gesturing toward Jake. "I know you get plenty of attention, though why you don't take advantage of that, I'll never understand. I mean, chicks at this school will—"

"Conner, focus," Noah interrupted.

"Okay, but you know what I mean. She's not the only fish in the sea. You're putting too much importance on this one girl because of some bizarre feeling you had *three years ago*."

"As much as I hate to say it, the man has a point," Noah said, joining them in the kitchen.

Jake sat up and leaned his chair back on two legs before remembering what had happened the last time he did that. He came back to the floor with a thunk.

"We're talking about Lexie Preston," Conner went on. "The unicorn who appears in our lives every few semesters and twists you up in knots until you can't see straight, but who you refuse to have an actual conversation with in case she won't agree to have your babies on the spot."

Jake scoffed. "I don't think—"

"No, you *do* think," Noah said, cutting him off. "And that's the problem. You were struck by lightning at our freshman mixer, and ever since then, you've been convinced this girl is your future wife. Of course you can't have a simple conversation, because in your mind, you already have grandchildren."

There was a long silence, during which Jake tried to find the holes in Noah's argument. Unfortunately, there weren't many.

"I wasn't struck by lightning," he grumbled, crossing his arms over his chest. It was true; nothing spectacular had happened the first time he'd seen Lexie. It hadn't been a Hollywood moment—no clap of thunder, no booming voice of God, no angel choir bursting from the heavens—but Jake had had the sudden, vague sensation that, for whatever reason, he would remember that exact moment in precise detail for the rest of his life. She hadn't even seen him, perched as she was on a teetering stool on the far side of the gymnasium. She'd been laughing, part of a crowd of new students all getting to know each other before the first day of classes. He didn't even remember why he'd looked up from the precarious tower of cheese fries he and Conner had been devouring at the time. And yet . . . he had.

And the rest, as they say, was history.

If history could be summed up as several years' worth of false hope on his part. Conner was right; there was no logical reason why Lexie Preston should be special. But Jake still couldn't shake the feeling that she *was*.

The corners of Noah's mouth quivered as he worked to keep a blank look on his face. "That's all you got out of that?" he asked, the humor evident in his voice.

"Shut up," Jake shot back, instantly feeling like he was back in the sixth grade.

"Look, has it ever occurred to you to just be friends?" Noah asked. "Just get to know her—the *real* her and not your made-up fantasy version. Maybe she is all you've got her cracked up to be, and maybe she isn't, but you're never going to find out if you keep acting like an idiot every time she walks in the room."

Jake scowled, and his mouth popped open to respond, but nothing came out. Grudgingly, he considered whether his friends might be right. It was much harder to talk to someone when you felt like your entire future was on the line.

"Just be friends," he repeated, as if testing the idea in his mind. He thought about the deep green of Lexie's eyes as they'd caught his, the electric current that had sparked up his arm when she'd touched him. "I can do that."

He took a bracing breath and glanced out the front window, watching cars of every color whizz past on the highway. Maybe it would be as easy as it sounded.

⪼⪻

"WE'RE STILL ON for tonight, right, babe? I'll be there in twenty," Colt said, his voice booming from where Lexie's phone sat at the edge of the bathroom counter. She applied another coat of mascara and examined her reflection critically.

"Yes, we are, but would it be so terrible to stay in? It's been a long week," she said, glancing longingly at the sweatpants that lay discarded on the tile floor.

"Exactly! That's why we need to get you out and shake the rust loose! You know how uptight you get when you're stressed."

Lexie's hand stilled as she reached for a tube of the matte pink lipstick Colt liked.

"I don't get uptight," she protested, glaring at her phone as if he could see her.

"You do, and you know it. So, let's pull the stick out and have some fun! Gotta take care of my girl, you know," he said, and she could hear the grin in his voice.

Lexie frowned, her brows coming together in a deep crease.

As if reading her mind, Colt broke the silence. "Aw, come on, babe. You know I'm just teasing. I love you, stick and all."

Somehow that didn't make Lexie feel any better, but there was no arguing with Colt. When he wanted something, he eventually got it. Olivia liked to say he could charm the pants off a nun—and Lexie was sure it wasn't a compliment.

She sighed, not bothering to hide her exasperation. Colt probably wouldn't notice anyway.

"I'll be ready when you get here," she said, knowing how much he hated to wait. "We're going to Barclay's, right?"

"Actually, I was thinking about the Taproom."

"The Taproom?!" Lexie blurted, her gaze jumping to her reflection. Her turquoise A-line dress was well-suited for an upscale restaurant but *not* for a college dive bar with a live band. "You told me we were going to dinner! I'm dressed for a sit-down meal."

"Well, change then. The band tonight is a solid nine, and I've invited some of the guys. Maybe wear that purple number from my birthday party?"

Lexie bit back a groan and rubbed her fingertips against her temples. She was not in the mood for loud music and "some of the guys." That inevitably meant pints of beer and shots of whiskey and exaggerated stories about the "good old days" when Colt and his fraternity brothers had still been tearing up the county.

Not that they didn't still tear up the county, but at least now they had to pretend to be upstanding businessmen during daylight hours.

"Look, babe, don't make it a big deal," Colt admonished, his voice changing slightly. It was a reminder that he'd made a decision and her only job was to comply.

Like always.

"Alright," Lexie said, caving.

Like always.

"Great. I'm ten minutes out, and I want to find a blonde bombshell when I get there!" he said cheerfully, and then he hung up.

Lexie's phone changed back to her lock screen and its photo of the two of them in the ornate lobby of the Peabody Hotel. That had been early in their relationship, back when she still thought she had a say in anything. Those were truly the "good old days." She sighed again and headed down the hallway toward her bedroom, unzipping the back of her dress as she went. She was going to have to hurry if she only had ten minutes.

She found the purple cocktail dress near the back of her closet, hidden with the other outfits she tried to avoid. Not that it wasn't beautiful—the shimmering violet fabric caught the light in a thousand ways as she pulled it off the hanger—but it certainly wasn't her style. It had been a birthday present from Colt. He'd hung it over a dressing room door, instructed her to "show it off," and then swiped his credit card at the register—all while ignoring her feeble protests.

Lexie stepped into the slick material, working hard not to tangle the thin straps that crisscrossed the back like shoelaces. It was harder than it sounded, and she had only just smoothed the cold fabric over her hips when she heard a knock at the door.

"I'm coming!" she shouted, adjusting the straps along her collarbone one more time and twisting to see her back in the mirror. The dress dipped low along her spine, and she was suddenly thankful she'd been using tanning lotion in the shower. She shifted, trying to pull the fabric higher, but it jumped stubbornly back into place.

The knock came again, more insistent this time. Lexie quickly grabbed a pair of silver stilettos, but then paused. If Colt wanted to hear a band, then he probably wanted to dance, too. She dropped the strappy sandals and reached instead for a pair with lower heels. Hurrying down the hall, she opened the door to find Colt waiting in pressed black slacks and a light-blue button-down shirt he'd rolled to the elbows. His collar was open, his tie from work probably tossed in the backseat of his BMW next to the sport coat he usually wore when seeing clients.

He let out a long, low whistle when he saw her.

"Give me a spin!" he instructed, reaching for her hand. She did as she was told, and the confidence he exuded filled her like a balloon. But it was short-lived. His sky-blue eyes darkened to cobalt, and a frown tugged at the corners of his mouth.

"You're not going to wear those, are you?" he asked, his eyes locking on the kitten heels that dangled from her hand.

She glanced down at them, the helium already leaking from her chest.

"They'll be better for dancing. You do want to dance with me, don't you?" she asked, keeping her eyes as wide as she could. Sometimes the doe-eyed approach could buy her a pass.

"Well, yeah, but not in those," he said. "Go find something else, the higher the better. I'm the only one of the guys who's still dating a college girl, and I hate feeling like I'm robbing the cradle."

He shooed her away like a persistent puppy, and Lexie held in another sigh as she padded back to her room to retrieve the shoes she knew he would like. She could already feel the nails that would stab the balls of her feet by the end of the night.

"Now *that's* what I'm talking about!" Colt said, obviously pleased when she returned to the living room four inches taller. "Now, let's get a move on, or it'll be standing room only," he said as she grabbed her clutch from the table. She didn't bother to mention that she would have been ready sooner if he hadn't changed their plans.

The Taproom was indeed bursting at the seams by the time they arrived. The man at the door nearly stopped them, but a slick flash of Colt's black American Express card had them inside in an instant. Lexie was immediately swallowed up by the pulsing beat of "Welcome to the Jungle" as the band on stage did their best Guns N' Roses impression.

Colt's fingers were cool along her lower back as he kept her close, working their way through the crowd until he spotted his friends holding down a table near the stage.

"Jase! Harding! How's it been?" he yelled over the music, slapping palms with the boys and yanking them forward for the international frat-boy chest bump. It was so stereotypical that Lexie had to fight not to roll her eyes. Instead, she fixed Jason Arnolds with her best "hands off" stare as he made a show of looking her over.

"Well, if it isn't Smith and Wesson, my best friends," he drawled, his eyes drifting up from somewhere south of her face. "Lexie, I do believe you get hotter every time I see you."

"Thanks," she said, her sarcasm drowned out by the sound system. Colt lifted his first shot of the night in her direction, a silent salute to tell her he was pleased.

At least that made one of them.

Nearly an hour later, the high-top table was littered with the boys' shot glasses, and Colt had fully transitioned back from daytime professional to college playboy—a metamorphosis that would fascinate social scientists everywhere. Lexie, still nursing her first strawberry daiquiri, had already seen him check out four of the waitresses and a group of girls dancing nearby.

A young woman in a white button-up shirt and a short black apron came to clear their empty glasses, and Lexie watched as Colt caught her by the elbow and leaned in to say something in her ear. His hand lingered on the woman's arm, even after she shook her head and started to walk away, and Lexie absently wondered why she wasn't more upset that her boyfriend of more than two years was blatantly flirting with other women right in front of her.

When had she learned to simply sit and take it?

"You could at least look like you're having fun," Colt said, sliding up to where she sat perched on a high stool. His hand moved automatically up her leg and came to rest along the curve of her hip.

"What did you say to her?" Lexie asked, shooting him a pointed glare.

"Who?"

"The waitress, just now," she said, and she jerked her chin toward the woman, who was still clearing a nearby table.

Colt rolled his eyes and threw back another shot, swallowing with a grimace.

"Nothing that matters. Come dance with me. Loosen up." He reached for her wrist, and she had no choice but to put her glass down and stand before he tugged her straight out of her chair.

"Do you think I don't notice when you flirt with other women? Or do you do it on purpose just to get to me?" Lexie asked as Colt led her onto the dance floor.

"Oh, don't be like that," he said, his voice impatient as he slipped his arms around her waist and toyed with the lacing across her back. "You know you're my number one. The rest is just a guy thing."

"Just a guy thing?" she repeated with disgust, stepping away, but he yanked her back into place, his hands drifting lower along her spine.

"What are you doing?" she hissed, reaching back to grab his wrists. She hated when he pawed at her in public.

"Looking for the stick," he said as she squirmed.

A quick glance told her Jason and Harding were watching, and she saw their smirks grow as though they were enjoying her discomfort. Everything Colt did was a show, and while she'd been flattered by the spotlight in the beginning, lately it felt less like she'd been chosen and more like she'd been captured.

"Colt, stop it," she said, her voice firm. She pressed both palms against his chest and pushed, but Colt was built like a linebacker and refused to be moved.

He chuckled, the low rumble rolling through her, and moved his hands back up in a rare moment of compliance.

"Kitten has claws tonight," he said, tugging her closer until there was no room to spare between his torso and hers. She could feel the slinky dress catching against his belt buckle as he moved with the beat of the bass guitar. "Put them away and play nice," he growled. "If you were willing to actually have some fun, maybe I wouldn't need to window shop."

She stilled against his chest, mentally wilting, and the voices in her mind began to chant a familiar chorus.

This is your fault.

What's wrong with you?

Why can't you just relax?

Maybe it really was that simple. He worked hard, after all. He deserved to have some fun. Couldn't she at least give him that?

Letting out a long breath, she softened.

"That's better," he murmured, and Lexie closed her eyes.

This she could do right, at least.

2

JAKE'S STOMACH RUMBLED as he reached the front of the line at the Redtail Cafe, one of several outdoor eateries dotting the edge of campus. The late August sun shone down through the trees overhead, painting a mass of hungry students with its dappled light. The cafe wasn't usually this crowded, but Taco Tuesday was always the exception.

"Three beef tacos, please, and a Dr. Pepper," he said, leaning over the counter to be sure the cashier could hear him above the chatter of three dozen conversations.

"Coming right up," the young woman said. She swiped his student card and then handed him a tray laden with food.

Jake took it and turned to scan the patio, hoping to see a familiar face or an empty chair. He found both, right underneath the giant iron clock that hung against the sun-warmed brick.

Lexie Preston.

Hers was a face he couldn't forget. It wasn't just the classic way her features came together beneath tousled blonde beach waves that made him want to reach for his camera. It was the way she always seemed to be tucked inside herself, like the best parts of her were still hidden beneath the surface. Jake wanted to be the one to bring them out, to turn each piece over carefully and examine it until he could sketch the ridges in his sleep.

Just be friends, he repeated to himself as he made his way across the crowded patio toward where she sat alone at a small cafe table. She had a textbook open in front of her, a yellow highlighter poised in one hand, and he second-guessed his plan of attack. What if she resented the interruption?

But another glance around the space confirmed that hers was the only table not already full, so he pressed on. At least he could use that as an excuse if necessary.

"Hi," he said, coming to a stop opposite her.

She finished the sentence she was reading and glanced up, a look of surprise crossing her face.

"Can I sit here?" he asked with an uncertain smile.

Lexie's eyes scanned him slowly, as if considering, before she nodded. The chair in front of him slid out as she pushed it with her foot, and he sank into it, reaching up to rub the back of his neck with his free hand. He took a deep breath and went for broke.

"I want to apologize for Friday. I was rude to you, and I'm sorry. It was the noise and the crowd and . . . just all of it, really. I promise I'm not usually a jerk." He glanced at her awkwardly, and his chest tightened as he waited for her to say something, anything. Finally, she gave a wry smile.

"I believe in second chances," she said. "Although, technically this will be your third."

Jake relaxed, but only slightly.

"The first time wasn't entirely my fault," he countered, picking up a taco and shifting it in his hands.

"So, you just want to blame gravity, then?"

Jake winced. "Something like that," he muttered.

Lexie shrugged and then leaned down to slide her high-lighter into her bag. "I'd like to say it happens to the best of us. Although, most people are smart enough not to tip a chair that's already on wheels."

Jake chuckled, unable to help himself. At least she had a sense of humor. "I deserve that," he agreed.

An odd look crossed Lexie's face, part surprise and part amusement.

"It's not often I find a guy who can laugh at himself," she said. "Maybe you won't be such a pain to work with after all."

Jake shrugged. "Nowhere to go but up."

❧

"HOW DOES A person get to be twenty-one having never seen *Ghostbusters*?" Jake asked nearly an hour later, his voice filled with disbelief. His legs were stretched out under the small table, though Lexie noticed he had angled them carefully to avoid touching her.

"Twenty-two," she corrected, "and I don't know. I just haven't."

"Okay, we have to fix this. Friends don't let friends live this way," he insisted, shaking his head.

Lexie studied him in the quiet beat that followed. Olivia wasn't wrong; Jake Tanner *was* cute. He gave off a definite cowboy vibe, with broad shoulders under a white T-shirt and dusty boots that peeked out from beneath faded Levi's. His mop of dark hair matched a beautiful pair of brown eyes, which made Lexie think of melted chocolate on a summer day. She was struck by the notion that a girl could easily sink into them and never find her way out.

She blinked, suddenly finding those eyes trained on her, and Jake cleared his throat awkwardly. He'd obviously caught her staring.

"What about *Back to the Future?*" he asked.

"Nope."

"*The Sandlot?*"

"Don't think so."

"*Star Wars? Please* tell me you've at least seen *Star Wars!*"

"Some of it," Lexie admitted with a shrug.

Jake shook his head slowly, as if he simply couldn't believe what he was hearing.

"This is so much worse than I thought," he deadpanned, and Lexie bit back a smile. "We really should start the marathon right now, but I have to get to work. Are you going in today?" he asked as he rose to his feet.

"Yeah, I am, actually," Lexie said, gathering her long-abandoned textbooks. "I'll walk over with you."

"Good, because we have to get to the bottom of this problem. Either your taste in movies is horrific, or you just had an incredibly stunted childhood," Jake said, waiting as Lexie rose to her feet.

She hiked her backpack higher on one shoulder and tried to ignore the sharp pain in her chest as the truth of his words hit home.

When they reached their office building, Lexie held the door while Jake helped one of the ladies from accounting with a stack of file boxes. He carried them up the short stairs into the building, loaded them onto a waiting handcart and then pulled the whole thing down the hall. The older woman was positively blushing by the time he finished, and Lexie couldn't hide a smirk as they climbed the stairs to the third floor.

"What?" he asked, returning her smile with a look of confusion.

"Nothing," she said, and she grinned wider as she shook her head. "I just think Mrs. Atkins might try to take you home if we stick around any longer."

Jake flushed, rubbing his neck in a gesture she could already tell was a nervous habit. Lexie decided in that moment to consider him "awkwardly adorable." It was a dangerous combination.

"I mean, come on," she teased, seeing an opportunity and jumping in with both feet. "I bet you've got the market cornered on little old ladies around here. Do they bring you homemade cookies?"

Jake's blush darkened, and though he kept his eyes straight ahead, Lexie could tell he was fighting back a laugh.

"I'm just being helpful," he protested. "What's wrong with that?"

"Oh, nothing! Nothing at all," Lexie went on, enjoying his reaction. "I'm just saying, if you ever need a date for Winter Formal, I'm sure any of the ladies on the first floor would go with you. Or offer you their granddaughters."

Jake laughed then, and something about the deep rumble warmed Lexie's heart. She couldn't decide what happened to the guy she'd met Friday, but she certainly liked this version better.

⟳⟲

"THANKS FOR COMING in on your day off. I could actually use another pair of hands," Lexie's boss, Julie, said later that week. She moved a stack of papers off the massive calendar that covered one side of her L-shaped desk and peered down at the notes that marched across it like tiny ants.

"Admissions is hosting a pep rally for the elementary school ahead of this weekend's football game. Andy's got the mascot on hand for photo ops, but we need someone to be responsible for him while he's in costume. You know, to make sure he doesn't trip over the kids and things like that," Julie said, looking up. "Do you have time to follow a giant hawk around for a few hours?"

"Anything you need," Lexie replied, glad for an extra chance to be useful. "I've actually never met Ronnie. It could be fun."

The school's mascot, Ronnie the Redtail, was a comical seven-foot-tall hawk who could usually be found tossing T-shirts into the stands at home games while wearing the school's signature colors.

"Fabulous. I'll show you where he is," Julie said, reaching for her bag.

A few minutes later, Lexie was directed down a hall off to one side of the alumni gym, where she found Andy waiting beside a closed door.

"So, you're the babysitter, huh? Oh, you're going to love this," he said.

"What do you mean?" Lexie asked, resisting the urge to peek through the door's small window just above her line of sight.

"Just trust me. It's a special treat," he said. He grinned as he rapped sharply on the door and opened it a crack. "Are you decent?" he called.

A muffled voice must have answered in the affirmative because Andy opened the door the rest of the way and gave Lexie a view she wouldn't soon forget. Pieces of Ronnie were scattered everywhere—extra feet and random feathers, enormous jerseys for both the basketball and baseball teams, two giant hats meant for a massive head, and, of course, the head itself. It looked like someone had blown the poor bird to bits.

"You owe me for this," a familiar voice said from the far corner, and Lexie's mouth fell open as Jake appeared wearing Ronnie's body from the neck down, complete with shoulder pads beneath the custom football jersey. He lifted his gaze from his oversized feet and froze, locking eyes with Lexie across the room.

Her hands flew to her mouth but failed to stop the stream of laughter that poured out.

"Ta-dah!" Andy shouted.

Lexie's giggles grew until she sank to the floor, her arms clutching her midsection. Every time she thought she had herself under control, she'd look at Jake standing there as half a bird and start all over again, tears streaming down her face.

"Why are you here?" Jake said, his face clearly pained. He shuffled forward, looking down at her over the edges of the costume.

"Oh, you haven't heard? I get to make sure you don't squash small children with your giant bird feet," Lexie answered as she rose to stand, her wide grin still running wild.

Jake groaned and looked at Andy, who was obviously enjoying the exchange.

"Put on your beak," Andy said as he lifted Ronnie's gigantic head from the floor and placed it over Jake's tiny one. He tightened the fasteners around the sides. "Let's go over the ground rules again. What is mascot rule number one?"

"No talking while in costume," Jake recited, his voice coming through the mesh that made up Ronnie's mouth.

"Yes, strike one for breaking that already," Andy said, grinning. "And you should be sure to . . . ?"

"Take extra big steps," Jake said, and Lexie could hear the scowl in his voice.

"Good, and also never . . . ?"

"Lean too far to one side, or I will fall down and not be able to get back up," Jake supplied, earning another burst of laughter from Lexie.

"Great," Andy replied. He consulted a list in his hand and then ran through another check of his photography bag. "Just walk around for a few minutes and get used to the weight of it all, then we'll get you through the door."

"This is a one-time thing, I assure you," Jake grumbled to Lexie. "The real Ronnie is sick, and I happen to fit the costume."

"Oh, you don't have to explain yourself to me," she said gleefully. "If you want to moonlight as a giant bird, you go right ahead."

Jake made several slow treks across the room, and Lexie pulled herself together long enough to help him make the turn at the end of each pass. Getting through the door was a bit difficult, requiring Jake to turn sideways and crouch to keep from knocking Ronnie's head off, but they managed it on the second try.

"Alright, kids. I've got to get in there, but you hang around the back doors until you hear your intro, then let him loose," Andy instructed, grinning at Lexie. "Don't let the kids climb on him."

When he was gone, Lexie turned to Ronnie and stretched up on her tiptoes to put her face in front of his giant beak. She could barely see Jake inside the dark costume, the only light coming from the mesh opening.

"Can you see anything?" she asked.

"Only what's right in front of me. No peripheral vision," he said.

"Okay, well, I'll be your eyes, then," Lexie replied. She ran her palm down the thick wing that covered his arm. "Where's your hand?"

"Almost at the end, there's a hole," he said, raising his arm to show her where a brown glove peeked out just under the wing tip. Lexie grabbed his hand and, after a moment, felt his fingers close around hers in a tentative grip. For some reason, it felt like she was holding on to an electric fence.

"Feel good?" she asked. "About going out there?"

"Yeah," Jake said, his voice faint from inside the costume. "Feels great."

There was an awkward silence before someone with a megaphone called for a drumroll.

"Sounds like your cue!" Lexie blurted, grateful for the distraction. She tugged Jake toward the double doors, choosing to believe that the heat creeping up her neck had everything to do with the crowd and nothing to do with him.

❧

"YES, MA'AM, I'VE been doing my laundry," Jake said, pacing in a circle outside the administration building, his phone pressed to his ear while his mother verified that he was actually a responsible, functioning adult. Even though he was barely half an hour from home, sometimes it seemed like Kathleen Tanner thought her only son had gone to live on the moon.

He stopped to lean against the warm brick, only partially listening as he watched several groups of students pass through the quad. He nodded politely to a few before catching sight of a familiar figure approaching through the afternoon sunlight.

"Hey, Mama, I've got to go," he blurted, feeling only slightly guilty for interrupting what he was sure was a riveting story about his Uncle Rob and a goat that got stuck in the fence.

"Oh, well, alright, honey. We'll talk soon," his mother said. She blew a kiss into the phone, like she always did, and Jake returned it quickly before hanging up. He slipped his hands into his pockets just as Lexie made the turn up the sidewalk toward where he stood.

"Hey!" he called, and her eyes darted in his direction, though they didn't warm as he'd hoped they would. Instead, she looked crestfallen, like someone had sneezed on her last cookie.

"What's wrong?" he asked when she reached him. There was a moment when he thought he saw truth flicker in her eyes before she shuttered them, pasting on a practiced smile instead.

"Just having a long day. How about you? Important phone call?"

She nodded toward his pocket, where his hand still gripped his phone, and Jake realized she must have seen him before he saw her. He liked the idea that she'd been watching.

"Oh, no, not really. Just my mom checking in. You know how that is," he quipped, reaching out to open the administration building's heavy outer door for her. Another shadow passed across her face, as if he'd said something wrong. Lexie went inside and crossed the wide entrance hall toward the stairs.

"Did you tell her they made you be Ronnie?" she asked a moment later, starting up as Jake followed behind.

"No, I forgot. It wasn't so bad, actually, once I got used to it. It was sort of fun being a celebrity for a while," he admitted as they climbed to the top floor. *Plus, I got to hold your hand for two hours*, he thought, remembering the way his whole arm had gone fuzzy.

"Maybe next time you'll get to walk with a cheerleader. Wouldn't that be something?" she added, though her voice was flat.

Jake shrugged, not at all interested. "Sounds like a step down, honestly," he admitted, following Lexie out of the stairwell and down the hall.

She stopped near the door to the marketing office and looked up at him with an odd expression, like she was trying to solve a puzzle without the box. He cleared his throat and took an awkward step toward the doors of the photography studio.

"I'll see you later, alright? If you're still around when I get done," he said, backing away.

"Yeah. Later," she echoed, still watching him with a thoughtful crease between her brows.

Jake wasn't sure he wanted to know what she was thinking.

But three hours later, he was still wondering.

What did she see when she looked at him? Was he just a guy who sometimes made her laugh, or did she see something more? If he wasn't her type, could he change her mind?

Editing Andy's pictures from the day before didn't help his train of thought. It was bizarre to see photo after photo of himself holding Lexie's hand, even if nobody else knew it was him. His palm itched with the memory. If only they'd been alone, maybe he could have come up with a reason to tuck those wispy blonde strands behind her ear and breathe in whatever made her hair smell like strawberries.

Jake sighed, rubbing his hand across his forehead. He couldn't be more pathetic if he tried.

"Jake?"

Lexie's soft voice came from beyond the partition between him and the door, as if his thoughts themselves had summoned her. Jake jumped slightly and quickly minimized the photo on his screen.

"Back here," he called. He heard her footsteps come closer until she appeared in his doorway.

"I'm finished for today, but I thought you might need some help before I go," she said, looking around his workspace. She picked up a small acrylic award from a shelf above his desk and turned it over in her hands.

"Association of Photographers Student Competition, Third Place, Southeast Region," she read, her eyebrows rising as she looked at Jake. "That's impressive."

He felt his neck get hot, and he automatically rubbed his hand across the back of it.

"I'm pretty proud of that one," he admitted, and Lexie nodded as she replaced the award on the shelf.

"You should be. You're good at what you do," she said. There was a trace of bitterness in her voice that Jake didn't like.

"Do you think you aren't?" he asked. "I read your stuff; you're a fantastic writer."

Lexie scoffed and was silent, scuffing the toe of her shoe against the warped edge of his plastic floor mat. The same unhappiness he'd seen earlier crept across her face, and Jake stood, intending to say something encouraging. But the words disappeared when her face tipped up and her emerald eyes met his. There was sadness etched along the edges of her mouth, and his fingers tingled with the need to reach out and brush it away.

He wondered what she would do if he touched her, if he leaned down and showed her exactly what he thought of her and everything she did. The image in his mind involved backing her up against the wall, and the urge was so strong he had to shove his hands into his pockets just to keep them to himself.

The sudden motion caught Lexie's attention, and she shook herself, stepping away and creating distance where there had been none.

"What can I help you with?" she asked, changing the subject and breaking the tense silence all at once.

Jake looked past her into the studio, taking a deep breath he hadn't realized he needed. He mentally catalogued the equipment in front of him.

"I've got the volleyball team coming soon, so if you'll pop open those reflectors, I'll set up the diffusers and stands," he said, pointing toward the open studio space. They worked together for a few comfortable minutes, Jake giving instructions as Lexie unzipped cases and handed him what he needed.

"Sit on the stool and let me get the settings right," he directed, taking a test shot of the empty chair. The strobes flashed quickly, momentarily flooding the backdrop with extra light, and Lexie obediently took a seat. Jake stood a few feet in front of her and took several more shots, adjusting the settings on both the camera and the strobes.

After a few minutes, Jake started to study the angles of her face and the shadows along her throat as if she were a still-life subject and not the main character in so many of his daydreams. He looked long and hard through the viewfinder, taking advantage of the silent permission she gave. Her green blouse made her eyes twice as vibrant, and her hair fell in effortless curls around her shoulders, yet her face was still nervous, as if she were expecting to be judged.

"Think about me," he said, the thought becoming words before he could stop it. Lexie cocked her head slightly, confusion flickering in her eyes, and Jake cleared his throat. "In the bird suit," he clarified.

As he'd hoped, her eyes lit up and her face split into a smile that brightened the room.

There she is, he thought, snapping the photo before the glow could fade.

"I will never forget that, not as long as I live," Lexie said, and Jake smiled, every bit of her reaction warming something deep inside him.

"I hope you don't," he said, letting the camera rest low against his chest. Lexie's eyes darted toward a point over his shoulder, and Jake turned to see a young woman in a crimson sports uniform leaning through the doorframe.

"Excuse me," the woman said. "Is this the right place for team pictures?"

"Yes, ma'am," Jake answered, a little too brightly. He glanced at his watch. "You're right on time. If you would, just put your name and details on the form by the door."

Several other team members appeared in the hallway a moment later, and Jake got caught in a jumble of questions and instructions. When he looked up, Lexie had slipped away, and he felt a physical pang of loss in the otherwise crowded room.

LEXIE SCROLLED BACK through her text messages as she crossed the quad. There wasn't any point in torturing herself, yet she couldn't seem to help it. Her father's words stung every time she read them.

LEXIE: Have you seen my article on Dr. Henry Thornton's new dementia trial? It's my first alumni feature!

DAD: Did you help him collect samples or analyze his trial data?

LEXIE: No, of course not.

DAD: Then what good is it? Anyone can write words.

Lexie stuffed her phone back into her pocket as she reached her car. If nothing else, she'd at least thought her father would be impressed that she'd met the man who was revolutionizing neuroscience as they knew it.

"Thanks for the encouragement, Dad," she muttered. "No time like the present to make your only daughter feel useless."

In truth, Dr. Garrett Preston III had never passed up that kind of opportunity.

3

"WHAT ABOUT THE animal shelter? Does anyone work there?" Lexie asked late Tuesday morning, holding the phone to her ear so she could listen to the voice on the other end of the line. For someone tasked with tracking student community service hours, this woman certainly wasn't much help. So far, all she'd been able to tell Lexie was that athletes and students who were members of Greek organizations completed the highest number of hours; however, she didn't have any information on when or where the hours were served.

Lexie thanked her and hung up in frustration.

"What was that all about?" Jake asked, coming into the break-room as Lexie crossed another idea off her list with irritation.

She looked up in time to see him lift a large box marked "photo negatives" onto the top of a long row of black file cabinets, and something in her brain stuttered as the muscles in his arms and back flexed beneath his T-shirt. The same thing had happened the other day when he'd been standing close enough for her to see all the shades of brown that ringed his irises. It was like a mental glitch that only happened when he was close by.

Jake gave her a funny look as he turned around, and Lexie realized he'd asked a question.

"I'm looking for students completing community service hours, but I'm coming up empty. So far, nobody I've talked to is part of a current project." She shuffled the papers in front of her and tossed back the last of a strawberry smoothie she'd grabbed after class.

Jake headed back into the hallway and returned a moment later with another box, lifting it up beside the first. This time, Lexie looked out the window, willing herself not to watch. It was rude to stare, after all.

"I can probably help," Jake said, leaning back against the row of cabinets. His stance did nothing to keep Lexie's attention off the tanned arms that crossed over his chest, and she mentally smacked herself. What was wrong with her all of a sudden?!

"I volunteer with parks and rec during the fall season. So do several other students," he went on, oblivious to her internal monologue.

"You do?" Lexie gasped, bringing her attention back to their conversation. "You're telling me I've been trying to track people down for hours when I could have just gone across the hall?"

Jake chuckled. "Happy to help. What do you need?"

"Well, I'd like to find out exactly what everyone is doing and why and how it impacts the community. Can I interview you?"

"Sure, and I can give you the names of a few other coaches I know," Jake said, pulling out the chair across from her as she reached for her voice recorder and turned it on.

Lexie stopped and looked up. "Other coaches? You're a coach?"

"Yep, kids' soccer," Jake said. He sank down into the chair and rested his forearms on the table. "I played in high school, and community service is part of my scholarship, so I figured it was a good match."

Lexie made a few notes on her pad. "So, what kind of time commitment is involved with being a coach?"

"Well, the season just started last week, so we'll have practices on Tuesdays and Thursdays for a month or so. Then, in October, we'll have games on Saturday mornings against the other teams in our age group. I'm with the four-to-six-year-olds this year, so it's basically bumblebee soccer," he said.

"It's what?"

"Bumblebee soccer," he repeated. "They're so little, they really just run around in a huddle wherever the ball goes—like bumblebees. There's very little strategy and no focus on positions. I'm just teaching them how to kick a ball with both feet and not use their hands."

Lexie nodded. "And what do you get out of it?"

Jake smiled and leaned back in his chair, crossing one ankle over his knee.

"Well, of course, it's required for my scholarship, so there's that. But honestly, I enjoy working with kids. I love soccer, and while I'm not playing at the college level, that doesn't mean I can't work on my skills by teaching another generation of players," he said. "The kids are hilarious, and they really remind you why sports are supposed to be about having fun and not just about trophies and titles and records."

Lexie nodded, remembering how natural he'd seemed with the elementary school students at the pep rally. Colt tended to grimace and walk the other way when he saw kids coming.

Not that she was making comparisons.

"I feel like I need to see Coach Tanner in action. You know, for the sake of journalism," she said, making the most serious face she could.

Jake laughed. "Anything you want, Lex," he said, his dark eyes trained on hers, and for the briefest second, she wondered if he was still talking about soccer.

❧

BY THURSDAY, LEXIE had everything she needed for her article. There was no *real* reason to attend a practice in person, and yet she still found herself parking outside the Cypress Valley Rec Complex at a quarter to six. Climbing out of her silver Infiniti, she scanned the large practice area for anything that would point her toward field three—but there wasn't a single sign in sight. The open expanse of grass beside the parking lot was dotted here and there with miniature soccer goals and teeming with people of all ages. Lexie stood beside her car, unsure what to do next, until a young woman in athletic leggings and an oversized T-shirt passed nearby.

"Stay with me, Hannah," the woman admonished, squeezing the hand of a little girl with a swinging brown ponytail. "We have to find Coach Jake and your friends before you go running off."

Lexie's ears perked up, and she fell in line with the young mother, who seemed to know where she was going. The practice area was enormous, and kids clumped together in color-coordinated groups, each set of bright T-shirts displaying the name of a local business sponsor. Hannah's shirt was black with gold lettering identifying her as an "AutoZone Blackhawk."

Finally, after weaving their way past the concession stand and through a snaking line of parents near the restrooms, Hannah released her mother's hand with a squeal.

"There they are!" she cried, racing toward where a cloud of

black-clad children was gathering with Jake as its center. He towered over them, and Lexie couldn't help but notice how his wide shoulders filled out his black coach's shirt. Her eyes automatically traced the line of his torso as it tapered down to comfortable athletic shorts.

She had a boyfriend, but she wasn't blind.

"Coach Jake, Coach Jake, look!" a little girl beside Hannah exclaimed, her shrill young voice lifting above the hum of activity. She thrust one small foot out expectantly, and Lexie smiled as Jake dropped to a crouch to admire her tiny pink cleats. Whatever he said made her bounce excitedly, and her blonde pigtails flopped in all directions. He chuckled and patted her shoulder before rising and scanning the field, his mouth moving silently as he counted the little black meteorites flying wildly in all directions. His gaze landed on Lexie standing near the goal, and his look of concentration melted into something else entirely.

"You made it! I brought you a chair in case you didn't have one," he said, closing the distance between them and steering her gently toward a tan camp chair near the midfield line. "I've got to get started, but I'll find you after, okay?" he said. Then he lifted a shiny whistle to his lips and gave a few quick blasts as he jogged toward the center of their designated practice area.

"Alright, Blackhawks!" he shouted, clapping his hands, and the kids gravitated toward him like tiny electrons. They obviously adored him, and Lexie couldn't help but smile as Jake patiently demonstrated the day's exercise by weaving his ball back and forth around a series of low cones. He exuded an easy confidence that Lexie envied.

"Little kicks. Keep control of your ball," he reminded the players as one little boy sent his ball out of bounds.

"That one's mine. He has too much energy for his own good," the woman in the next chair said. She leaned over with a friendly smile. "I don't think I've seen you on the sidelines before. I'm Tabby."

"I'm Lexie, and this is my first practice," Lexie responded. "I'm writing an article about some of the student coaches from CVSU."

"Oh, Coach Jake is fabulous! Jordan loves him," Tabby said.

Lexie reached for her bag and retrieved a pad of paper and her voice recorder.

"Can I ask you a few questions for my story?" she asked, leaning toward Tabby as she flipped to a blank page. A grin from the other woman was all the answer she needed.

"Be my guest!" Tabby said, laughing, and Lexie instantly liked her.

Forty-five minutes later, they were still talking, though Lexie had long since put her equipment away.

"So, is there any reason you chose to observe this particular practice? Because, you know, Samantha over on field eight is a student coach, too," Tabby said, pointing toward another field.

Without thinking, Lexie glanced to where Jake was showing his players how to pass their soccer balls to each other. When she looked back at Tabby, there was a mischievous twinkle in the older woman's eye.

"But don't get me wrong," her new friend added, waggling her eyebrows, "the view is definitely better over here."

Lexie's mouth dropped open. "It's not like that!" she protested, but Tabby rolled her eyes with a grin.

"Honey, please. You've been watching him like you think he'll run away while you're not looking," she said. "Not that I blame you. I'm happily married with three children, but that doesn't mean I don't have eyes."

Lexie felt her cheeks heat, and Tabby settled back into her chair, satisfied.

"Uh-huh. Say what you want, but you've got reasons," she said.

Lexie shook her head silently and looked back at Jake, who waved when he saw her watching.

"Jake and I are coworkers and friends. Besides, I'm already seeing someone," she said, giving Tabby the most serious expression she could muster. Tabby reached across the gap between them and patted Lexie's arm, giving her such a motherly look that Lexie's chest tightened.

"Lexie, take this from a woman who's been around the block a time or two: life is too short to spend it with a man who doesn't know your worth. So, unless this boyfriend looks at you like you hung the moon and stars, leave him behind. Because from what I can tell, that boy right there"—she nodded toward Jake, who looked away suddenly as if he'd been caught—"he does."

⁓

"ALRIGHT, BLACKHAWKS! GREAT job today," Jake shouted, releasing the players to their parents. "Same time, same place next Tuesday, alright?"

An affirmative sound rippled through the crowd as mothers and fathers gathered their gear, collected their children and started the trek toward the parking lot.

"I hope to see you again, Lexie," Tabby said. She snagged her son's arm as he tried to slip past her. "It was great talking to you, and good luck," she added with a wink, slinging her camp chair over one shoulder and turning to take in Jordan's excited post-practice chatter.

Lexie waved and remained in her seat, fiddling with her bag on the ground while the crowd thinned. A few parents had lingered to talk to Jake, who still needed to pack up the gear he'd brought with him. Lexie stood and wandered over to a cluster of small soccer balls, kicking each one hard in his direction. They rolled to a stop several feet from his bag, but at least they were in the right vicinity. She jogged out to the far boundary line and tapped the last ball with her foot, sending it a few feet across the grass. Following lazily, she used first one foot, then the other, dribbling the ball between them as she'd seen the children do during their drills.

Back and forth, back and forth, she slowly made her way toward midfield, keeping her eyes on her ballet flats. Suddenly, a white tennis shoe darted into her line of vision and swept the ball out from under her. Looking up, Lexie watched Jake dribble it effortlessly toward the small net and then launch it into the goal with a swift kick. The ball hit its mark with an audible swish.

"Goal!" he shouted, throwing his hands in the air.

"No fair!" Lexie called, her hands on her hips. "I wasn't ready."

"Oh, really? Is that why it was so easy?" he taunted. "Fine, I'll let you try again." He snatched the ball from the net before trotting back to her and dropping it at her feet. "If you can get it past me, we'll consider that a win."

"Just past you? That's it?"

"That's it."

Lexie narrowed her eyes, sensing a trap, but she took the bait anyway. Sweeping the ball to the left, she tried to arc around Jake, but he easily stole from her again and headed downfield in the opposite direction. Lexie huffed and shook her head.

"Okay, I should have expected that. Let's go again," she said. "But you have to give me more room."

He smirked and kicked the ball back. Standing several yards away, he spread his arms wide and gestured to the empty field.

"What are you waiting for, Preston? Nobody's stopping you!"

Lexie set her face in determination, ignoring his taunt, and struck out to one side. She could see him standing at the edge of her vision, waiting, and she suddenly felt like a mouse being stalked by a cat. All at once, he was inches away, knocking the ball out of her path and taking off toward the goal behind her. He did a few spins on the way, obviously proud of himself.

"Show-off!" Lexie shouted.

Jake stuck his tongue out in childish victory, his self-satisfied grin lighting up his face, and a whole swarm of butterflies took flight in Lexie's belly. His teasing shouldn't have affected her so deeply, but it did. She huffed out a breath and raked her hands through her hair before pulling a rubber tie off her wrist and securing her soft waves into a low ponytail. It was time to change strategies.

"Oh, this is getting serious!" Jake called, his voice filled with laughter. "Are you going to show me how it's done?"

Lexie narrowed her eyes and bit the inside of her cheek, trying not to give him the satisfaction of making her laugh.

"One more time, but I'm going to take it from you, *and* I'm going to score," she said as she closed the gap between them.

One of Jake's eyebrows popped up, his expression skeptical. "Yeah, I doubt that."

"Oh, I'm sure I can find a way. You have no idea what I'm capable of," she said, swishing her hips and moving closer until she was all but leaning against him, her palms flat against the curve of his shoulders.

Jake went very, very still, his eyes wide, and Lexie could have sworn he stopped breathing. An unfamiliar sense of power surged through her blood as she realized she had his undivided attention—something she hardly ever got from Colt. She almost hated to misuse such an incredible gift.

Almost.

Taking full advantage, she shoved Jake hard with both hands. He stumbled backward, and she snatched the ball from between his feet. Lexie kicked it hard and ran with all her might to catch up.

"That was dirty!" he shouted, his voice thin as he raced up behind her. There was a moment of confusion when the ball got tangled between their feet, and Lexie latched onto his arm just above the elbow, trying not to fall.

"I never figured you'd cheat," he said.

"Well, you figured wrong!" she replied, kicking the ball out of the scuffle and darting beyond him. But Jake lunged forward, and his arms closed around her from behind just before he lifted her off her feet. Lexie struggled in vain, laughing as the ball rolled out of range.

"What is *this*?" she said, smacking his forearms where they remained locked around her waist.

"Payback," he replied as he set her down.

Turning, Lexie found his face lit up with a cheeky grin, and her stomach turned over. He wasn't extraordinarily tall, maybe five foot ten to Colt's six foot plus. It would be so easy to—

Whoa! Where did that come from? she asked herself, alarmed by the unexpected image of Jake's lips pressed against hers. But she couldn't seem to push it away, not with him looking at her like that.

"*. . . like you hung the moon and stars.*"

Tabby's words echoed in her mind, and it was suddenly very hard to breathe. Jake's eyes went soft around the edges, full of a gentleness she never saw in Colt's icy blue ones, and Lexie felt herself being pulled into them like a shell drawn out to sea. His hand brushed along the back of her arm, sending a shiver all the way to her toes and making her painfully aware of how close she was to doing something stupid.

"Jordan's mom!" she blurted, surprising them both. Confusion spread across Jake's face as his brows knit together, and Lexie took the opportunity to step back. "Great quotes from Jordan's mom," she said, struggling to find a complete thought in her scrambled brain. "She loves you. The kids! The kids, I mean. *They* love you. Thanks for your help."

"No problem," Jake said slowly, though he still looked bewildered. He paused for a moment, scanning her face, before turning to gather the discarded soccer balls. There were a few moments of silence as Lexie cast about for something else, *anything else* to say, desperately trying to forget the way she'd started to lean into him.

After he'd packed his equipment, Jake stopped next to her, toying with the cinch strap on his equipment bag.

"I usually grab ice cream on the way home from practice. Would you like to come?" he asked, his tone casual. But he didn't meet her eyes.

Lexie took a long, slow breath.

Jake *looked* like the kind of guy who had smooth, practiced pickup lines at the ready, who could collect girls like trading cards if he wanted. But the more time Lexie spent with him, the less she felt like that was the case. She'd seen girls flirt with him on more than one occasion, but Jake seemed to shy away from that kind of attention more often than not. He certainly didn't soak it up like it was his birthright the way some guys did.

Well, the way *most* guys did.

Now, she wasn't completely certain how to interpret his invitation. If he was asking her out, she should say no. But if he wasn't asking her out . . . she should still say no. She obviously couldn't trust herself where he was concerned.

Colt would tell her to say no.

Suddenly, Lexie could hear the grit in Colt's voice as he justified himself.

It's just a guy thing. . . . Don't be like that. . . . Pull the stick out.

And she didn't care what he would say.

"Sure, that sounds like fun!" she answered, ignoring the warning voice that told her it was a bad idea. She was a grown woman, after all. She could handle it.

❧

JAKE SAT ACROSS from Lexie outside the local Dairy Queen and did his best not to laugh as she battled a hole near the bottom of her waffle cone.

"Plug it with your finger," he said, pointing to the gap where her strawberry ice cream was escaping.

"I can't, it keeps breaking!" she said with dismay as the cone cracked farther up the side. "I'm heading for a full containment breach!"

Jake laughed, scraping the last of his hot fudge sundae from the bottom of his paper cup.

"Here, see if this helps," he said, handing the cup to her.

Lexie unceremoniously dumped her dripping concoction into his empty container, shaking a few drops of ice cream from her sticky hands.

"This makes me think about animals that adapt so they can't be eaten. You know, like porcupines and poison dart frogs," she said, cleaning up with a pile of napkins he'd grabbed at the pickup window.

"How exactly did you get from ice cream cones to poison dart frogs?" he asked, not bothering to hide his amusement.

"You know, the way they make themselves inedible. This cone is fighting back."

Jake shook his head. "I'm starting to think your mind works in strange and mysterious ways."

"Oh, you have no idea. Once, I had a dream that was part Harry Potter, part Wizard of Oz, and it was incredible."

"I'd watch that movie. Did it have both the Wicked Witch of the West *and* Voldemort?" he asked, raising his drink to his lips.

"Yep, married with kids, actually. And let me tell you, green-skinned, no-nose babies are not attractive."

Jake pitched forward, barely containing the Dr. Pepper that threatened to spray across the table and make her messy situation even worse. He wiped his mouth with the back of his hand and swallowed.

"Sorry. I probably should have waited until you weren't mid-sip," Lexie said, grinning.

Jake laughed, feeling his cheeks stretch until they hurt. This was the best first date he'd ever had. But was it actually a date? She'd driven herself and refused to let him pay, so maybe not. But it was certainly date-*adjacent*.

It wasn't *not* a date, at least. And he was willing to work with that.

"There's probably some telepathic link straight to Copper Hill that's going to tell my mother I spit on a woman, and she'll be here in less than twenty minutes to beat me with a wooden spoon," he said.

It was Lexie's turn to laugh, and Jake loved the way her whole face changed. If she'd been a distraction on the sidelines, it was nothing compared to sitting across from her now.

"What's your mother like?" she asked, taking a sip of her remaining ice cream as if it were a milkshake.

"Well, she's pretty much your typical Tennessee housewife. She used to be a kindergarten teacher, but then when I came along, she stopped working to stay home and keep me out of trouble. She makes the best lasagna in the world and likes to grow tulips in these huge flower beds in the front yard. She says she wants the place to look like those fields in Amsterdam," he said, lacing his fingers behind his head.

Lexie's eyes followed the movement, catching somewhere near his shoulders before jumping back to her dessert. Jake smothered a triumphant smile as a blush rose in her cheeks.

Definitely date-adjacent.

"So, you're an only child?" she asked, keeping her attention on her cup.

"No, I have a younger sister, Ashlyn; she's a sophomore at CVSU. I also grew up within ten miles of my nine first cousins, so the house was always full."

"*Nine* cousins?" Lexie asked. "Wow."

"A lot more if you count second cousins, too. There are currently four generations of Tanners in Mason County," he said proudly. "My grandfather is the oldest of Grandpa Jacob and

Grandma Ruby's four boys. Then he had four kids himself, including my dad, so there are a lot of us."

"I grew up in a big house all by myself," Lexie said wistfully. "I can't imagine having siblings or cousins running around all the time. It must have been fabulous to always have someone to play with."

Her faraway expression tugged at Jake's heart.

"So, what do your parents do?" he asked, desperate to learn more about her. The sadness that flickered through her eyes was unexpected.

"My dad is a doctor, a surgeon, actually."

Jake let out a low whistle and leaned back, propping his feet up on an empty chair. "What kind of surgery?"

"Cardiothoracic," she said, wincing like she'd said a bad word. "He's the surgeon-in-chief at Vanderbilt."

Wow, Jake thought, though he didn't expect that was the response she wanted.

"I've heard they have hard schedules," he offered instead, trying to tread carefully.

Lexie picked at the soggy pieces of her cone.

"Yeah, they do. He wasn't around much when I was growing up, but I think that was intentional."

Jake frowned. "What about your mom?" he asked, hoping for a better answer.

"Well, she was a waitress when she met my dad, and I'm pretty sure he married her just to make my grandparents angry—his one act of defiance." Lexie cleared her throat, her attention returning to her bowl. "She died in a car accident when I was fifteen."

Jake felt like he'd been punched in the gut. How was he supposed to respond to something like that? He cleared his throat and leaned his forearms on the table, filling the silence with motion.

"I'm sorry. I'm really on a roll with my questions tonight."

"It's okay," she said, offering a sad smile. "How are you supposed to know if you don't ask?" She stood and tossed the dregs of her ice cream cone into the trash. "I should probably call it a night."

Jake watched her gather her things, feeling her impending absence more keenly than he'd like. He reached out on impulse and caught her hand as she passed his chair, surprised by his own audacity.

She stopped and looked toward where his fingers looped around hers.

"I'm really glad you came. I've had fun," he said, lifting his gaze to her face. Those brilliant green eyes drifted up to his and lingered.

"Yeah, it was fun," she said. "I'll see you at work, okay?" She gently pulled her hand free and walked toward her car, then slid inside.

Jake forced himself to stay seated, knowing that if he stood, he'd probably do something stupid—like try to stop her. He watched her back carefully out of her parking space before pulling onto the main drag. Then he flexed his fingers a few times, noticing a sticky spot where he'd held her hand.

It was proof she had been there.

Proof there was hope after all.

"WHERE HAVE YOU been?" Olivia asked, looking up from the textbook in her lap.

Lexie pushed the door shut behind her and dropped her purse onto a kitchen chair. "Playing soccer with Jake."

"Doing what with who now?" Olivia asked, setting down her pen and giving Lexie her full attention.

Lexie sighed. "It wasn't a big deal, Liv. He helped me with a story, we played soccer, and then we got ice cream."

Olivia blinked several times before closing her book and swinging her feet off the couch. She patted the now-empty cushion with her hand.

"I'm sorry, but I'm going to need more information."

Recognizing when she needed to fold, Lexie sank down beside her friend and started talking. When she mentioned kicking the soccer ball around the empty field, Olivia laid a hand on her arm.

"Lex, please tell me you know he was flirting with you."

"What? No, definitely not," Lexie said, though she felt guilt creep up her neck anyway. "It was just good fun."

"Lexie," Olivia said, letting her name hang in the air. "Guys don't play keep-away soccer with girls just for the fun of it. And then he asked you on a date!"

"It wasn't a date! We're just friends. We work together. That's all," Lexie protested, though it was too much, even to her own ears.

"Did he drive?"

"No."

"Did he pay?"

"No!" Lexie said, feeling vindicated.

"Did he try to?"

Lexie paused, remembering Jake's insistence that she let him buy her cone. He'd even gone so far as to snatch her five-dollar bill and hold it above her head. But she'd put her foot down and demanded to pay for herself, and he'd eventually given in—albeit reluctantly.

"Yes," she said miserably, unable to ignore the truth any longer.

Olivia lifted one eyebrow. "Does he know you have a boyfriend?" she asked.

"No," Lexie moaned, dropping her face into her hands. "It's never come up."

"What do you mean, 'It's never come up'?" Olivia repeated. "There's never been a place to simply drop Colt's name into conversation with a guy who is obviously interested in you?"

"It's not . . . He isn't . . . It's just that . . ." Lexie stammered, searching for a way out.

She just hadn't wanted it to end. The way Jake always looked at her like she was something worth having, the way he acted like spending time with her was more important than anywhere else he needed to be. . . . It had been so long since anyone had treated her that way. She'd only wanted to hold on to that feeling for a little while longer.

Olivia just smiled. "He seems like a good guy."

"*Colt* is a good guy," Lexie said reflexively.

Olivia patted her friend's knee. "Maybe sleep on it," she suggested. "But either way, you're going to have to tell Jake the truth. It's not fair for him not to know."

Lexie felt another sharp pang of guilt. She wasn't the kind of girl to play games or string a guy along; it had just gotten out of hand. She sighed, tilting her head back against the couch.

Leave it to her to ruin a good thing.

JAKE NARROWED HIS eyes, concentrating on the advertisement he was creating for the university magazine. He nudged the photo three clicks to the right, then four clicks back to the left. Truth be told, he'd been done for twenty minutes. Now he was just stalling.

Get up! he told himself, but somehow, the instructions weren't reaching his legs.

"I was wondering if you'd like to go to dinner with me sometime," he mumbled under his breath, testing the words. "Is there any chance you'd . . . No, that sounds worse."

"Ask her to go *out* with you, not just to dinner."

Jake jumped to his feet and turned around, surprised to find Andy standing with his shoulder against the edge of the partition.

"There's less ambiguity that way. Dinner could be a friend thing, but '*out with you*' is definitely a date," Andy added with a grin, his arms crossed over his chest.

"How long have you been standing there?" Jake demanded.

"Long enough."

Jake groaned, wiping one hand down his face. "Is there any chance you could stop sneaking up on me? Maybe announce yourself when a guy's obviously thinking out loud?" he snapped, yanking his bag off the floor.

"As your boss, I am outraged by your attitude. As your friend, I advise you not to yell at your boss."

"He'll get over it," Jake muttered as he pushed past him.

Andy only chuckled. "Lexie is a lucky girl," he said with a smirk.

Jake's eyes went wide. "How do you even know that's who I'm asking?" he asked, his eyes darting toward the door in case the girl in question magically materialized.

"Everyone knows. You don't fall out of your chair for just anybody," Andy said, and Jake groaned again.

Exactly how obvious had he been?

He left the studio and crossed the hall to the main office suite, pausing with his hand on the door.

"Would you like to go out with me sometime?" he repeated, grudgingly admitting it did sound better. With one final exhale, he pulled open the door and smiled at Ms. Patterson, who sat at the front desk.

"Is Lexie still here?" he asked, though he already knew the answer.

The secretary nodded and pointed her pen toward an open area where the interns worked, and he thanked her without stopping. The clacking of computer keys grew louder as he approached where Lexie sat hidden behind her own partition.

"Hey," he said, rounding the corner into her cubicle.

She startled slightly and looked up at him, her eyes wide.

"Oh, hi," she said as she brushed a lock of hair out of her face. She seemed nervous, and not in a good way. It was more like . . . dread.

Jake felt his brows pull together.

"You alright back here? I meant to stop in earlier and see how your article was going, but I got busy," he said, waiting for her body language to change. "The new magazine spreads are pretty good, if I do say so myself."

But Lexie didn't seem to relax, no matter how long he talked. Not knowing what else to do, Jake plowed ahead.

"So, I really enjoyed hanging out last night. I was wondering . . . Well, I wanted to ask if you might—"

"Where's my girl?"

An unfamiliar voice came from the far side of the room, and Lexie jumped to her feet, nearly knocking her keyboard to the floor.

"Colt! What are you doing here?" she blurted, obviously surprised to see the tall young man who was striding into the room as if he owned the place. Jake stepped back as she pushed roughly past him.

"What? Can't a man surprise his girl at work?" The newcomer wrapped one arm possessively around Lexie's waist, and Jake's stomach dropped when the guy's mouth crashed down onto Lexie's without hesitation.

So . . . not her brother, then.

Good manners told him to look away, but he couldn't seem to do it. He took in every detail: the way Lexie stood stiffly, the way she seemed to pull away first, the way her eyes flicked straight to his when she opened them.

"So, this is work, huh?" the guy asked as he looked around the room. He kept one arm around Lexie, as if he thought she'd run away—and, honestly, she looked like she might. His gaze drifted until it landed on Jake, who could almost feel ice water wash over him.

"Hey, man, how's it going? I'm Colton Derricks with Derricks Pharmaceuticals," he said, crossing the room with Lexie in tow.

Jake could feel the anxiety radiating from her. Colt, it seemed, could not.

"Colt, this is Jake Tanner. He's one of our photographers," Lexie supplied, looking quickly from Colt to Jake and then back.

"Nice to meet you," Jake said, and he reached out to shake the hand that was offered. Colt seemed to make it a point to grip harder than necessary, and Jake worked to keep his expression neutral. He could have been Lexie's cousin and a guy like this would still march in and pee on everything in sight. There was no point giving him more ammunition.

Definitely not who he would have imagined for her.

That's because he's not you, you idiot.

"You as well," Colt said, still holding on. "Though I wish I could say I'd heard all about you."

"Jake takes the photos for my stories," Lexie said, jumping in. She smoothed her hand down the sleeve of Colt's dress shirt, as if soothing a child.

Colt gave Jake a last once-over and released his hand, turning back to Lexie.

"That's great, babe. I hope he does as he's told." Colt's smile was tight, and Jake grit his teeth to keep words from tumbling out. Nothing he could possibly say about this guy would be nice.

That did not change when Colt tugged Lexie tighter against him and kissed her again, making an obvious show of drawing it out. Jake clenched his jaw and looked out the window. He couldn't leave anyway, since they were blocking his path to the door. Besides, he didn't want to give this guy the satisfaction of walking away.

"What do you say we get out of here?" he heard Colt ask Lexie, his voice pitched low. "It was great to meet you, *Blake*, but I've got to get my girl home," Colt added at a normal volume, turning away without waiting for Lexie's answer. He grabbed her laptop bag off the back of her desk chair and slung it over his own shoulder, turning with her toward the door.

Lexie glanced back as she was propelled out of the office. Her eyes found Jake's, and she held his gaze for a moment before Colt started talking again, saying something about a sale he'd made earlier in the day. Then they were gone.

Jake leaned back against the wall and cursed his own luck. Of course Lexie Preston was with someone; why had he ever assumed she wasn't?

Because she seemed into you. And because she's never mentioned him.

Ever.

At all.

Jake ground his teeth and pushed to stand, figuring the happy couple had had enough time to make it to the elevator. Why couldn't she have said something? It wasn't that hard to drop into conversation. She'd probably gone home and laughed at how desperately transparent he'd been on the soccer field. He'd almost kissed her, for goodness' sake, and she couldn't have warned him?

She did start babbling like a crazy person, his memory reminded him, but he roughly pushed the thought away. Breaking a tense moment was not the same as coming out and saying "Jake, I'm sorry, but I have a boyfriend."

He was still fuming when he reached the parking lot and yanked open the door of his old pickup truck. A car horn blared to his left, and he looked up in time to see Colt wave from the driver's seat of a shiny, black convertible, his face stretched into a victorious grin as he passed in a cloud of dust.

Jake watched the BMW disappear over the rise, feeling bile churn in his gut. Why would Lexie ever want someone like him when she could have a guy like that? Sure, Colt was a tool of the highest order, but he could give her things Jake never could.

Give her a little more credit, would you? his brain chided, and Jake instantly felt guilty. Lexie wasn't that kind of girl. Sure, she came from money, but she didn't seem to live for it. Even so, Jake couldn't help but wonder if she would ever really be happy with less.

And right then, he sure felt like a whole lot less.

4

"WHY DID YOU have to do that?" Lexie snapped. She smoothed her hands over her hair to keep it from flying every which way, since he'd insisted on putting the top down on his convertible.

"Do what?" Colt asked, his face full of false innocence.

"Be a jerk for no reason," she replied, her anger building as she mentally replayed the last ten minutes. "Jake is my friend, and you acted like a dalmatian that found a fire hydrant."

She wasn't really surprised—that was how Colt always acted when he found her talking to other men—but she'd been hoping Jake wouldn't experience it firsthand.

"Your friend, huh? That's interesting," Colt said, cocking his head as if considering her words. "I hear about everything you do with Olivia and Kate and Robin. Is there some reason you've never, not once, mentioned the existence of this guy you work with in any of your stories from the past three weeks? Seems like if he were just 'a friend,' then I would have known about him before I waltzed in and found him pinning you to your desk."

"He wasn't pinning me to my desk!" Lexie huffed as she secured her hair with one hand and turned toward him. "And we *are* just friends. I'm allowed to have those, you know. I don't have to tell you about every single one of them."

"You have to tell me about the ones who are into you."

"You think every guy is into me!"

"That's because they are!" he shot back, and Lexie could tell he was getting angry. And maybe he had a right to; he wasn't that far off, after all.

But then again, didn't trust go both ways?

"Why do you have such a problem with this? I don't get to pick my coworkers any more than you do, and I've seen your sales rep roster. Some of those women are gorgeous, and I've never complained about that."

"I have a *problem*," he said, smacking his hand on the wheel, "with you prancing around letting every guy in the county drool over what's mine."

Lexie knew she shouldn't push him, but this time, her words refused to stay bottled up.

"What's *yours*?" she spat, letting her hair go so she could gesture with both hands. "First of all, I don't *prance* anywhere, and second, I am not an object to be owned! I do not *belong* to you or anyone else. And third—"

Colt's hand snapped up and grabbed her wrist, squeezing hard enough to make her wince. He stopped the car at a red light, and his eyes were cold as he leaned toward her.

"I would wrap up this little temper tantrum, if I were you," he said, his voice grating over her skin.

Lexie held his stare and forced herself not to shiver.

"You are mine if I say you're mine, and I don't share. You got that?"

Lexie simply blinked, too angry to let him win but too smart to disagree.

"I'll take that as a yes," he said, throwing her arm to the side as the light turned green. He settled back into his seat and continued toward her apartment. "I was thinking about Barclay's for dinner tonight, since we skipped it last time," he said, as if nothing were wrong. "It can be just us. No boys."

Lexie simply rubbed her wrist and stared silently out the windshield, letting her hair whip across her face. At the next light, Colt put the top up and reached across to tuck the errant strands behind her ears.

"Baby, don't be like that. You can hardly blame me," he said, running his thumb along the curve of her jaw before dropping his hand to her leg.

She looked over, studying the side of his face as he drove and feeling her frustration slowly drain away. He wasn't entirely wrong. The line between her and Jake—the boundary between friends and more-than-friends—had gotten fuzzy, and that was her fault. She'd just have to keep him at arm's length from now on. Colt wasn't perfect, but he deserved that much, at least.

"I love you," Colt said, catching her watching him.

"I love you, too," she answered automatically, remembering a time when those words had felt like a fairy tale come true.

These days, they just felt like words.

JAKE KICKED BACK in a threadbare lawn chair, his shoulders braced against the warm brick of the house and his grass-covered sneakers propped on the splintered porch railing. A few bats chased mosquitoes through the branches of a tulip poplar tree nearby, their silhouettes flashing here and there across the gaps of summer sky that had slowly faded from gold to crimson. Someone down the street was grilling, and the smell of roasting hot dogs made his stomach growl.

"The yard looks good," Conner said, letting the cockeyed screen door snap shut behind him as he sank into a mismatched chair.

Jake gazed out over the perfectly mown grass that only hours before had been a jungle of overgrowth. It had been so long, he'd had to mow twice. Then, he'd used the Weed Eater on every stray blade he could find before dropping to his knees and attacking a long-neglected flower bed on the back side of the house. Every muscle in his body ached, but he still wasn't satisfied. The place was still a dump; it would always be a dump. It wasn't the kind of place a girl like Lexie would ever set foot.

Conner offered him a long-necked bottle, the Coca-Cola logo faintly visible in the fading light, and Jake twisted off the top and took a long, cold swallow.

"I thought you'd be out on the town by now," Jake said, rolling the bottle between his hands.

"So did I, but I lost rock paper scissors, so here I am," Conner said, taking a drink from his own bottle. "We were afraid you might get the chainsaw out next."

"I can use a chainsaw just fine," Jake muttered darkly, and Conner snorted.

"The last time you tried trimming that tree, you nearly put a hole in the roof."

"That's because neither of you idiots would come out here and help me," Jake snapped, setting his bottle on the faded porch boards below his chair. "Besides, the place is already falling to pieces. I doubt we'd even notice a hole in the roof."

Conner chuckled. "Well, you're the one who lives upstairs, so if you want a skylight, then be my guest."

Jake snorted, the sound unexpected, even to him.

"You know, the house wouldn't look quite so bad if you and Noah would stop trying to destroy each other. Haven't you had enough of this prank war? I mean, seriously, I found him knocking holes in his bedroom walls the other day."

Conner snickered, his whole body shaking. "You have to admit, that was a good one."

"It was psychotic! Who hides a speaker in the drywall and plays creepy voices at all hours of the night?" Jake said, shaking his head in disbelief. "How do you think of these things?"

Conner howled with laughter, and Jake rolled his eyes. It had been a pretty good prank. Even he'd gotten a kick out of watching Noah slowly lose his mind.

"Relax. We're just getting a head start on the demolition," Conner said, taking another swallow. "Although I will be sad to see this old place go. Dad is thinking about putting a duplex here instead." He looked wistfully around the yard, as if remembering all the cookouts the boys had hosted in the past two years.

"And besides, Noah deserved it," Conner continued, getting back on topic. "That bucket he dumped on me the first day? It was olive oil! It took *ages* to get it all off. I was slippery in unspeakable places for a week!"

Jake shuddered, glad to be merely a third-party bystander to his friends' hijinks.

"Just remember to leave me out of it," he said, reaching for his soda again. He took another swallow as a bat swooped low, chasing a moth that fluttered around the outdoor light.

Conner grunted in agreement.

They sat in companionable silence while the last of the day's light faded, until Conner moved as if to stand.

"Lexie is seeing someone," Jake blurted, feeling some of the tension drain out of him.

Conner settled back into his chair. "She tell you today?"

"Nope," Jake said, letting the word pop from his lips. "I was in the middle of asking her to dinner when some guy waltzed into the office and tried to swallow her face."

Conner winced. "Ouch."

"Yeah. The rich frat-boy type; a real piece of work, from what I can tell."

"And you didn't know?"

"Does it look like I knew?" Jake said, lolling his head to one side so he could look at his friend head-on.

"So, she's never said anything?"

"Not a single thing." Jake drained what was left of his Coke and leaned forward to set the bottle on the porch railing. "I mean, how hard would it have been to give me a heads-up? Just a simple 'my boyfriend and I' would have done it, you know? Anything to tell me not to make a fool of myself like an overeager puppy dog."

"Maybe it isn't serious," Conner said, rolling his drink between his palms.

"Well, I don't think *Colt* would agree," Jake spat. Just saying the guy's name left a bitter taste in his mouth.

There was a long silence, broken only by the cooing of a nearby dove and the slam of a car door down the road.

"In my experience, a woman who's happy in her relationship will find a way to mention it," Conner said, tilting his head back to stare at the sky. "And a woman who isn't . . . won't."

Jake considered this, his mouth pressed into a hard line. Lexie certainly hadn't been pleased to see her boyfriend, at least not in an obvious way. But then again, maybe she just didn't enjoy public displays of affection.

Or being treated like property.

Or maybe Jake just didn't know her at all.

He grunted, feeling agitation rising in his chest again. If it were simply about Lexie not wanting *him*, he thought he could get over it. But why would she want a guy like *that*?

Conner cleared his throat. "I wasn't going to mention this, but one of Jasmine's friends has actually been asking about you."

Jake puffed out a breath, leaning his chair back on two legs and trying to remember Conner's latest fling.

"Yeah? Which one?" he asked.

"Macy, the redhead from that barbecue we went to."

Jake searched his memory and came up blank.

"She brought the watermelon?" Conner supplied.

That did it. This was the girl who found out Jake liked watermelon and spent the rest of the evening hovering nearby to make sure he never ran out. He'd almost had to beg her to stop.

He stifled a groan.

"I know, I know, she was a bit over the top, but I promise she's usually cool," Conner reassured him. "I think you just made her nervous." He waggled his eyebrows, and Jake laughed skeptically.

"I highly doubt that."

"Well, I mean, you're not me, but you're alright."

Jake reached over and socked his friend in the arm, but Conner only laughed as he rose to his feet.

"Just think about it. If you're interested, I can get you her number."

Jake took a deep breath and tipped his face toward the dark sky. "I'll think about it."

⁂

"LEX? LEXIE? ALEXIS!"

Lexie jumped, hearing her name repeated with rising irritation as Robin smacked her palm on the tabletop between them.

"Are you even listening?"

"Yes! No. Sorry," Lexie stammered, rubbing her fingertips across her forehead. All she could focus on these days was the growing knot in her stomach. A crease formed down the center of Robin's brow, but she didn't press the issue. Instead, she simply picked up where she'd left off.

"As I was saying, we need to reserve our cabin if we're going to the mountains this year. Is everyone still okay with leaving right after finals?"

"I've already told my parents I won't be home that week," Olivia said, sliding into the raised booth beside Lexie. She was lucky to have a seat at all since the Hawk's Nest was particularly packed, even for a Friday evening. The humid September night seemed to have driven everyone inside for ice cream floats and burgers in old-fashioned plastic baskets.

Robin nodded, obviously pleased. "What about you, Lex?"

"I'll have to check with Colt," Lexie answered, swirling her straw in her chocolate milkshake.

Robin, Kate and Olivia shared a glance that was as heavy as it was silent, and Lexie pasted on a too-bright smile.

"We might be going to see his parents that weekend. Have you ever met the Derricks?"

"Have you ever met Colt?" Kate muttered, taking a long pull from her straw.

"What's wrong with Colt?" Lexie asked, feeling her smile wobble. All three of her friends answered at the same time.

"Well . . . he's just . . ."

"Very charming! Gorgeous, of course . . ."

"But he can be a little . . ."

"Sometimes he's . . ."

"Oh, just spit it out!" Lexie snapped, looking at the girls around her. Robin and Kate gave Olivia pointed stares, and Lexie's best friend sighed.

"We just think Colt could be nicer to you sometimes," Olivia said, obviously choosing her words with care.

"Remember when you were *rocking* that orange dress at your birthday bash, and his first words when he saw you were 'that's not your best color'? What boyfriend says that?" Kate blurted, waving her hands in the air emphatically.

Lexie's chest tightened with the memory.

"And didn't he tell you your new job was good playtime? Like you're a child he sends to daycare?" Robin butt in, dunking a few crispy french fries into a puddle of ketchup.

"He didn't mean it that way," Lexie mumbled, feeling her face get hot.

Kate opened her mouth to say something else, but the jukebox in the corner interrupted with the opening notes of "Sweet Home Alabama."

"I love this one!" Robin gasped as she latched onto Kate's forearm. "Dance with me!" she demanded, half-dragging her friend out of the booth with another look at Olivia—one Lexie heard loud and clear. It said "You handle this."

The girls joined a growing crowd of Cypress Valley students on the makeshift dance floor between the restaurant booths and the pool hall. Olivia and Lexie watched them go.

"You know they mean well. We wouldn't say anything if we weren't concerned," Olivia said, squeezing the top of Lexie's leg.

"What's to be concerned about?" Lexie snapped, her ego still stinging. "Colt is allowed to have opinions. He should be able to share them."

Olivia stayed silent, snagging an onion ring from Lexie's basket.

Lexie leaned back against the vinyl booth cushion, absent-mindedly watching her friends jump and sway to the beat of the music. Her gaze drifted over their heads toward the pool tables at the opposite end of the restaurant, where she saw a familiar smile. Jake was leaning against a cue stick, one ankle crossed casually over the other as he watched a pretty girl line up her shot.

The knot in Lexie's gut tightened instantly.

Their relationship had shifted dramatically over the past week. Where there had been a sense of camaraderie, there were now tense silences and awkward glances—that was, when Jake acknowledged her at all.

It was probably what she deserved, but that didn't make it hurt any less.

Jake's date knocked one ball into a side pocket and a second into the far corner before throwing her hands into the air victoriously. Jake tossed his arm around her shoulders in a familiar sort of way, and Lexie could almost hear his laughter from where she sat, like a memory played on repeat. Whoever the girl was, she was soaking up his attention like a sponge, flipping her hair over one shoulder and standing with her hip popped to the side.

"What are you watching so intently?" Olivia asked, leaning against her friend's shoulder to follow her gaze.

Lexie jerked her eyes back to their table and then rummaged through her basket as if trying to find the one perfect onion ring.

"Nothing in particular," she said, trying to keep her voice neutral. What Jake did in his personal life was none of her business. Why should she care who he dated, or if he dated at all? But even so, something sharp pressed against her breastbone when she glanced up and saw the pretty girl bump Jake with her hip as he bent flat over the pool table. He paused his shot and turned his head, narrowing his eyes at the girl, who laughed.

"You know, if seeing him with someone else bothers you this much, that probably should tell you something," Olivia teased, as though she'd found the answer to her own question.

Lexie dragged her attention back to her friend.

"I don't know what you're talking about," she insisted, her grip tightening on her glass.

"Sure you don't," Olivia said. She rolled her eyes. "And I bet you don't care at all that Miss Priss just planted a big one on your boy."

"She *what*?!" Lexie exclaimed, jerking her head up.

"Down girl! I was only teasing," Olivia said with a satisfied smirk.

Lexie closed her eyes and fought the hot flush rising in her face.

"Although I think you've proven my point," her friend added before crunching another onion ring.

Lexie ignored her and tried not to watch Jake prowl the edges of the pool table, studying his options. The girl didn't take her eyes off him as he moved, her face full of challenge, and Lexie was struck by the sudden urge to yank her cue stick out of her stupid hands and beat her with it.

Which was ridiculous, because what did it matter if some floozy chick threw herself at Jake? Good for him. Maybe he'd take her home at the end of the night.

A wave of nausea washed over Lexie, and she put her last onion ring down. The fried food was obviously getting to her.

JAKE DRUMMED HIS thumbs against the steering wheel of his truck as he headed northwest along a series of back roads that might as well have been tattooed onto his skin. He could have driven this route between Cypress Valley and Copper Hill with his eyes closed, but instead, he watched the bean fields fly by and wondered what his mother might be cooking for dinner.

He was *not* going to think about Lexie. Enough was enough. She was with someone, and he was going to move on with his life. End of story.

And yet the scrap of paper Conner had given him with Macy's number on it still sat in the cup holder of his center console, untouched since he'd jammed it in there last week. He just couldn't bring himself to call a girl he already knew he wasn't interested in, even just to have fun; he wasn't a "just have fun" kind of guy. Noah and Conner gave him endless grief for it, but Jake believed you could meet a person and instantly know whether or not they would fit into your life. He couldn't explain exactly *how* you could know, only that you could.

And Macy the watermelon girl just wasn't the one.

Twenty minutes later, he pulled into a long, dusty driveway that wound across acres of soybean fields, finally parking in front of a two-story farmhouse, its green roof and shutters crisp against classic white siding. His truck had barely come to a stop before a brown basset hound stood up from his sunning spot on the wide front porch and threw his head back, baying as though to wake the dead.

Gomer trotted down the porch stairs, his ears flopping with every step, and made a circuit of the truck, stopping to smell all four tires. Jake descended from the driver's seat and crouched to give the dog a good scratch behind his ears.

"Is that who I think it is?"

Jake looked up as a woman in blue jeans and a floral top pushed through the front door and stepped onto the porch, her white apron covered in streaks of bluish-black. "Hi, Mama," he said, his voice taking on a softer quality that only came out here on the farm. This was where his roots grew deepest.

"Don't you 'Mama' me," the woman called. "I don't know who *you* are! I sent my little boy to kindergarten just this morning."

Jake smiled as he stood and jogged over to the porch. He mounted the steps and wrapped his mother in a bear hug. She smelled like sugar and blackberries, scents that hinted at jam-making in progress.

"Well, alright then. I guess you can come inside," she said, feigning reluctance. "Your daddy will be in later."

Jake nodded, looking toward the field where he could hear the sound of heavy machinery. His father, uncles and cousins were hard at work planting winter wheat, and he felt a familiar pang of guilt for not being there to help. Farming was a family business for the Tanners and had been ever since Grandma Ruby's father bought the first acres in the early 1900s.

"Don't do that," his mother said sharply, her eyes missing nothing. "I know what you're thinking, and we're not going to discuss it again. There are plenty of strong young men around here to carry on with, and another one would just get underfoot."

Jake pressed his lips together, familiar with the sentiment but still feeling its sting. Thankfully, three of his cousins had been born with soil in their veins and seemed happy to carry the family business into the next generation. For that, he was grateful.

"Now, what would you like for breakfast?" his mother asked, shooing him through the open screen door and toward the kitchen. "And don't tell me you ate something at school, because I know those protein bars and sugary cereals just don't cut it."

It was nearly ten o'clock in the morning, but Jake chuckled, knowing that protest would be worse than futile. If there was one thing Kathleen Tanner did well, it was feed people, and if you didn't eat willingly, she would hound you until you changed your mind. He watched her unhook a large pan from a rack above the stove before reaching into the refrigerator for eggs. Truth be told, his stomach had started growling the moment he'd turned into the driveway.

"Where's Ash?" he asked, turning to look out the picture window into the backyard. A tall row of sunflowers reached for the sky along one side of the garden shed, while a flock of birds harvested the seeds that had fallen to the ground.

"Your sister has a new 'beau,' as Grandma Ruby says," his mother announced, obviously pleased. "Do you remember Tommy Garland from a few farms over?"

Jake turned, his brows raised. He texted his sister a few times a week and saw her on campus periodically. She definitely hadn't mentioned a boyfriend.

"Of course I remember Tommy; he was the same year as me in school. Don't tell me she's taken up with him?" He scoffed. "Tommy was the biggest idiot I'd ever met until Conner James came along."

"Well," his mother said, smiling, "Tommy has turned into a respectable young man. He's finishing up business school in Hampton and works at an office down the street from where Ashlyn teaches at the daycare. They make a smart couple, if I do say so myself."

Jake made a face, trying not to picture his baby sister making a "smart couple" with anybody.

"Anyway, I expect they'll both come for dinner tonight," his mother finished as she flipped a few pieces of bacon. They sizzled loudly in the hot pan, and Jake did all he could not to drool.

"How did Brooklyn's campus visit go yesterday?" she asked, without looking up.

"Well, I had to peel her off some guy on a motorcycle, so I'd say she had fun."

His mother's hands stilled over the stovetop, and her eyes cut over to him suspiciously. Jake laughed.

"Mom, seriously, I took her to dinner at the Hawk's Nest and lost miserably at pool. I'll have to throw her in the pond the next time I see her, but she enjoyed herself," he said, leaning back in his chair. It was a bad habit he just couldn't seem to kick.

"Good. Christy and Rob will be glad you took care of her. That's what cousins are for, you know," his mother said, retrieving a plate and glass from the cabinet to her left. "So," she went on, leaving an obvious pause, "your girlfriend was okay with you taking another young woman to dinner?" She cut her eyes toward him again, a hopeful smile flickering on her face.

Jake knew exactly what she was fishing for.

"No, Mama. There's no girlfriend," he answered, leaning forward again so that all four legs of his chair were back on the floor.

His mother rapped the wooden handle of her spatula against the counter with an intensity that made him jump.

"Jacob Ryan!" she said, exasperated. "You are a kind, decent, handsome young man with excellent career prospects and an almost-finished college degree. You explain to me right this minute why you can't seem to find a nice young woman to bring home to your mama."

Jake started to laugh but stopped short when he found the business-end of his mother's cooking spoon pointed in his direction.

"This isn't a laughing matter, young man. I didn't raise you to be a perfect gentleman just to waste all those good manners on a hunting dog," she said, shaking the spoon as she spoke.

Jake worked hard to keep his amusement contained; he'd seen enough of that spoon as a child.

"I know you're still young, but one of these days, I'd like to have grandchildren," she went on. She turned back to the stove and loaded a plate with scrambled eggs and crisp bacon.

"Sounds like you'll have Ashlyn and Tommy for that," Jake quipped, letting his grin rip open. His mother pressed her lips together, and he knew she was trying just as hard not to laugh. Her eyes softened as she brought his plate to the table and set it down in front of him.

"Jacob, I just want you to find someone who makes you happy, who lights up your heart and makes you glad to come home at night. I want to know that someone will take care of you after I'm gone."

Her words made something tug inside Jake's chest the way only a mother's could.

"I'll find her, Mama. And I'll let you know the moment I do," he promised, trying not to think about Lexie.

His mother ran her thumb across his cheek the way she had when he was little.

"See that you do. Now," she said, changing the subject as she turned away, "take your food and go see your great-grandmother. She knows you're here, and your presence is expected in the throne room."

Jake chuckled at this mention of Grandma Ruby's add-on suite, where she'd been holding court since moving in with his parents almost five years before. Picking up his heaping breakfast plate, he leaned in to kiss his mother on the side of her head.

"I love you, Mama."

"I love you, too, pesky boy," she said, returning to her jam jars.

Jake smirked and stole a handful of freshly picked blackberries from a basket on the counter, quickly darting out of reach of the wooden spoon his mother still held in her hand. Heading down the hall, he popped the berries into his mouth one at a time, letting the late-summer sweetness burst against his tongue. The last closed door muffled the familiar whistle of the theme song from *The Andy Griffith Show* as Jake stopped to knock.

"Grandma Ruby, it's me!" he called loudly, opening the door a crack. Grandma Ruby was ninety-four years old and seemed to be very hard of hearing, except at times when it suited her to be otherwise.

"Come in, dear," came the reply, and Jake entered the softly lit room to find his great-grandmother's tiny frame half-absorbed by a reclining chair in front of the television. Despite her currently prone position, her suite sparkled in the morning light and smelled like a whole bottle of lemon furniture polish. Grandma Ruby, as usual, had been hard at work.

She smiled when he appeared, her wrinkled face taking on new light. Jake set his plate on her coffee table and stooped to kiss her forehead, soaking in the cool feel of her papery hand against the side of his face. Grandma Ruby had nearly thirty great-grandchildren from her four boys and their offspring, but she and Jake had always been particularly close. The first Tanner boy of his generation, he was named for her late husband and, truth be told, looked a lot like him, too.

"Let me see you," she said, taking his chin in her small hand and turning his face from side to side. "You've forgotten how to shave, I see."

Jake rubbed one hand over the week-old scruff that darkened his jaw.

"You'll look like a bear soon, if you aren't careful," Grandma Ruby said, though her eyes were playful.

Jake laughed, sinking onto the sofa while she used a remote control to bring her chair back to a sitting position.

"Tell me what you're up to these days," she ordered. "And don't leave anything out! You know how I love all the nitty, gritty details."

Jake grinned and reached for his breakfast plate. He settled it on his knees and began to eat, pausing between bites to tell Grandma Ruby about classes and his senior portfolio, about shooting from the sidelines at football games and coaching bumblebee soccer. He talked about his favorite new photographs and the magazine he hoped to work for after graduation, and the whole time, Grandma Ruby studied his face with the intense concentration of someone searching for the truth.

"And there's a girl," she said as he finished. It was not a question but a statement of fact.

Jake rolled his eyes toward the ceiling, setting his now-empty plate on the coffee table and flopping back against the couch.

"Why does everyone think there's a girl?"

"You've got that look," Grandma Ruby said confidently, her thin mouth curving into a smile. "I raised four boys; I know that look. Don't lie to your grandmama."

Jake crossed his legs at the ankle and frowned down at his boots for so long that Grandma Ruby reached for her walking stick and used it to rap him lightly across the shins.

"Ouch! Alright, yes, there's a girl," he admitted as he sat up.

"And?" Grandma Ruby prompted.

"And she's dating a guy who thinks he's entitled to whatever he wants, including her—some rich jerk who will inherit his daddy's multimillion-dollar company," he said bitterly, scuffing his boot across the floor. He may or may not have Googled Derricks Pharmaceuticals in a fit of insecurity, though it had done nothing but remind him he could work his whole life and never measure up.

Grandma Ruby pursed her lips. "I don't see the problem."

Jake stared at his great-grandmother, open-mouthed. "She's with somebody. He owns an entire company," he repeated uselessly. "What would she ever want with me?"

"So, you're telling me this girl of yours is so shallow that the size of a man's wallet is more important to her than his character?"

"Well, no, but . . ." Jake trailed off, surprised by the sharp question. Lexie wasn't that kind of girl; he was sure of it. "Okay, so what am I supposed to do?" he asked.

"That's easy, Jacob," Grandma Ruby replied with a soft smile. "You show up."

5

LEXIE SLOWLY MOVED to the shoulder, her car thumping wildly with every inch and her dashboard flashing like a carnival game. After turning on her hazard lights and cutting the engine, she eased her door open and circled around to the back of her Infiniti, finding exactly what the fancy sensors said she would.

A flat tire.

Fabulous.

Just another shiny sprinkle on a perfectly exhausting day. The phone call with her father wasn't even cold yet.

"It's time to get your act together, Alexis! How long will you insist on dragging this family down with you?"

Lexie sighed, trying to relieve the pressure in her chest. Nothing she did was ever good enough. Not the years of formal cotillion classes she'd endured with a smile, not her college scholarships or honors standing, not her coveted internship position.

She couldn't even manage to *drive* correctly.

A visible piece of metal poked out from the rubber, and she nudged it with the toe of her shoe, wincing as the hissing noise got louder. She glanced first one way and then the other down the empty back road, shading her eyes from the glare of the setting sun while she considered her options. Her first call was to INFINITI Roadside Assistance, which of course came standard with the car. After giving her location to the operator, there was a long pause that made her stomach feel heavier with each passing second.

"Ma'am, I'm so sorry, but our closest location to you is more than an hour away, and all the attendants are currently on other jobs," said a friendly woman's voice, and Lexie could hear the sympathy in her voice. "It could be two hours or more until they reach you. I'm happy to put you on the list if you'd like, but is there anyone closer who might be able to assist you? I'd hate for you to wait that long."

Lexie sighed and pinched the bridge of her nose, trying to ward off the headache she knew was coming.

"I'll find someone, thanks," she mumbled, hearing the apology that followed before the line disconnected. Scrolling through her frequent contacts, she hovered over Colt's name.

Colt was not a tire-changing kind of guy. He was a hire-a-tire-changing-guy kind of guy, and besides, he was in Dyer County for dinner with a new client. He would probably send one of his buddies to get her, and the last thing she wanted to do was sit on the side of a dark, lonely, two-lane waiting for Jason Arnolds.

She called Olivia instead and got her voicemail, remembering at the last minute that her roommate was in a late study session.

"Alright, Lexie," she said out loud, not caring if the cattle watching from beyond the fence thought she was nuts. "You're a smart, resourceful young woman. You just have to take the screws"—she furrowed her brow, not sure that was the right word—"off the old tire and put on the new one. How hard can it really be?"

She threw her shoulders back, walked purposefully to the trunk and then popped it open. Seconds later, she stood staring down at the clean, beige trunk liner, feeling stupid. Of course it was empty; she'd known that. It's not like she loaded her groceries around a spare tire, just waiting to be useful.

"Okay, think. If you were a spare tire, where would you be?" she asked herself, glancing back up at the cattle who stood chewing their cud without comment. At least she had company.

Gathering her long hair into one hand, she quickly bent to check beneath the car. Nothing looked promising. She stood and scanned the empty expanse of her trunk again before reaching inside and feeling along the closest edge.

"Yes!" she shouted as she found a small perforation where she could insert her fingers. She tugged the bottom of the trunk up, revealing a compartment that mercifully held a small tire. Then she shoved her hands underneath and managed to wrestle it out of the trunk and lean it against the fender.

"Look at that!" she told the cows. "I'm not totally useless after all!" Breathing hard after the unexpected effort, she planted her hands on her hips and tried to think of what she needed next—some sort of tool, obviously, though she wasn't sure what she was looking for. But it wouldn't have mattered anyway, since there was nothing else in the hidden compartment. She went to rummage in her glove box—nothing useful there either.

Lexie tipped her face toward the sky and reminded herself that the frustrated tears she could feel gathering wouldn't do anyone any good. She'd be even less competent if she started blubbering like a child. Muttering under her breath, she weighed her phone in her hand. There was an obvious option she hadn't tried. Colt wouldn't like it, but then again, Colt wasn't there.

She frowned at the ruined tire, which now resembled a deflated party balloon, and scrolled back through her contact list. He was probably busy, and even if he wasn't, he probably didn't want to talk to her—judging by the last week of radio silence.

Lexie took another deep breath and dialed anyway.

"Hey," Jake said, answering on the fourth ring. His voice was guarded, but he didn't sound angry, so that was something, at least.

Lexie leaned against the side of her car and closed her eyes, as if focusing on the dark insides of her eyelids would make the whole night easier.

"Hey. I know this is probably a huge imposition, and I'm really, really sorry to ask, but I was wondering if you . . . well . . ." She trailed off, hating how awkward it felt to ask him for help when a week ago she wouldn't have hesitated. But she couldn't just stand outside all night.

"Yeah?" he asked.

"How much do you know about changing a tire?" she blurted before she could overthink it anymore.

"A good bit," he answered.

She waited for him to go on, but he didn't, and her cheeks flushed in acknowledgement of the fact that *she* hadn't learned what he obviously considered common knowledge.

"If you've got a flat, I'm sure your boyfriend can change it for you."

Lexie felt another wave of tears surge to the surface and wished, not for the first time, that she could go back in time and be upfront with him from the beginning. She really had messed everything up.

"This isn't really his thing," she said, her voice small as she tried to keep it steady.

"But you think it's mine?" Jake answered, and Lexie hated the distance in his voice. She couldn't think of a single thing she wouldn't do to make it sound the way it always had before.

"I know you're upset with me, and I know I'm asking a lot, but I really just need help right now," she said. Then she clamped her lips shut and held her breath to keep a sob from escaping. The last thing she wanted to do was let him hear her cry.

There was a moment of silence, and she could imagine his exasperation on the other end of the line. Why would he take time out of his evening to come rescue a stupid girl who'd made him look ridiculous? Why had she even asked?

"Where are you?" His soft question broke the silence, and in it, she almost heard the old Jake.

"Out on Bishop Road, north of the big granary," she said, the words rushing out in relief as a tear finally broke free and made its way down her cheek. She swallowed hard and wiped it away, willing the rest to stay right where they were.

Jake gave a low whistle. "What are you doing all the way out there?" he asked.

"Just driving. Trying to clear my head, come up with new ideas, find inspiration," she said with a groan. "But I don't think that's what's stuck in my tire."

"Do you have a spare?"

"Yes, I found it."

"Okay. Do you have a tire iron?"

"A what?"

The question came automatically, and Lexie cringed, trying not to imagine what Jake was thinking. But if he laughed, she didn't hear it. Instead, she heard a door snap shut and a creak of metal that might have been his tailgate closing. Then, she heard the rumble of an engine.

"I'll be there soon, Lexie. It's fine."

"Okay. Thank you," she said, though her throat was still tight as they hung up. She closed her trunk and climbed up to sit on it, forcing herself to take one deep breath after another. But all she managed to do was listen to the voices that floated on the empty air—the ones reminding her how incapable she really was.

After what felt like an eternity, a pair of headlights appeared near the end of the lonely stretch of road. Lexie watched them grow closer with each passing moment and eventually turned to shield her eyes as Jake's truck came to a stop on the shoulder. The lights flicked off, and he jumped from the cab before pushing his door shut.

The guilty twist reappeared in Lexie's stomach as she watched him approach, his face just as shuttered as it had been all week. She thought about the disarming smile he'd given the girl at the Hawk's Nest and suddenly wished she knew how to earn one for herself. It used to be so easy; she hadn't even had to work for it. But now, everything had changed.

"Thanks for coming," she said, wringing her hands in her lap.

Jake stopped a few feet away, his hands in his pockets, his gaze steady on hers.

"No problem," he said. "It's not like I'd just leave you out here."

He wasn't cold, exactly, but he definitely wasn't the Jake she missed so much. The thought that she might never see that side of him again made her eyes burn, and she looked away before he could see her fresh layer of tears. She gestured vaguely to her left, where the evidence of her efforts lay on the ground.

"I found the tire, and I thought I could figure it out. I know it can't be that hard, but I just don't have the tools to do it." She could feel herself babbling. Just the fact that he was *there*, when he could have been anywhere else, made it hard to breathe again.

Jake must have seen the pain on her face because his expression changed, melting from cautious to concerned in a matter of seconds.

"Hey," he said softly, coming closer. "Are you okay?"

Lexie shook her head hard as a single tear ran down her cheek. She dashed it away with the back of her hand.

"I'm fine, it's fine. It's just a tire," she said, though her voice wavered. She sucked in a breath and held it, trying to force the flood back behind its containment wall before she lost control completely. A sob still jumped out before she could swallow it.

"Lex?" he said, reaching out to touch her arm.

That simple gesture tipped the scales, and Lexie released a shuddering breath as the dam broke.

"Hey, come here," he said, tugging her off the back of her car. As soon as her feet hit the ground, he pulled her into his arms, wrapping her tight and anchoring her against his chest.

Lexie buried her face in his shoulder, not wanting him to see her fall apart even though it was inevitable. Jake's thumb swept across the base of her neck in a soothing motion that only made her cry harder. Her father would have told her to pull herself together, and Colt would have said she was embarrassing him. But Jake simply held her while her gasping sobs ran their course, letting her tears soak through the cotton of his shirt until it stuck to his skin.

Her body drank in the pressure of his arms, drawing comfort from his presence. Everything about him was solid, from the shoulder she cried on to the way he took her weight when she could barely stand. Finally, her heart began to slow, and she matched her breathing to the steady rise and fall of his chest beneath her hands. She quieted enough to notice the way the clean, crisp scent of soap and detergent mixed with something that was uniquely Jake, though she couldn't identify any specific elements within it. He smelled . . . *safe.*

That was the only word that came to mind as Lexie breathed him in, feeling herself relax in a way she hadn't in a long time.

"Better?" he asked at last, and Lexie felt the word rumble through him as he spoke.

She made an affirmative sort of noise but didn't move, letting herself revel in the way his hand had drifted into the hair at the nape of her neck. He was warm in the chilling evening air, and she wanted nothing more than to sink into him and tell him everything. It had been so long since someone had held her like this—like she was precious and protected. She hadn't realized how much she'd missed it.

The girl from the pool hall was lucky.

Lexie felt a sharp stab of guilt at the base of her heart. That girl was probably waiting for Jake to get back, and here Lexie was, smearing makeup all over him. He'd probably even smell like her perfume when he got home. She wiped her fingers beneath her eyes, knowing she probably had mascara everywhere, and took a step back. Jake's hold broke reluctantly, like he wasn't quite ready to let her go, and when she looked up, the depth of emotion on his face took her by surprise. There was a single frozen second where they stood there, neither one daring to breathe. But then he blinked, and the moment shattered.

"I'm sorry," she said with an embarrassed laugh. "I'm such a mess."

He shook his head, his eyes never leaving hers. "Don't be sorry, Lexie."

His voice was rougher than usual, and his hands balled into fists at his sides, as if he were fighting to control them. He continued to stare for a moment, his jaw clenched tight, and Lexie's chest contracted again—this time for an entirely different reason. She opened her mouth, not quite sure what she planned to say, but Jake turned toward his truck before whatever it was could come out.

He rummaged around in the passenger's side of the cab before flipping on his headlights and returning with several tools she only vaguely recognized.

"So, this is an easy swap, just on and off," he explained, suddenly all business. Just moments ago, he'd done nothing but stare; now, he didn't seem able to meet her eyes.

Lexie nodded mutely, still steadying herself as he knelt in the dust beside her fender. She felt like if she took a single step, she was going to throw herself at his feet and do something mortifying, like beg him to hold her again.

As if she hadn't already embarrassed herself enough.

"You're lucky you didn't lose control of the car," he said, fitting a tool onto the bolts holding the old tire. He leaned his weight against what Lexie guessed was a tire iron and forced it to turn. Glancing up, he caught her watching, and she saw his throat work as he swallowed hard.

"Nobody ever taught you to do this?" he asked.

Lexie felt heat in her cheeks again as she shook her head, and Jake gave a decisive nod.

"Alright then. Come here."

Lexie was caught off guard by this unexpected turn of events, but she did as she was told, closing the gap between them and lowering herself to the ground at his side. She kept her attention firmly on the tool he put into her hands, trying to ignore how close he actually was.

"This is a tire iron," he said, and she caught a trace of humor in his tone. Obviously, he was starting at the *very* beginning. "You have to loosen the lug nuts before you raise the car so the tire has resistance against the ground," he explained. "You move in a star pattern to keep everything balanced. I did this one, so you'll start here," he said, pointing.

Lexie put the tire iron where he indicated and pushed. When it didn't move, she rose up on her knees for better leverage, but the lug nut still wouldn't budge. He'd made it look so easy.

"You'll need to put your full weight into it. You're so tiny," he said, and she paused. "Tiny, but mighty," he amended quickly, and this time, he definitely sounded amused.

"I don't think I can do this," Lexie said as she tried again, her arms shaking with the effort.

"Here, let me help."

Jake rose to his knees and placed his hands carefully beside hers, though he made sure not to touch her. This time, the nut moved easily, though Lexie knew without a doubt it wasn't her doing.

"You loosened it," he said.

Lexie turned her head and caught him smiling—the same

way he always had before—and it made her heart stutter. If she'd had any more tears, they would have flowed out in relief.

Maybe she and Jake would be okay after all.

He helped her with one nut after another, and Lexie stopped trying to avoid bumping into him as they worked side by side. Nothing else mattered right then. It was just her and Jake and that busted tire—them against the world. For once, she wasn't worried about how she looked or how she carried herself; she wasn't worried about impressing anyone or living up to someone else's expectations; she wasn't worried about not being enough. She just *was*.

It was a feeling she never had with Colt.

Jake talked her through positioning the jack beneath her car and cranking it, and the Infiniti rose slowly off the ground with jerky movements. After a while, Lexie realized he'd never once said she should have already known how to do this or that she was lacking in any way. He simply gave her the skills she didn't have, without question or accusation, and that made her feel like she could conquer anything.

With the lug nuts gone and the tire off the ground, Lexie reached to remove the old wheel. Jake's hands brushed over hers as he did the same.

"Maybe let me get this," he said. "They can be pretty heavy."

"I can do it," she insisted, and Jake looked at her with something that was almost admiration.

"Alright, Wonder Woman. You can do it," he said, moving back—though Lexie noticed he didn't go very far.

She yanked on the tire and immediately pitched forward when it plummeted to the ground. Jake's hands darted out and grabbed her shoulders, keeping her from smacking her forehead on the fender.

"See? I told you I could do it," she said, panting as she sat back on her heels.

Jake was grinning from ear to ear.

"I never doubted you," he answered. "Although, I do think gravity helped a little."

Lexie smacked his shoulder with the back of her hand, forgetting to second-guess herself. This was the Jake she'd wanted.

"I've missed you," she said, the words slipping out before she could censor them. Jake stilled, his expression frozen, and Lexie cleared her throat. "I've missed *this*," she clarified as she gestured between them. "I hated this last week."

A muscle in Jake's jaw twitched, and he swallowed hard. "Yeah. I hated it, too," he admitted.

"I'm sorry," Lexie went on, casting her eyes toward the ground. "I should have told you. I just . . . didn't know how."

Jake sighed and rubbed one hand across the back of his neck. He obviously knew what she meant.

"It's okay, Lex. We're good."

"Yeah?" she asked, more hopeful than she should have been.

"Yeah," he confirmed, bumping his shoulder against hers.

"Thank you for coming out here," she said again, picking up a few lug nuts and rolling them in her palm while he reached for the spare tire. There was a long silence as she debated whether or not to ask the question that had imprinted itself in her mind, but friends talked about this kind of thing, didn't they? And that's what she and Jake were—friends.

"Did your date from Friday go well?" she finally asked, trying to calm the jitters in her belly. It didn't matter what he said. Not really.

A deep crease formed on Jake's brow as he stopped. He seemed to be studying the side of her car as if it might answer his next question.

"My . . . what?"

"The girl from the pool hall? She's pretty."

He blinked several times, as if the words weren't registering.

"Last Friday? I was there with friends. You were with somebody? Sorry, I just assumed . . ." Lexie trailed off, unsure why he didn't understand. Maybe she'd been wrong about him after all. Maybe he went out with so many girls that he didn't remember them all.

The thought made her stomach clench.

"Last Friday . . ." Jake seemed to be thinking hard, and then his face smoothed out. The corners of his mouth flickered, like he was fighting a smile. "Oh, you mean Brooklyn," he supplied. His attention seemed to shift back to positioning the new tire.

Lexie tried to ignore the way his fingers brushed across her palm when he retrieved the lug nuts, leaving licks of fire in their wake.

"Brooklyn," she repeated, testing the word. "You looked comfortable together."

Jake glanced over, and their eyes met for a fleeting moment.

"We should be. I've known her since I was four."

Lexie's eyes widened, a little puff of air escaping her lips. "Four? Wow. You definitely have some history then, huh?"

A knowing smile settled on Jake's face as he turned the handle on the jack and lowered her car back to the asphalt.

"You could say that, yeah. Here, all I'm doing is the same steps in reverse," he said, changing the topic abruptly. But Lexie didn't want to learn any more about changing a tire. She wanted to know about Brooklyn. The girl Jake had known all his life. The girl who smiled and teased and challenged him. The girl who—

"Lex?"

Jake's voice brought her mental avalanche to a sudden stop.

"Yeah?"

"Brooklyn is my cousin."

Now it was her turn to struggle.

"Your cousin?"

"Yes, one of nine, remember?" Jake smirked as if he knew exactly what she'd been thinking. "She was here for a campus tour. She'll be a freshman next year."

"Oh." Lexie took a long breath, one that suddenly felt easier, and tried not to show how relieved she was. After all, there was no reason she should care one way or the other.

But you do, a small voice sing-songed, and she quickly silenced it.

Jake used the tire iron to tighten the lug nuts, saying nothing as she watched. After a few minutes, he cleared his throat.

"So, how long have you been with Colt?" His voice was casual, but Lexie saw his shoulders tense as he asked.

She blew out a breath.

"I'm sorry about the way he treated you," she said, avoiding the question. "Sometimes he can . . . Well, you saw how he was. He shouldn't have been a jerk."

Jake shrugged as he began gathering his tools into a pile. Then he leaned back on his heels and dusted his hands on his jeans.

"As long as he isn't a jerk to you. That's what matters," he said, rising to his feet. He reached a hand down to help her up, and she took it, trying not to watch the way the muscles in his forearms bunched as he pulled her to her feet. It was fully dark now, and his face was unreadable in the harsh glare of his truck's headlights.

"I'll follow you home to make sure the spare doesn't burst, but don't get above forty-five miles an hour," he warned, walking over to open her door. "And I can go with you to get a new tire tomorrow, if you want."

Lexie wiped her hands on her jeans, then nodded as she slid behind the wheel, choosing not to analyze the lump that had formed in her throat. Jake thumped his fist on the roof of her car and started to turn away, but then stopped mid-step.

"And Lex?" he added.

She stopped breathing as she looked up at him and waited for his next words.

"You can always call me. For anything."

Lexie watched him where he stood motionless, his face half in shadow, and nodded again, unable to answer. Her eyes jumped to the rearview mirror as he made his way back to his truck, and she tracked him while he climbed inside. When his lights flashed, she pulled slowly onto the roadway and headed toward her apartment.

And when her cell phone vibrated in the center console—Colt's name lighting up the screen—for the first time ever, she ignored it.

JUST SHOW UP.

That was Grandma Ruby's big advice.

Show up. Be consistent. Be the better man.

Jake couldn't see his knuckles, but he knew they were white against the steering wheel as he followed Lexie's car down the dark road. Of all the things that might have happened, he'd never expected to catch her as she'd fallen to pieces like the world was ending.

But he'd do it again in a heartbeat.

He was glad he hadn't asked what was wrong. If she'd said it was Colt, he'd probably have done something he'd regret later.

Jake wasn't a hot-tempered person. It took a lot to get him worked up, and yet somehow, just thinking about the way Colt had taken Lexie from the office—from her *job*, like he had the right to dictate her life—made Jake want to put a hole in a brick wall. Not to mention the fact that *she'd let it happen*. That part really got under his skin. How could she not see she deserved so much better? He shoved his hand back through his hair, wondering what Lexie was thinking in the vehicle in front of him. It had taken every ounce of willpower he'd possessed not to pull her forward and kiss her until she couldn't remember her own name, much less why she'd been so upset in the first place.

And there was a tiny piece of him that thought, just for a second, that maybe she'd wanted him to.

He cranked up the radio, unwilling to let himself get sucked back into that daydream. She was someone else's girlfriend, and he did have boundaries. Even if he sometimes wished he didn't.

But one thing was now painfully clear, regardless.

He was in love with her. Not just intrigued by or interested in or curious about her, but totally, absolutely, irrefutably in love with her. The nameless feeling he'd been carrying for years was now a concrete certainty that had taken up residence in his chest and refused to leave.

Of course, he couldn't tell her that, not while she was with Colt. So, he'd just have to say it some other way and hope she was listening.

6

"WHY ARE YOU *looking at me like that?*" *Lexie's shoulders bumped the door of the old darkroom as he came closer.*

His eyes darkened to the color of Hershey's syrup as his hands hit the wood on either side of her head, caging her in. He didn't say anything, but the look on his face spoke volumes.

"Jake, why are you looking at me like that?" Lexie repeated, feeling oddly breathless. Somehow, he'd taken all the oxygen from her personal space when he'd stepped into it.

His laughter was soft in her ears as he settled one forearm against the door. His other hand dropped to her waist, and his fingers tightened against the curve above her jeans.

"That depends. What do I look like?"

The low timber of his voice made Lexie shudder, but in a good way, and her hands found their way to the front of his T-shirt, tugging him closer.

"Like I'm a snack, and you missed breakfast."

A rumbling sound rolled out of him as he dipped his head and brushed his mouth up the side of her neck.

Lexie felt the shiver all the way to her toes.
"Well, I am pretty hungry."

Lexie woke with a start, sucking cool air deep into her lungs, unsure what had disturbed her. Her sleep-fogged brain gradually registered the sound of her cell phone, and she rolled toward it and managed to answer before the call went to voicemail.

"Hello?" she said, pushing her hand across her forehead and into her hair. Her heart was still racing, and she sounded like she'd just run an eight-minute mile.

"Hey, babe! This is your wake-up call!" Colt's voice filled her ears, even as Jake's face still hovered behind her eyelids.

Lexie groaned and peeked at her alarm clock. "Colt, it's barely six thirty."

"I know, sweetheart, but we need to leave by nine if we're going to make it to my parents' house on time. Last time we were almost late."

Lexie scrubbed her palm over her closed eyes. It was the first Sunday of the month. She'd almost forgotten. Her mind was still leaning against a rough wooden door with Jake's breath against her skin.

Colt said something else, but it got lost in the fog of her daydream.

"I said, be sure to wear the earrings I got you for your birthday," he repeated, an edge to his voice now, and Lexie jumped, remembering that he was still on the phone.

A wave of guilt crashed over her. Here she was, dreaming about another guy while Colt was trying to be considerate. She really didn't need two and a half hours to get ready . . . but that was neither here nor there.

"Of course," she said automatically.

"And Mother thought that dark dress you wore last month was depressing."

"She what?" Lexie asked, suddenly feeling slightly more awake. Mrs. Derricks had complimented her outfit! Several times, actually. Which, now that Lexie thought about it, should probably have been a sign.

"She said it looked like you were dressed for a funeral."

Lexie closed her eyes and stifled a yawn.

"Are you even listening?" Colt asked, his irritation coming through loud and clear. "You seem very distracted."

"Yes, I'm sorry. It's just very, very early," Lexie said, sneaking another peek at the clock and hoping it had changed.

"Well, forgive me for disturbing you. I didn't want to wait for you to finish curling your hair or whatever else you women have to do every time you leave the house," he snapped, and Lexie flinched. How had she already made him angry? She'd only been awake for five minutes.

"I'll be ready. Don't worry."

"Good. I'll be there at nine," he said sharply, and then he was gone.

Lexie dropped the phone onto her pillow without looking at it and rolled over, closing her eyes.

Jake's heart pounded against her chest, his body heat making hers rise as his hand slid up her rib cage.

"Now, where were we?" he asked.

Ugh. Lexie's eyes flew open again. Where *were* they?

Nowhere. That was where they were.

Jake was kind and gentle and considerate. He left comic strip clippings and Post-it note doodles on her desk every day. He sometimes randomly disappeared from work and returned with strawberry smoothies from her favorite cafe. He was a good friend, and nothing else. That ship had sailed when she'd embarrassed him; he wasn't likely to come back begging for another round.

She had Colt, and he was . . . well . . . Colt. He was brash and arrogant, confident and cocky. He made decisions for her and didn't ask for her opinions. But he took care of her. And he loved her.

Didn't he?

That was the million-dollar question.

Lexie stared at the textured ceiling above her bed, the details barely visible in the early morning light.

Colt *said* he loved her. She'd waited her entire life to hear those words, and even though love didn't feel the way she'd always hoped it would, it wasn't something she could just walk away from. Plus, her father had made it very clear that Colt was the only good choice she'd ever made, and who was she to argue? She didn't have any real evidence to the contrary.

Knowing she'd never get back to sleep, Lexie slung her legs over the edge of the bed with a groan. She moved quietly down the hall to the bathroom and filled the tub with steaming water, thinking she might as well enjoy herself since she had so much time. She made a mental note to thank Colt for that, managing not to roll her eyes as she did.

"DO YOU REALLY have to go all the way to Hampton just for breakfast?" Olivia asked, sitting on the edge of Lexie's bed almost two hours later.

Lexie unwound a long, golden ringlet from her curling iron and arranged it over her shoulder, giving herself a critical look in her dresser mirror.

"It's tradition. The first Sunday of every month is brunch at Penbrooke," she said, referring to the Derricks' large home about an hour from Cypress Valley. It not only had a name but also a set of tennis courts, a driving range and an infinity pool complete with a lazy river. It was basically a resort destination.

"You'd think they'd give you a break since you're not actually family. It's just pancakes," Olivia replied unhelpfully.

Actually, it was a four-course social experience with everyone who was anyone within Derricks Pharmaceuticals, including the entire executive team and their families. Lexie's presence was expected by default. The heir to the throne must have his princess, after all.

"You know how they feel about appearances" was all she offered Olivia, keeping the finer details to herself.

She knew exactly how it would go.

She and Colt would climb out of the car in his parents' driveway, and Colt would appear at her side like the attentive, adoring partner he was meant to be. He would put on his most charming smile and look at her warmly, maybe even leaning down for a kiss if he thought anyone might be watching from the front windows. She'd look up into those crystal blue eyes, and her heart would remember a day when she'd thought this entrance came from a Hollywood movie rather than a well-choreographed sleight-of-hand show.

And then they'd go into the lion's den, where glittering women using pretty words would pick her apart and show her every flaw she'd ever tried to hide, all while smiling graciously and asking if she'd like more champagne.

Lexie yanked the plug for the curling iron out of the wall, grateful for something to do with her hands.

"It's only a few hours. I'll be back soon, and then we can go out with Kate and Robin," she said, meeting Olivia's eyes in the mirror as she put on the extravagant earrings Colt had given her months ago. The heavy pear-shaped diamonds swung in their delicate pendants with every movement, already threatening to give Lexie a headache. She popped open a second jewelry case and removed a glittering tennis bracelet from its velvet resting place. The stones sparkled, even in the artificial indoor light, but as she pulled it out, her eyes jumped from the expensive gemstones to a small brown oval resting nearby. She picked it up, turning it between her fingers.

The penny had been flattened in one of those souvenir machines at the children's museum in nearby Willow Creek. Lexie rubbed her thumb over the small princess now stamped into the copper where President Lincoln had been. She could still feel the brush of Jake's hand as he'd slipped it into her palm during a staff meeting—like a secret only they would share. She started to set it back down, but as an afterthought, tucked it into her pocket instead.

"Hey, would you fasten this?" she asked, turning to Olivia and extending her wrist with the dangling diamond bracelet. Olivia stood with one eyebrow cocked, her gaze darting up from Lexie's pocket.

"What's with the penny?"

"What?"

"The penny. The one you just caressed with your eyes and put in the pocket of a designer dress," Olivia prompted, fastening the bracelet as requested.

Lexie fought back the blush that crept into her cheeks.

"It's just a penny. For good luck," she hedged, but Olivia only smirked.

"This lucky penny wouldn't happen to be part of your new collection, would it? Like the doodles taped to your mirror and all the comic strips on the fridge?"

Lexie rolled her eyes with effort, then slipped her feet into a pair of strappy silver sandals and fastened the tiny buckle around each ankle.

"I don't know what you're talking about."

"Oh, you don't? Well, I guess we can get rid of these, then," Olivia declared, reaching over to her friend's bedside table and grabbing three four-leaf clovers, each carefully dried and pressed.

Lexie felt the blood drain from her face. "No!" she shouted.

Olivia paused with the treasures suspended over the trash can and eyed her friend in triumph.

"They're from Jake, aren't they? All these things are from him?" she asked, laying the fragile plants carefully where she'd found them. She picked up a small plush frog wearing a tiny Cardinals baseball cap—the kind of toy that might have come from an arcade game. She squeezed it, and it croaked.

Lexie, on the other hand, didn't answer.

"Come on, Lex. Colt gives you expensive jewelry that you wear once a month, but these things . . . these are important to you," Olivia said as she sank back down onto Lexie's bed with a softer look on her face. "Why can't you come out and admit it? You like him. You really, really like him."

"Who?" Lexie asked, adding a spritz of perfume to the insides of her wrists.

"Jake!" Olivia all but screamed. "Don't play dumb with me. Why are you still going to family brunch with Colt when you'd rather be here with someone else? Why waste your time?"

"It's complicated," Lexie said.

"No, it's scary," Olivia corrected, crossing her arms stubbornly over her chest. "I know you, Lex. I know you don't like to make waves. But I also know you have the good sense to see that something's wrong with this picture."

Lexie ignored her and twisted around to see her back in the mirror.

"Colt will be here soon. Check me over and make sure I don't have any snags," she instructed, turning in a slow circle so Olivia could make a final inspection. Swirls of tiny silver sequins spread across the front of her pink cocktail dress, making Lexie feel a bit like a disco ball as she twirled.

"You're avoiding the issue," Olivia observed.

"How perceptive of you," Lexie said, her voice flat as she picked up her purse and made her way to the living room.

A single glance at the hallway clock showed she was right on time and, true to form, so was Colt. She could hear his heavy footsteps on the landing as she reached the door, and she opened it before he could knock. He looked impeccable, his tall, broad frame dressed in a dark sport coat and matching pants. The indigo in his shirt brought out the blue of his eyes, and Lexie couldn't help but remember how handsome she'd thought he was on the night they'd met.

Fresh out of her first year of college, the attention of the most charming man in the bar had turned her head, and she'd relished the jealous whispers of other women as Colt had claimed every dance, ignoring his friends and making her feel like the luckiest girl in the room. After that, he'd started calling, sending flowers and pretty gifts to her apartment, and showing up to spirit her away to expensive restaurants in Memphis and swanky hotels in St. Louis. Only a year out of college himself, he'd already had the air of a successful young businessman. It had all felt too good to be true. Why would a guy like him think she was special? No one else ever had.

It wasn't until later that he'd started criticizing her appearance, bossing her around and finding ways to make her feel small. But by then, she'd been in too deep to turn around.

"Take what you can get, my dear. Men are not generous with their hearts."

She could still hear her mother's voice as she said those words, though it had been nearly seven years since they'd been spoken aloud. Lexie had seen the truth of them play out in her parents' marriage until the day it ended, and she'd yet to find a relationship of her own that could prove her mother wrong.

She blinked, and the memory of Colt the night they'd met gave way to the man now standing in front of her, whose eyes darted over her body before he'd even said hello. Lexie felt herself brace for impact.

"You look perfect," he said, and the genuine tone of his voice nearly knocked her over. She sighed in relief.

"Thank you," she said. She could feel his praise in every fiber of her being, and she did another little twirl, relishing his attention.

"I mean it, babe! This color really complements the diamonds."

Lexie's steps faltered slightly. Had he just complimented her or the jewelry?

"All that extra time I gave you really made a difference, huh?" he said, clearly pleased with himself.

Lexie's expression hardened until it felt like she was wearing a mask. She glanced back into the living room and saw Olivia sitting silently on the couch, pretending not to pay attention, but Lexie knew better. She caught the twist of her friend's mouth that clearly meant she had something to say but was holding it back, and it made Lexie sad. Olivia was smart-mouthed and fearless. When had she started hiding what she thought?

Colt reached past Lexie and grabbed the door handle with a cursory wave of acknowledgement to her best friend.

Olivia did not return it.

"We'd better get going. Simon Anderson is going to be there today, and I'd like to catch him up on the latest trends we're seeing with the new respiratory inhaler," Colt said, taking Lexie's hand. He obviously didn't notice she wasn't paying attention. He led her down the stairs to the parking lot, and she caught sight of her reflection in the fresh layer of wax on his BMW. Her eyeliner made a perfect wing, her flyaways were all tamed and she looked like she could grace the cover of a glossy magazine.

"Take what you can get, my dear."

Ugh.

She should have gone back to sleep.

"ALEXIS, DEAR, DO we need to have Maria sew your pockets closed?" Harriet Derricks asked, her tone playful but her eyes sharp. She glanced pointedly to where Lexie's hand had disappeared for the umpteenth time.

"I'm sorry, Mrs. Derricks," Lexie said, reluctantly pulling her fingers away from the flattened penny and leaving it behind.

"Young people are so fidgety these days," Colt's mother said. She laughed in a way that invited the women nearby to join her, and several of them did.

Lexie stood as still as she could on aching feet, keeping her hands folded primly in front of her and doing her best to pay attention. But as Mrs. Derricks went on and on about yet another charity art auction, her words began to sound like bees buzzing around Lexie's ears. She snapped back to attention when she heard her name again.

"So, Alexis, are you excited about graduating in the spring?"

One of the wives, whose name Lexie couldn't remember, looked at her expectantly.

"It's terrifying, to be honest," she answered. "The idea of finding a real job next summer is a bit daunting."

Colt's mother laughed, a false, tinkling sound that grated on Lexie's skin.

"Oh, dear girl, don't be coy. We all know how these things work," Mrs. Derricks said, gesturing with her wine glass. "I mean, look around. You can't honestly believe you're going to need a job, do you? Colton is more than able to support you in whatever style you'd like." She looked at the other wives with a knowing expression. "Frankly, I'm surprised you're even going to finish. After all, it's the men who need the diploma; all you need is the ring."

Lexie forced a tight smile as the women around her twittered like birds, all jostling to agree at once. The idea of becoming Colt's wife wasn't new, though it seemed the only people who hadn't discussed it at length were Lexie and Colt themselves. She looked across the mansion's immaculate courtyard to where he stood talking with a group of older men. He was far and away the most charismatic young man present, and the gentlemen around him visibly hung on his every word. A cluster of giggling girls in pastel dresses talked behind their hands, sneaking not-so-covert glances in his direction as they did.

Lexie should have been thrilled that *this man* was hers, but instead, she just felt tired—tired of pretending, tired of never quite being enough, tired of hoping for a change that never came. She smoothed her hands over her dress again, feeling the outer ridge of the penny beneath the shimmering material.

"Take what you can get, my dear."

What she was getting was a handsome husband and a gorgeous future.

So why did that not feel like enough?

LEXIE WATCHED WEST Tennessee life flash by the windows as she and Colt headed north to Cypress Valley several hours later. The crisp, blue October sky showcased wispy clouds, like cotton stretched between a child's fingers. Small-town main streets flew banners advertising festivals and farmers' markets, and endless acres of soybean fields were dotted with barns of every shape and size.

"Dad says if I keep up my current sales trend, I'll be a shoo-in for the Young Salesman's Award this coming spring. Just think, second year in a row!" Colt crowed, smoothing his hand over the lapels of his coat.

Lexie absently thought he looked a lot like a bird preening its feathers.

"That's wonderful, sweetheart," she said, more because she knew it was expected than anything else. She wasn't completely certain what his job as a pharmaceutical sales rep entailed, but to hear him talk, you'd think he personally invented the lifesaving drugs he sold.

Colt kept talking, but Lexie's mind was still on the party they'd just left and the endless line of similar events that waited in her future. Did she really want to spend the rest of her life as an accessory to his success, pretending to listen and trying to forget she'd ever had dreams of her own? Her mother had done that tirelessly for years, and look where she was now—in an early grave at a fancy cemetery that no one ever visited.

A soft curse from Colt caught Lexie's attention, and she turned to him.

"I've got to stop for gas," he muttered, suddenly changing lanes. He made a sharp turn into a station at the southern edge of Cypress Valley, and Lexie's clutch slipped off her lap and clattered into the space beside the center console. Colt pulled into the closest gas pump before shutting off the engine. "I'll be right back," he said, and he unfastened his seat belt and climbed from the car.

Lexie twisted sideways, peering into the thin crevice where her purse had fallen. Catching a glint of the case's metallic exterior, she wedged her hand into the gap, but instead of her cold, hard wallet, the tips of her fingers brushed something soft. She automatically grabbed whatever it was and pulled it out, surprised when a wad of lacy black fabric pooled in her hand.

Unfolding it, she found an expensive pair of women's underwear.

Lexie's breath caught in her chest, and her surroundings seemed to fade until all she could see was the material in her hand. Her breathing slowed until it was just white noise in her own ears, as if all other sounds had ceased.

There was underwear shoved under the seat of Colt's car.

Sexy, silky women's underwear.

There had to be an explanation.

Maybe he'd bought them for her and they'd fallen out of his shopping bag. Maybe he'd driven a friend home from the airport and her carry-on had come open. Maybe—

The gas pump shut off with a dull thunk, jolting Lexie into action, and she shoved the panties back where she'd found them. She snatched her clutch from the crevice in the same movement and straightened just as Colt's door opened.

He slid behind the wheel and ran one hand through his hair.

"I can't believe we still have to pump our own gas. What do the attendants do all day?" he complained, oblivious to the way Lexie kept her eyes trained straight ahead, unable to look at him.

There wasn't enough air in the car. Lexie took one shallow breath after another, counting slowly to one hundred in her mind. She didn't know if she was angry or in shock or embarrassed—or maybe all three at once—but she was afraid that if she opened her mouth, she would scream.

She was becoming her mother after all.

7

THE TEXT MESSAGE came as Lexie crossed the quad alone, stopping her in her tracks. She looked wildly in all directions, but Jake was nowhere to be seen.

Lexie smiled for the first time in two days and resumed her path toward the bell tower. It was her favorite outdoor study spot, and she sank onto one of the wrought iron benches at its base before scanning the sidewalks in all directions. Jake was always behind a camera, and with a telephoto lens to his eye, he could be almost anywhere.

JAKE: Because you are.

She laughed weakly. This almost felt like flirting.

But, of course, it wasn't. Because they didn't do that anymore.

Lexie rolled her neck, trying to relieve the tension in her muscles. Jake was right; she *was* tired. Every time she closed her eyes, she saw Colt with another beautiful woman—dancing, kissing, touching. The highlight reel was endless. She dreamed about life as Mrs. Colton Derricks, finding unfamiliar lingerie under the bed and between the sofa cushions, and she woke drenched in sweat and jittery with anxiety.

Her phone vibrated again.

JAKE: Look up.

She did, and at first she saw nothing. But then something high in the bell tower shifted, and she saw the long lens of a camera peek from an opening in the belfry.

Surely not . . .

"Jake?" she called, her voice the only one drifting through the quiet quad. She thought she heard a faraway chuckle, muffled by the building itself.

"Yes, ma'am?" he answered, and his head poked out several stories above her.

Lexie laughed in surprise.

"Hold on, I'll come and get you," he called, his hands cupped around his mouth. A few minutes later, a door at the base of the tower opened. Lexie had tried it a few times in the past, out of curiosity, but it had always been locked.

"How did you get in there?" she asked as Jake waved her over.

He grinned and gave a cheeky shrug.

"There are perks to being me," he said, his eyes twinkling, and Lexie just shook her head, trying to ignore the rolling sensation in her belly when he smiled. She looked past him to a narrow metal staircase that twisted around the inside of the building.

"Actually, this is a great place to get aerial photos and video footage, so I have special access," he explained, gesturing for her to start the climb.

Lexie gripped the slender railing tightly, feeling a rush of nerves as she tested her weight on the first step.

"It's solid, I promise. I've been up and down this thing a dozen times, and you probably weigh half what I do," he said from behind her.

The outer door clicked shut, and they were plunged into semidarkness, lit only by exposed bulbs that protruded from the brick wall every forty or fifty feet along the staircase. The spaces between were filled with shadows, and Lexie could almost imagine the stairs ascended into fathomless space.

"Trust me, Lex. The climb is worth it," Jake said, and his voice was both too loud and too soft in the small space.

Every hair on the back of her neck stood on end, and she willed herself not to turn around. She had a feeling that if she did, he'd be standing entirely too close. So, instead, she took a deep breath and started up into the gloom.

Jake's feet shuffled on the stairs behind her, every step making the metal staircase vibrate slightly, and while they didn't speak, Lexie was hyper-aware of his presence. They climbed for what felt like eons, and her knees screamed in protest. Finally, she reached the top of the stairwell. The bulb here had burned out, and she stood in the humid darkness, staring at what seemed to be a solid wall.

"The knob is down here somewhere," Jake said, reaching around her to run his hand along the wood. His chest brushed against her back as he searched, and Lexie could feel his breath skate across her shoulder. He kept his other hand on the railing, though if he'd lifted it, she would have been standing in his arms.

She heard his breath hitch and wondered if the same thought had occurred to him as well.

"Here!" he blurted at last, finding the knob and turning it sharply. He sounded almost relieved as the cooler outside air rushed in and Lexie moved forward, putting space between them.

She stepped into a circular room with open windows that looked out over the campus in all directions. Jake's gear—two camera bags and a tripod—was laid out on the floor.

"You carried all that up here by yourself?" she asked.

"Nah, I have a secret army of lawn gnomes that do all my heavy lifting."

If Lexie hadn't been trying to catch her breath, she would have laughed, but instead she leaned against the stone wall and looked out one of the large windows. The sill was at chest height, but the opening soared far above her head in a pointed arch. There was no glass, and Lexie fought the urge to lean over and look straight down.

"This is amazing," she breathed, gazing out over the green sea of tree branches below them. The bell tower was the highest point on campus, and she could see all the way across the long quad to the football stadium on the eastern edge. To the north and south were the angled roofs of academic buildings and dormitories, and to the west was an open expanse of field where the agricultural programs kept livestock. The green pasture was full of black dots that were probably cows, but from this distance, could be almost anything.

"I had to sign all kinds of liability waivers to be allowed up here, so don't get too close," Jake warned from across the room.

"Will you get in trouble for bringing me up?" she asked, looking over her shoulder.

Jake shrugged.

"Probably. So, just don't tell anyone, okay?" Then he laughed. "Actually, I think one of Andy's first instructions was 'no girls in the tower.' "

Lexie ran her hand along the rough stone windowsill.

"So, I'm the first girl who's been up here?"

"Well, I don't know about that for sure, but you're the only girl who's been up here with me," Jake said, and Lexie thought she saw a flush creep up his neck as he rearranged his equipment.

She wandered over to where he knelt and lowered herself down beside him. Sitting against the wall, she peered up to the ceiling of the belfry, which was strangely empty.

"Where are the bells?" she asked, cocking her head.

Jake settled himself at her side, leaving a purposeful gap between them, and looked up.

"Not sure. I know one of them broke a while ago, so they started using pre-recorded music instead."

"What a shame. I had this whole Quasimodo thing going on in my head."

Jake snorted. "You thought there was a hunchbacked guy jumping up and down up here every hour?"

A grin stretched across Lexie's face. It felt good.

"Not hunchbacked, necessarily. Could just be a crazy guy who likes bells."

"And what would he do up here all day?" Jake asked incredulously.

"I don't know. Maybe he takes pictures of people as they walk by," she said, glancing at him from the corner of her eye. "Because that's not creepy at all."

Jake laughed—just a quick exhale of breath—and shook his head sheepishly. "Alright, point taken," he said.

Lexie caught his eye, and they both chuckled. She leaned her head against the warm stone behind her and closed her eyes, soaking in the quiet sounds of life above the treetops. It felt like the most natural thing in the world to simply sit in silence with Jake as the afternoon rolled forward. Birds twittered in nests just outside the windows, and more than one flew into the empty space and perched high above, looking down on them with interest.

It was the first time in forty-eight hours that Lexie's brain was still.

"I heard a song on the radio this morning that made me think of you," she said finally, her eyes still closed.

"Yeah?"

She couldn't see Jake, but she could feel his full attention on the side of her face.

"Yeah. It was one of those country songs about childhood sweethearts. Something about a little boy chasing a girl around the playground, and then they grew up and got married and lived happily ever after." She sighed, hearing her own wistfulness. "You strike me as a third-grade-sweetheart kind of guy."

Jake gave a self-deprecating sort of laugh. "Not exactly," he said. "I still thought girls were icky in the third grade. Present company excluded, of course. I'm sure you were never icky."

"Oh, of course not," she said, turning to look at him. "I was delightful."

"I actually broke up with my first girlfriend on her parents' answering machine," he admitted, rubbing the back of his neck with a grimace. "I got myself all psyched up to call and tell her I didn't want to be her boyfriend anymore, and then when I got the machine, I panicked. I word-vomited my whole spiel after the beep and hung up. A few days later, her mom mentioned it to my mom, who mentioned it to my dad, who dragged me across town, walked me up to her front porch and rang the bell."

"He did not!" Lexie gasped, her eyes wide.

Jake smiled ruefully. "Yes, he did. He stood there until she came to the door, and then he went and sat in his truck while I prayed with all my might for the earth to swallow me whole. Later that night, he gave me a long lecture about how being a man means owning the things I've done, both good and bad, and taking responsibility for how my actions affect other people. It's not one I've forgotten."

"How old were you?"

"Fourteen."

Lexie felt her heart tighten, wishing every young man had learned the same lesson. Jake must have seen a change in her expression because his humor transformed into something else.

"What is it?" he asked, his voice soft.

Something about the tenderness in it made Lexie want to reach for his hand, which now rested on his knee, only inches away. Her fingers tingled with the desire to move, but she folded them into her lap, unwilling to give in. She stared silently out one of the huge windows, watching a hawk circle in an updraft. Jake didn't push her, but she could feel him waiting patiently at her side.

"Nobody taught my father that," she said at last. "I'm not sure he's ever made a mistake that he believes was actually his fault, including the night my mother died."

Jake drew in a sharp breath but said nothing, so she went on.

"He cheated on her for years, parading his mistresses in front of her like show ponies, one after the other. That night, I heard them arguing. She asked what she could do better, what he needed that she wasn't giving him. She begged him not to go back to his girls, but he left anyway. He brushed her aside like lint off his jacket, and he grabbed his keys and shut the door without even saying goodbye. She drank most of a bottle of tequila and then got in her car to go after him. I stood in front of the door and begged her not to leave. But she said, 'Lexie, a woman's got to fight for her man. One day you'll understand.' And then she left.

"I fell asleep on the couch waiting for her, and I answered the door when the policeman came. He wouldn't tell me the truth, because I was a minor, but I knew. I knew she wasn't coming back. Turns out they'd found her car halfway down an embankment, wrapped around a telephone pole. She was so drunk she probably didn't feel a thing."

Lexie felt Jake's hand slide over hers, his warm fingers curling around her palm as he balanced it on her knee. He had calluses across the pad of his hand, and they scraped against her skin in a way that made her whole arm tingle. She stared down at where his tanned skin contrasted sharply with hers and wondered why she felt more comfort in that small gesture than she did during entire evenings with Colt.

Jake didn't say anything, but she knew he was listening intently.

"My father had to go downtown and identify her body, and he played the shell-shocked husband the whole time," she went on. "I heard him telling people afterward that he had no idea why she would have been drinking or why she'd left the house. I'm sure he never once considered he might have been to blame."

Lexie wiped her free hand across her cheek, though the motion was unnecessary. Oddly enough, she could tell this story without breaking down. It only left her numb.

"She always said a woman has to fight for her man, but what I want is somebody who fights for *me*." Her voice finally wavered on the last word, and she scoffed. "Isn't that pathetic?"

Jake's hand tightened around hers without hesitation, and he cleared his throat. "No," he said. "You deserve to be the most important person in someone's life. You shouldn't settle for anything less."

Lexie huffed, pulling her hand away and picking instead at the fraying knee of her jeans. It was too much to be connected to him just then—too raw. She couldn't fathom being the most important person to anyone. She'd learned long ago not to aim that high.

"I think Colt might be cheating on me," she said without preamble, blurting it out before she could decide not to. The only answering sounds were the buzzing of bugs and the distant shouts of students passing far below. She chanced a glance at Jake and found him watching her closely, his brow pinched in the middle.

"You think, or you know?" he asked softly.

Lexie wrung her hands in her lap and rolled her lips together, willing herself to say what she knew in her heart was true.

"I know," she said, and the unexpected weight of disappointment settled on her chest. It wasn't really because Colt had been unfaithful, though that certainly hurt. It was because she had let herself end up in this place where she said she'd never go. She'd watched from the outside so many times, made so many naive judgments about the way her mother lived. Now, she was getting a taste of what it felt like on the other side. Walking away wasn't nearly as easy when it was your own life you were turning upside down.

"So, are you going to leave him?" Jake asked, his voice rough.

Lexie looked at the urgency in his eyes, something that bordered on desperation, and wondered why that question was so hard to answer.

His gaze clouded over as her silence stretched on. "Lexie?"

There was pain in his voice, like her next words meant everything.

"I don't know," she whispered.

Jake blinked several times, clearly processing. "You don't know?"

"I don't know! Maybe I'm overreacting."

"Overreacting?" Jake asked as he gestured emphatically with both hands. "He's been with another woman, and you think leaving him might be overreacting?" His eyes searched hers like he might find an explanation within them, like he might understand what she was thinking if he could only see it for himself.

"There is such a thing as forgiveness, you know," Lexie spat, the words coming hotter and harder than she'd intended because she'd heard them before. And she'd hated them then, too.

"Well, yeah, but does he deserve it? I've seen the way he looks past you when you talk, the way he acts like you're supposed to worship the ground he walks on. You deserve better than that!" Jake said, his volume rising.

"It's not that simple, okay?" she cried. She scrambled to her feet, and hot shame pricked at the corners of her eyes as she crossed to a far window and leaned her forearms on the sill. The warm stone beneath her arms grounded her when all she really wanted to do was float away.

After a beat, she heard Jake's footsteps crossing the hard floor. He stopped beside her in the narrow gap, his arm pressed against hers from shoulder to wrist as he leaned out the same window, taking in the same view.

"Tell me why not," he said, though it wasn't a demand. Instead, there was an unexpected gentleness to the words that somehow let her open the door she'd always kept closed.

"Because he's stayed," she said, staring resolutely over the treetops so she wouldn't have to see Jake's judgment. "Because he made room for me when nobody else ever has. Because he says he loves me, and I want to believe him. Because he might be the best I get."

There was a long silence during which only the birds spoke, and Lexie fought hard against the urge to look at Jake. She didn't want to see the pity she knew was written on his face. She didn't want to be a girl he felt sorry for.

After what seemed like hours, he shifted slightly, and Lexie felt his arm trade places with hers, his bicep filling the space beneath her shoulder and his hand trailing down to where hers dangled over the emptiness beyond the window. He linked their fingers together, as if he'd done it a thousand times, and the simple motion took Lexie's breath away. All she could do was stare down at the place where his warm palm touched hers, her chest too tight for words.

"Lexie," he said, his voice soft enough that she had to concentrate to hear him—not that he didn't have her full attention anyway. "You are so much more talented, more amazing, more incredible than you know. You deserve someone who notices when you change shampoo because your hair doesn't smell like strawberries anymore, who loves the way you bounce when you get excited and would do anything to make that happen. Someone who knows you play classical music when you're stressed and would keep your favorite tracks on his phone, just in case you ever need them. Someone who will fight for you every day for the rest of his life."

He lapsed into a silence so heavy that Lexie turned to look at him. She found his eyes studying her face, indecision painted on his features.

"Do you love him?" he asked finally, and Lexie felt her whole body lock up.

"I don't know," she said, wishing she had a better answer. "I don't think I know what love looks like."

Jake swallowed hard. "Maybe you're not looking in the right places," he said.

For just a moment, Lexie let herself get lost in his eyes the way she'd always known she could. He was hiding nothing from her. There were no pretenses, no qualifiers, no fences erected to keep her out, and something in the back of her mind recognized how precious that was.

Jake must have realized it too because he stepped back, disentangling their fingers in a way that left her oddly chilled. He held her gaze for another second, looking away as the speakers above their heads began to chime the hour. The pre-recorded music was deafening by proximity, and Lexie suddenly realized life was moving on without her far below.

"I'm late," she said, sure he couldn't hear, but she grabbed her bag and darted toward the stairwell all the same. Her first steps on the old staircase were hesitant as something inside her urged her to stay, but soon she was flying down as fast as her feet would carry her.

JAKE WATCHED THE staircase door shut behind Lexie as the sound of the bells faded, and he let his eyes drift closed. He felt raw, like every nerve had been torn from his body and put on display.

Stupid, stupid, stupid.

Why had he said all those things? Here he was, the guy who couldn't take no for an answer, who brought her sad little presents like a magpie and took advantage of her vulnerability to lay his heart at her feet.

What had he been thinking?

He turned and braced both hands on the windowsill, taking one shaky breath after another and trying not to dwell on how warm she'd felt nestled against him in that exact spot not two minutes before. It didn't matter that she'd fit perfectly. It didn't matter if some instinct said she was made for him. None of it mattered if she chose someone else, someone who wasn't nearly good enough for her.

Jake didn't feel good enough either, but at least he would *try*.

When his heart finally slowed to an acceptable pace, he knelt to pack his gear. He folded the tripod and secured the legs, counted his memory cards and tucked them away, replaced the lens caps and wiped down the camera body. But he was in no hurry to leave. The downstairs door had locked behind Lexie as she fled, and he was safe in his fortress of solitude. At least up here, high in the sky, he could avoid the inevitable repercussions for a while longer.

Killing time, he flipped the Canon on with his thumb, watching the screen turn white as it powered up. He scrolled through the most recent set of photos, and images from the quad below passed in quick succession as he looked for the shots he wanted.

At the end of the series, he found Lexie. He'd photographed her even before she'd realized he was watching. She looked anxious and withdrawn, like a turtle hiding inside its shell. The images were crystal clear, and the pain on her face made his heart ache all over again. *This* was what Colt did to her. This was what it looked like when an amazing woman felt worthless.

His stomach tightened, and his hands clenched reflexively. What Colt needed was a good beating. And maybe a few red-hot knitting needles stuck in memorable places.

Jake flipped through the images that followed, watching Lexie look at her phone and smile. *That* was because of him.

The very last picture, the one where she'd found him at last, showed her looking straight up into the camera, her face a mix of surprise and amusement. She'd been glad to see him. Maybe even excited. *He* had put that light in her eyes.

Jake studied the image for a long time, wondering if Lexie would ever look at him that way again.

8

"LEXIE, ARE YOU out there?"

"Yes, ma'am."

"Can you come here, please?"

Lexie pushed back from her desk and made her way toward her boss's office, stopping short in the doorway.

"Take a seat," Julie said, and Lexie sank slowly into one of the cushioned chairs on the nearside of the desk, trying to hide her nerves. Julie was an amazing boss, the kind interns everywhere hoped to have, but she was also an uncompromising editor with a vicious red pen. Lexie's work often looked like it had been bled upon by a small animal, a sight she had a hard time getting used to.

"I realized recently that you and I have never taken time to chat about your career goals," Julie explained before taking a sip from her cup of coffee. "What are your plans after graduation?"

Lexie took a slow breath, biting the inside of her lip. She hated this question, mostly because she never had a good answer. If she did what everyone else wanted, she'd be hosting an endless number of charity dinners. If she did what she wanted . . . Well, she didn't know what that was yet.

"My father has mentioned a job opening in the research office at Vanderbilt. I would be drafting information about new drugs and protocols, describing them in layman's terms," she said.

"I see. And is that something you feel passionate about?" Julie asked, her head cocked as she watched Lexie intently.

Lexie got the feeling she didn't miss much.

"Well, a job is a job, right? Plus, you don't know my dad. I think my options are limited." Lexie tried to keep her tone light, though the weight of her words pressed down on her chest like an anvil.

Julie took another sip of her drink, studying Lexie carefully over the brim of her cup before slowly setting it down on the desktop between them. She leaned forward, her forearms on the table, and gave Lexie a kind smile.

"I know how daunting it is to cross that graduation stage and suddenly feel like you're floating in space without a tether. The problem, especially for talented students like you, is that there are almost too many options. And there are *always* options, Lexie, even if other people try to make us feel like there aren't. You're the one who has to live your life; only you can decide which path you take," Julie said, settling back in her chair as if she hadn't just dropped a truth bomb the size of Texas right in Lexie's lap.

"When you find your passion, it shows in your work. Take this, for example," she added, shuffling through a stack of papers before pulling out a few pages that had been paper-clipped together. Lexie's stomach flipped when she noticed her name on the top sheet.

Julie cleared her throat and began to read aloud.

"Though his work is often unseen and unpraised, Henry Wallace says he takes pride in each and every brick he lays. He has poured his blood, sweat and tears into hospitals, daycares, office buildings and museums, leaving his fingerprints across West

Tennessee in a way most people can only imagine. Wallace and his team hide in plain sight, making our most familiar landmarks what they are today with very little acknowledgment or thanks—changing the landscape so many of us call home, one brick at a time."

Lexie's breath hitched as Julie laid the pages on her desk without a word, smoothing them out with her hands.

"Where did this come from?" Julie asked, and Lexie took a long breath. This wasn't an article she'd been asked to write, and she wasn't sure if her boss appreciated her intern going rogue.

"Well, I was working on the story you wanted about the new research center, and I ran into Mr. Wallace while he was mixing mortar. I asked what he was doing, and I found out he's been involved in more than 150 building projects in this area. He's a CVSU graduate, and since our magazine is about alumni, I thought it would be worth a shot to tell his story, too."

"But the building's architect is also an alum. Why not focus on him?" Julie asked, her piercing eyes locked on Lexie's.

"Well, honestly, everyone knows his name," Lexie said, "but nobody talks about the men who lay the bricks, and without the bricks, the building wouldn't be finished. It wouldn't be as strong or as beautiful. So, I thought it would be different to take a look at the 'little people'—the ones who don't get the same recognition as the guys on top."

Lexie clamped her mouth shut, forcing herself to stop babbling. She wove her fingers together in her lap and waited. Interns wrote the filler material for the magazine but never the feature articles. It was a huge presumption to have submitted an article when she hadn't been asked.

Julie regarded her in silence for a few moments longer, and Lexie started to squirm.

"Lexie, this isn't work I would expect from an intern," Julie said, and Lexie's heart plummeted. The Henry Wallace piece was the best story she'd ever written. If that still wasn't good enough, then . . .

"This is next-level writing. *This* kind of storytelling is your passion," Julie continued, a proud smile stretching across her face. "You've taken someone we honestly would have overlooked and made him the star of the show. You made us connect with him on a fundamental level. If you keep up this kind of work, they'll be giving you my job in May."

Lexie felt tears of relief flood her eyes, and she took a shaky breath.

"You really think so?"

"About my job? They can try, but I'll warn you, I'm not going anywhere without a fight," Julie said, a twinkle in her eye. "But yes, I truly believe the human-interest side of reporting is a path you should consider long-term. There are plenty of places for a writer with your talent to land—places that will let you find the soul of your stories in a way medical research might not."

Lexie felt something loosen in her chest, like maybe her future wasn't as tied down as she'd always thought.

"Do you think you might use it?" she asked, realizing her biggest question had never been answered.

Julie's eyes warmed as she responded. "Lexie, we're not only going to use it, we're going to put Henry Wallace on the cover."

Lexie's face split open in an uncontainable grin. Her name would appear on the cover of the university magazine! No other intern could say that. Not one.

"Congratulations, dear. I'm proud of you," Julie said, pushing up to stand. Lexie hurried to her feet, still beaming, and shook her boss's outstretched hand. "I'll see you at the donor dinner tonight, yes? You and Jake will man the door," Julie added.

The wild cartwheels Lexie was turning in her mind came to a screeching halt.

Jake.

She wanted to run and tell Jake. She wanted to throw herself at him and scream and feel his arms around her while he told her he'd expected nothing less. Something in her chest wobbled, and Lexie stifled the urge to rub her hand over her sternum.

"Yes, ma'am," she said, voicing the words without really hearing them.

She'd successfully avoided Jake in the three days since the bell tower. Or, maybe he'd successfully avoided her. But either way, that would end tonight.

Lexie made her way back to her desk and reached absentmindedly for her cell phone. A single text message from Colt lit up the screen, reminding her about helping his mother with a charity event she was planning for next month. Lexie's finger hovered over the message, her big news begging to be shared, but after a moment, she slid her phone back into her pocket, the message unanswered. She wouldn't tell Colt just yet. She would keep her victory safe for a while longer, tucked close to her heart where no one could sully it.

THE SPACIOUS ALUMNI ballroom was dressed to impress, as were the guests within it. Precious stones glittered from delicate fingers, wrists and ears; cufflinks caught the light; and real glassware had been polished to perfection, waiting in precisely placed settings on every table. A string quartet played softly in a far alcove, and members of the catering staff—students desperate for overtime work—drifted through the crowd in pressed blacks and whites, balancing towering trays of hors d'oeuvres at carefully practiced angles.

Lexie tucked a strand of hair behind her ear as she worked the door, directing each new arrival toward where Jake stood behind a tripod. She kept waiting for him to look at her, but he'd barely acknowledged her since she arrived. Lexie could feel her skin tingle as if his attention were a physical craving she needed to satisfy.

All because of a cheap bottle of shampoo.

It was such a stupid thing, so small that she wondered if she were making a mountain out of a molehill. She'd been using the bottle for weeks without a second thought, but now . . . now it was all she could think about.

The label called it "green apple orchard."

"You deserve someone who notices when you change shampoo because your hair doesn't smell like strawberries anymore."

Strawberry. That had always been her go-to favorite . . . until the day she'd run out.

Had Jake noticed? Is that what he'd meant when he'd said—

A loud tinkling sound jerked Lexie's mind back to the room as the director of donor relations stepped up to the podium, clinking a fork against an empty glass.

"Ladies and gentlemen, thank you all for joining us today. If you would please take your seats, dinner will be served after a few words from our chancellor," he said, gesturing graciously toward the empty tables around the room.

As guests found their places and settled in, Lexie took up a post near the back wall where she could survey the crowd and have a clear view of Chancellor Carmike as he made his remarks. The lights came down, and a hush fell over the room, broken only by the hurried click of the hallway door as it admitted a last-minute arrival. Lexie watched the movement as a single gentleman was escorted to an empty chair a few tables away, but she barely got a glimpse before he was hidden from view.

"You're in my spot," a voice whispered from over her shoulder, disrupting her train of thought. Jake's low rumble made goose bumps appear along the back of Lexie's neck, and her stomach turned over.

"Your spot? I was here first," she whispered, mindful of the crowd.

"Nope, this is my spot. I scouted it earlier. You'll have to pick somewhere else," he said, opening the legs of his tripod.

"Well, I'm not moving, so you'll have to make do," Lexie answered. She tried to smother the smile that wanted to sneak across her face, but she was only partially successful.

Instead of leaving, Jake positioned his camera directly over her shoulder, making a point of trying to occupy the same physical space as Lexie. It was ridiculous, but nobody was watching. All eyes were on Chancellor Carmike as he began to speak, and Lexie fought to keep hers there as well.

It was harder than it sounded, since she could almost feel Jake breathing down her neck. He was *right there*, and try as she might, Lexie couldn't absorb a word of the chancellor's remarks. Instead, she listened to the rhythmic click of the camera shutter as Jake worked silently in the darkness, and she tried not to think about that same sound coming from the bell tower and all the words that had followed it.

"I heard about your cover story. Congratulations," he said suddenly, his hushed voice disappearing into the shell of her ear. "I'll try not to say 'I told you so.' "

Lexie was glad now for the darkness that covered the heat she felt spreading across her cheekbones.

"Thanks," she said, turning slightly. She caught a glimpse of his profile at the edge of her peripheral vision. "Will they use any of your photos?"

"Some of them."

"Good," she whispered, unable to say more. It felt like her throat was too tight for words. The opening speech ended, and a trio of violinists took the stage while dinner was served, but Lexie barely noticed. Instead, she stood motionless, acutely aware of the inches that separated her from Jake.

She needed to know for sure if she was right. Lots of girls used strawberry-scented shampoo, and lots of girls bounced when they were excited. It was probably just a coincidence; he could have been talking about almost anyone.

But the other thing . . . that had been oddly specific.

Lexie leaned back slowly, a millimeter at a time, until the back of her shoulder touched the side of his arm.

"Jake?" she whispered, turning her face toward him but keeping her eyes on the stage. If she was wrong, if she was completely overthinking this, she didn't think she could stand to see the truth on his face.

"Yeah?" he answered, so close she could feel heat radiating from beneath his navy dress shirt.

"Can I see your phone?"

"Mine?"

His confusion was palpable, but Lexie nodded. "Yeah."

She felt him shift as he reached into the pocket of his slacks, and she saw a dim flash of light as he flicked the screen on and entered his password without question. Lexie instantly thought about the last time she'd asked to see Colt's phone. He'd acted like she wanted nuclear launch codes. Now, she looked down almost reverently as Jake passed the device to her, recognizing this exchange for what it was—an act of trust. She could feel him watching silently as she flipped through his apps, but he made no move to stop her from seeing anything she wanted.

It was a freeing and powerful feeling.

She found his music library, opened it and scrolled through an artist list that was more eclectic than she'd expected. But finally, near the bottom, Lexie found something that made her stop. Hiding in plain sight beneath a collection of Van Halen's greatest hits was her favorite album of Vivaldi concertos, the same ones she often played when she needed to decompress.

"Someone who knows you play classical music when you're stressed and would keep your favorite tracks on his phone, just in case you ever need them."

If she hadn't been waiting for it, Lexie would have missed the sharp inhale from over her shoulder that told her Jake knew what she was looking at and why.

The trio on stage finished, and polite applause broke out as the musicians rose to their feet.

"Thank you," she managed, handing Jake's phone back to him. She chanced a glance up into his face. The stage lights reflected in his eyes as he looked directly at her like she was the only person in the room, and a feeling of enormous relief warmed her from the inside out.

"Maybe you're not looking in the right places."

As if he'd read her mind, Lexie felt Jake's knuckles brush hesitantly along the back of her arm in silent confirmation, and the hope in his eyes was almost overwhelming. She had to remind herself to breathe.

With a sharp squeal of the microphone, Chancellor Carmike reclaimed the podium and began to announce the winners of the annual donor awards, and Jake yanked his attention back to the stage. Lexie cleared her throat and shifted on her heels, her body flush with adrenaline.

"I need water," she mumbled, not sure if Jake could hear, before carefully stepping away from his tripod and blazing a trail toward the rear catering door. Safely in the hall, she leaned against the wall and filled her lungs with cool air, desperately trying to clear her head. Whatever this was with Jake didn't feel like just a crush anymore. It didn't feel like he'd given up after all. It felt like—

"Would you like to explain what's going on?"

An unexpected voice made Lexie jump, and her eyes flew open to find Colt looming over her, the lines of his face sharp and angry.

"Where did you come from?" she blurted, taken completely by surprise.

"About three tables away from where you've been embarrassing yourself for the last half hour," he said, his voice almost a snarl as he glared down at her. Even in her heels, he was still half a foot taller, and he was using every inch to his advantage.

"I got stuck in traffic, which apparently gave you permission to act like a dog in heat."

Shock and anger flooded Lexie's system, and the sound of her hand against his cheek was as much a surprise to her as it was to him. The smack echoed off the slick tile of the empty hallway, and Colt's face quickly cycled through a series of reactions, starting with disbelief and ending in purple-tinged outrage. She didn't have time to process what she'd done before his hand was on her, gripping her upper arm with a crushing force.

"Let go!" she demanded, trying to yank her arm from his hold, but Colt ignored her efforts entirely, steering them both down the hall with single-minded focus. "Let go, or I'll scream," she heard herself say, though it was like listening to someone else—someone with more courage than she usually possessed.

Colt stopped suddenly, letting her stumble.

"You do, and you'll regret it. I promise you that," he hissed, his teeth clenched tight. The look in his eyes made Lexie's blood run cold. He'd been angry with her plenty of times before, but never quite like this.

Another yank on her arm made her yelp, but she clamped her lips together and focused on keeping her feet underneath her as he kept going, all but dragging her behind him. She knew she should scream anyway. She should make sure everyone in the banquet hall could hear her. But then somebody would come, and he'd make it look like this was somehow her fault. He'd humiliate her in front of her boss, in front of the chancellor, in front of Jake . . .

Her bravado leached away as she realized what Jake would think if he saw her like this. Jake, who seemed to think so much of her, who seemed to care. He'd see how damaged she really was.

"Do you have"—Colt tested the handle of a closed door and found it locked—"any idea"—he turned a corner and rattled the knob of a second room, cursing when it wouldn't budge—"how much trouble you are?"

The third door finally opened, and he exhaled sharply, shoving Lexie inside ahead of him. She caught herself against the edge of a conference table and turned quickly, scrambling past several rolling chairs in an effort to put distance between them.

"I'm working. This is my job," she said, trying to find the confidence she'd felt earlier, but instead, she heard the waver in her voice as she backed away.

"Really? Fooling around in dark corners is part of your job? I think you'd probably earn more if you gave some old geezer a lap dance."

Lexie's mouth fell open. "I was hardly—"

"Do you have any idea how humiliating it is to watch *my girlfriend* rub up against some guy not twenty feet away and disgrace herself in front of a hundred people?"

And just like that, something inside Lexie snapped.

"Excuse me?" she shouted, no longer bothering to keep her voice down. "What about the way you undress women with your eyes, slipping tips into their blouses like you don't think I can see you? What about the underwear in your car, Colt? Who do those belong to?"

There was a crash as he shoved a chair out of his way, sending it toppling.

"How dare you go through my car!" he raged, rounding the head of the long conference table and advancing on her.

"*That's* what you're upset about? Not the fact that I caught you with your hand in the cookie jar? Not the fact that your word means nothing?" Lexie couldn't remember the last time she'd been this angry. Let the entire faculty come in right now and hear the whole sordid story. She didn't care anymore. "Real men don't roll around in backseats with women who can't even be bothered to put their underwear back on when they leave!" she spat. "Could you not find anyone classier, or did they all turn you down?"

She'd barely said the words before her cheekbone smashed against the tabletop in a blinding flash of pain. Colt reared up behind her, both her wrists in his hands as he twisted them toward her shoulder blades.

"That," he panted, "was too far."

Lexie tried to throw him off, but he was bigger and broader and stronger in every possible way. Every motion tore at her shoulders as the edge of the table bit into her hips, and she fought to catch her breath.

"You think you can flaunt what's mine, make me a laughingstock in front of the whole county, and then come in here and disrespect me like that? I am the greatest thing that's ever happened to you. Nobody else is going to put up with your endless issues the way I have all these years! Your own father can't stand to be in the same room as you for more than five minutes!"

"Colt, stop!" Lexie pleaded as his weight pressed down on her. Her tears pooled on the table beneath her cheek, and she hated them almost as much as she hated the man causing them. Colt continued pouring his words out like gasoline on a fire, but Lexie only caught the highlights.

Forgettable . . .

Disappointing . . .

Worthless . . .

"Hey!"

A voice sounded from the hall, followed quickly by the crashing of the door against the wall, and Lexie felt both relief and shame wash over her. Of course, of all the people in the building, it would have to be him.

"Let her go!"

Colt's grip disappeared, easing the fire in her shoulders. Lexie heard Jake's voice again, loud and angry, followed by the smack of skin against skin. There was another loud crash and then a blur of motion as Colt darted toward the door. Lexie scrambled back against the wall and sank to the floor with her knees pulled against her chest, making herself as small as possible.

"Lex! Are you okay?"

Jake dropped to his knees in front of her, and his cool fingers traced the edges of her face. A sharp sting cut across her cheek, making her gasp.

"Stay here."

The growl that came from his throat was completely foreign, as was the anger on his face, and Lexie instinctively clamped her hand over his arm as he started to stand.

"Let him go," she whispered, wincing as every motion made her shoulders ache.

"But he—"

"Please, Jake!"

Jake's attention snapped toward where Colt's heavy footsteps were fading down the hall, and Lexie saw the conflict raging on his face. But the fury in his eyes melted as they traveled over her again, taking in all the details she knew she couldn't hide.

"Okay. Okay, Lex. I'm not going anywhere," he said, cupping his hand under the good side of her face. He settled next to her with his back against the wall and scooped her into his lap. "I'm sorry I took so long, Lex. I'm so, so sorry," he murmured, still breathing hard.

Lexie tucked her face against the side of his neck and let out a shuddering breath, one that picked up speed as her adrenaline rush faded. For the second time, she broke down, her tears soaking through Jake's shirt as she clutched it in her hands.

And for the second time, he simply held her while she cried.

"YOU HAVE TO go to the police," Jake said, pacing the living room of Lexie's apartment. He felt like a caged animal, his muscles itching to destroy something. "I'll go with you. I'm a witness. I'll tell them—"

"Jake, stop," Lexie said, her voice flat as she curled herself around a pillow on the couch. She accepted a steaming cup of something from Olivia, who sank down beside her and rubbed a gentle hand over her back. It was the blankness in her eyes that bothered Jake worse than anything—the way she hadn't said more than two words at a time since they'd climbed into his truck half an hour ago. It made something inside him start to boil.

"Lexie, you have to do something about this! You have to have him arrested. You have to—"

"It's not worth it," she said, using that same hopeless tone.

"Not worth it? Of course, it's worth it! *You're* worth it, Lex! You still don't get it, do you? I—"

Olivia jumped up off the couch and stormed toward him. "No, *you* don't get it!" she insisted, catching Jake off guard as she jammed a finger into his sternum.

His eyes widened as he stepped back instinctively, throwing an anxious glance at Lexie, who was studying the contents of her cup as if they foretold the future.

"She doesn't *have* to do anything! And the *last* thing she needs right now is a man with a hero complex trying to run her life!" Olivia declared.

Jake locked eyes with Olivia, who looked madder than he'd ever seen her, and he was suddenly very concerned about his own well-being. He wouldn't put it past her to take a swing at him, and he couldn't bring himself to hit a woman.

The knuckles on his right hand throbbed, and he flexed his fingers cautiously. Nothing seemed to be broken, but the last three were an ugly purplish color that had only grown darker in the last hour. He just hoped he'd left a similar mark on the side of Colt's face.

"Why would I waste another second dealing with you when I could have anyone I want? There's nothing that makes you special!"

Jake had heard those words from the hallway, and everything after them was a blur of noise and motion.

The door that had cracked against the drywall when he'd shoved it open.

The jolt in his arm when his fist had connected with Colt's jaw.

The lurch in his stomach when Colt had shoved him backwards over an office chair.

The twist of panic when Lexie had slipped to the floor.

His first thought when he'd walked in was . . . Well, it was bad. Jake's stomach rolled just remembering the way Colt had been braced behind Lexie's small body, holding her down against the table. He looked at her now, sitting silently on the couch, and the anger in his chest began to ease. Olivia was right; he couldn't *make* Lexie do anything. He could only support the decisions she made for herself.

"Yeah, okay," he said, casting his eyes toward the floor.

"Stand down, cowboy," Olivia added, her voice softer this time, though she held her ground. "Go home."

Jake bristled again at the thought of leaving. "I'm not going—"

"Yes, you are," Olivia interrupted, and her tone left no room for argument.

Jake looked at Lexie again before heaving a sigh that left him drained and exhausted. With a glance at Olivia, who shrugged as if in consent, he stepped around her and made his way across the small living room. He reached the couch and sank to the floor in front of it, bringing himself eye level with Lexie.

"Lex?" he started, waiting for her to look at him, but those beautiful green eyes stayed fixed on her drink. He grazed his fingertips along the left side of her jaw before lifting her chin in his direction. Her eyes followed by degrees, finally finding his and holding on. "Anything you need, Lex. Whatever you decide, you've got me, alright?"

She nodded, and though it was only a few millimeters of motion, he felt it.

"Do you want me to go?" he asked.

Another nod, the smallest movement that somehow chipped away a piece of his heart. He wanted her to reach for him, to need him, to want him to stay. He'd thought maybe something had shifted earlier, before everything had unraveled.

But maybe he'd been wrong.

He gave a small nod of his own, trying hard to understand.

"Okay, then," he said, rising to his feet. On the way, he threw caution to the wind and leaned down, brushing his lips across the crown of her head.

It wasn't a kiss. Not really. But it would have to do.

"I'll check on you tomorrow" was all he said as he crossed back to the door, passing Olivia on the way out. He ignored the knowing look in her eyes, choosing instead to keep the moment tucked away as if it were his alone.

"Jake," Olivia said as she stopped him with a hand on his arm. She glanced back toward Lexie before lowering her voice even further. "Just be patient."

Jake sighed again, wondering if being patient would be the thing that killed him.

JAKE TEXTED LEXIE first thing in the morning.

JAKE: Hey, how are you doing?

LEXIE: I'm fine.

JAKE: Can I come over?

LEXIE: No.

He stared at her message for a full thirty seconds before letting out a deep sigh. He was already in his truck prepared to head to her place, but instead he started the engine and made the turn toward Copper Hill. When he finally made his way up the winding driveway of Tanner Farm, the front yard and porch were quiet. Not even Gomer came out to greet him.

However, the house wasn't completely vacant. The *Green Acres* theme song drifted down the hall from Grandma Ruby's apartment, and Jake followed it until he was standing in the open doorway. He arrived just in time to watch his great-grandmother drag a kitchen chair over to her small counter. She looked up, eyeing a cabinet over the fridge with obvious intent.

"Oh, no you don't, young lady!" he said playfully, striding across the room to stand between her and her destination. "If you climb on this chair, my mother will hang us both from the rafters in the barn."

"Now, don't you go bossing me," Grandma Ruby said, twisting her sweet face into a scowl. "I am not as feeble and frail-minded as you think I am."

"It's not your mind I'm worried about; it's the rest of you," he insisted as he pushed the chair back to the table. "Now, tell me what you need, and I'll get it."

He followed her directions to retrieve a large punch bowl and several etched crystal glasses, which apparently would make a special appearance at Sunday dinner that week. After setting them carefully on the counter, Jake turned to wrap his great-grandmother in a hug, knowing she wouldn't be able to hold her scowl for long. When he stepped back, her face had softened, though it changed again when she caught sight of the hand that was still wrapped protectively around her upper arm.

"Tell me this was for a good cause," she said, poking gently at his bruised knuckles with practiced skill.

Jake winced and pulled his hand away. "What are the chances you'll believe I shut it in a door?"

Grandma Ruby raised one thin eyebrow. "You forget I raised four hot-headed American boys. I've seen it all, and *this* was not a door."

Jake pursed his lips and looked down at his knuckles, closing his fingers into a tight fist before relaxing again. They didn't throb the way they had the night before, but the bruises were still glaringly obvious. Grandma Ruby made a tsking noise with her mouth, shaking her head slightly.

"The boyfriend, huh?"

Jake grunted, still looking at his hand, and Grandma Ruby apparently took the noise as confirmation. She shuffled slowly to her armchair and lowered herself into it.

"I can't help but notice you don't have any other marks on you," she said, missing nothing, as usual. "Is his aim that bad?"

Jake grimaced and sank onto the couch in his usual place.

"He shoved me over a chair and ran. Apparently getting caught making a scene was worse to him than hurting a woman," he grumbled, still irritated. Part of him wished Colt had put up a better fight, if only so he'd have had an excuse to beat more of that smug face to a pulp.

"And you didn't go after him?"

"No, I had to check on Lexie," Jake said, suddenly unsure he'd made the right choice. But Grandma Ruby smiled, her wrinkled features brightening like a soft candle had been lit behind her eyes.

"You put her well-being above your pride," she said, beaming. "It sounds like you did exactly right."

"Well, Lexie doesn't seem to see it that way. I think she wishes I hadn't been there at all."

"Of course she does."

Jake furrowed his brow, trailing two mental steps behind his great-grandmother. She smiled softly and shook her head.

"You men never learn, do you? You all expect a woman to fall gratefully into your arms when really, sometimes, we just want to curl up and lick our wounds in private. Is this Lexie of yours a strong woman? Does she have a good head on her shoulders?"

"Yes. She's brilliant."

"Then do you think she might be embarrassed to have needed help at all? That she couldn't handle it herself? Maybe not every reaction she has is about you."

Jake stared down at where his fingers hung laced between his knees, feeling chastened. He *had* imagined Lexie's reaction was all about him, but that may have been selfish.

"If she's not upset with me, then why won't she talk to me? Why won't she let me fix it?"

"Because you *can't* fix it," Grandma Ruby said. She used a remote to recline her chair back into a more comfortable position. "It seems to me this girl has a lot of soul-searching to do, and nobody else can do it for her. Does she know how you feel?"

Jake scrubbed the heels of his hands across his face, remembering the way Lexie had looked at him after she'd gone through his phone, the way she'd shivered when he touched her arm.

"I think so," he said. He glanced over to where his great-grandmother sat patiently.

"Well, then this is the hardest part," she said. "Now, you wait."

9

L EXIE SPENT SUNDAY morning watching the messages roll in.

> **COLT:** I love you. Can we talk about this?

> **COLT:** You know I didn't mean it. You shouldn't have pushed me.

Missed call from Colt Derricks.

> **COLT:** You brought this on yourself. Grow up and take responsibility for your mess.

> **COLT:** I know you're reading these!

Missed call from Colt Derricks.

> **COLT:** It's been two days, Lexie. Let's be adults about this and move on.

Missed call from Colt Derricks.
Missed call from Colt Derricks.

COLT: Lexie! Answer your phone and stop being a child!

As juvenile as it was, she felt a surge of satisfaction every time she hit "ignore," imagining Colt's face contorting in fury as his calls were sent to voicemail again and again. He was used to getting everything he wanted, but she was tired of giving it to him.

It was nearly noon, and she still hadn't gotten out of bed. The warm cocoon she'd created was soft and safe, and she saw no reason to venture into the ugly world beyond. Saturday, she'd immersed herself in work. Midterm exams were coming up fast, and for a while, that had been enough to distract her from the daytime soap opera her life had somehow become.

But Sunday was pity party day—table for one.

She silenced her phone, tossed it onto her nightstand and snuggled deeper into the blankets, only to be disturbed a moment later by a knock on her bedroom door.

"Lex? Can I come in? I have snacks," Olivia called from the hallway, and Lexie's stomach growled as if on command. If it had been anyone else, she would have played dead.

"Yeah, come in," she said, not bothering to sit up as her best friend slipped into the room.

Lexie peered out through a gap in her blanket fortress and watched Olivia look around, undoubtedly taking in the piles of textbooks, open notepads and stray scraps of paper that littered the room. She pushed aside a collection of highlighters on Lexie's bedside table to make room for a mug of something topped with whipped cream. Then, she sank carefully onto the bed, balancing a giant bowl of popcorn in her lap.

"So," Olivia started as she tossed a piece into her mouth, "what's the plan? Are we committing murder or arson? Because I'm down for either."

An unexpected bark of laughter burst from Lexie's mouth as she considered her friend's expressionless face.

"Olivia Nicole, you are truly scary sometimes," she said.

But Olivia only shrugged. "Look, you treat my best friend the way he did and see how it works out for you. My dad is Special Forces, and both my brothers are marines. I bet they know people."

Lexie snorted again, pushing herself up to sit against her upholstered headboard. She reached for the mug Olivia had set on the bedside table and smelled rich hot chocolate wafting from beneath the column of curled whipped cream. After taking a small sip, she licked the cream off her upper lip before swiping her finger through the column and eating that, too.

"I wasn't sure what you'd be in the mood for, so I also have four pints of ice cream—various flavors, of course—brownie bites, Cheetos, Pringles, chocolate pretzels, gumdrops, jelly beans and a monster bag of Pixy Stix, just in case," Olivia said, ticking the items off on her fingers as she spoke.

"What did you do, raid a gas station?" Lexie asked.

"It's important to have energy before committing a felony. Everyone knows that."

Lexie grinned and took another long slurp of her hot chocolate before stealing a handful of popcorn from Olivia's bowl. She crunched in thoughtful silence, savoring the perfect combination of warm sweetness and buttery salt.

"I've been doing a lot of thinking, and, to be honest, I don't want to commit a felony," Lexie said, staring into her cup.

"That's okay. I'll take one for the team," Olivia quipped, but Lexie stopped her with a sad smile.

"No, I mean, I don't want to punish Colt; I don't want to dwell on him. I just . . ." She took a long breath, choosing her words thoughtfully. "I just want to move on, you know? I just want to tell myself the past two years never happened. I just . . . How did I get here, Liv?" Lexie asked, suddenly pivoting the conversation. "How did I get to this place where I'm basically dating my father? Somehow, I went out and chose a guy who is all the things I grew up hating about my dad, and I couldn't even see it!"

Olivia focused on her handful of popcorn, putting one piece at a time into her mouth.

"I think maybe you didn't want to see it," she said, finally meeting Lexie's eyes.

"But you did?"

"Well, I hoped I was wrong."

"Why didn't you tell me?" Lexie blurted, setting her cup down.

"Would you have believed me? You were starstruck in the beginning, Lex. You thought he'd had the moon special-ordered and engraved just for you. And I was happy for you, I really was! You know how cynical I can be about the whole 'falling in love' thing. I didn't want to project that on you," Olivia said, looking guilty.

Lexie leaned back against her headboard and tipped her face toward the ceiling. The crying she'd done Friday night—first in Jake's arms and then with Olivia—was enough to last a lifetime. There were no tears left for Colt; he'd finally met his quota.

"You also told me he didn't hurt you anymore," Olivia added quietly. It wasn't an accusation, simply a statement of fact.

Lexie sighed. "It was always little things, and never in public," she admitted, though she felt oddly numb about that statement. "Friday was the worst time."

"I'm just glad Jake went looking for you," Olivia said, and Lexie watched as her friend's eyes scanned the greenish-purple bruise along the crest of her cheekbone, courtesy of the conference room table.

"I wish he hadn't," Lexie said, her voice barely a whisper.

"Lex, it could have been worse—"

"I know, I know, and I'm grateful. I am. I just wish he hadn't had to see how broken I am."

"Lexie, that boy does *not* think you're broken," Olivia said with conviction. "You should have seen the way he was looking at you. He went to bat for you, and if you'd even thought the words, he would have gone out and finished the job. As it was, I thought he was going to sleep on the landing. I almost had to walk him down to his truck and make sure he got in it."

Lexie groaned, her face hot with embarrassment. "He could have been hurt. He could have lost his job. He could have been arrested, and for what?"

"For *you*, sweetheart," Olivia said, a smile on her face. "That boy would slay dragons for you without batting an eye."

Lexie sighed, suddenly conflicted. Regardless of how Jake might feel, she didn't want to be that girl who just jumped from one man to another—no matter how shiny his armor might be. There was something to be said for finally standing on her own two feet.

Olivia, as usual, seemed to be reading her mind.

"I'm not saying you should leave Colt for Jake," she clarified. "I'm saying you should leave Colt for *you*. Anyone who comes after that is just incidental."

Lexie cradled her mug in both hands, silently watching the last of the whipped cream melt into the hot chocolate.

"Jake respects you, Lex, and that's huge," Olivia said. "You told him to leave, and he left, even when he didn't want to. He found out you had a boyfriend, and he backed off, even though we both know he's been crushing on you for ages. And when you needed him, he was there, and he didn't ask for anything in return." She picked up the flattened penny where it rested next to Lexie's alarm clock. "You could definitely do worse is all I'm saying. Figure yourself out, but don't punish yourself for stumbling upon somebody better than Colton Derricks. Maybe it's time the universe finally gave you something good."

Lexie mulled this over as she watched her friend trace the edges of the copper oval with her thumb. Suddenly, her thoughts were interrupted by a loud knock on the front door.

"That must be the pizza," Olivia said. She rose to her feet and headed for the hall without another word, though what she'd already said had found its mark.

Lexie nestled back under her comforter, distractedly listening to her friend move through the apartment and slide the chain lock on the front door. She jumped when she heard a shout.

"What are *you* doing here?" Olivia yelled. "Get out!"

"I'm not leaving until I see her," Colt growled, and his voice sent a shiver down Lexie's spine.

"I have a baseball bat, and I am not afraid to use it. Now get out before I start swinging," Olivia threatened, and Lexie leapt from the bed in a rush. She'd imagined seeing Colt again would be difficult, but right at that moment, she decided enough was enough.

"What do you want?" she demanded, striding down the hallway as if she were wearing Kevlar armor and not a faded T-shirt and flannel pajama pants. She stopped near the kitchen table, leaving ten or fifteen feet between herself and where Colt stood by the open door.

"I want you to stop throwing a fit and answer your phone!" he raged, gesturing wildly with both hands. "I want you to grow up and remember you have responsibilities. You missed that committee meeting yesterday about floral arrangements or whatever else it is my mother is so obsessed with, and now all she can talk about is what poor taste I have in women. I'm sick of it!"

Suddenly, all Lexie could see was a spoiled child stomping his foot in a candy store, and all the aggravation from the last two years welled up in her chest, lending her confidence.

"*Women*? Well, I'm glad she knows it's plural. I'd hate for her to think her only son is a responsible family man," she spat.

Colt's mouth popped open, and his eyes flashed, making the fading purple bruise along his cheekbone pop in contrast. Lexie traced the edges of it with her eyes, silently thanking Jake for marring Colt's usually perfect complexion, if only temporarily.

"Did you tell her we have matching war wounds?" she went on, her voice dripping with venom. She turned her head and held her hair back to give him a good view of her face. "I'm sure she'll be proud to know how I got mine."

Colt pressed his lips together and took another step into the room.

"Put on some clothes and get in the car. This is ridiculous," he said. There was a deep warning in his voice, but Lexie ignored it.

"No," she said. "In fact, I'm not going anywhere with you ever again."

Colt's face froze as he processed her words. "Excuse me?"

"Don't play stupid. You heard me," Lexie hissed. "Go find yourself another plaything. I'm done."

"And I'm done with this tantrum!" he yelled. "I don't have time for you to sulk. You want to make a point? Fine, you've made your point. Now, get dressed and let's go!" he ordered, fire crackling behind his eyes.

But Lexie crossed her arms over her chest and held her ground. She was glad adrenaline was still on her side, because just beneath the buzz of anger she felt a growing sense of nausea. She'd never put her foot down with anyone before, and she honestly wondered if she might get sick. From the corner of her eye, she saw Olivia duck into her own bedroom, then reappear seconds later with a baseball bat hanging casually from her hands.

Colt saw it too and rolled his eyes. "Seriously? You're going to beat me to death? I'd like to see you try," he taunted, throwing Olivia an unimpressed glance.

"Oh, she's serious, trust me. You should go," Lexie said, glad her voice was still steady.

Colt took another step as his hands clenched into fists at his sides. "You throw me out of here, and I'm not coming back," he said, his jaw set in a hard line. "Is that really what you want?"

"That is *exactly* what I want."

"Oh, really? So, you want me to have you arrested for grand larceny? Because you've got about eight grand in jewelry that belongs to me," he said, his voice smug, as if he expected her to be impressed by the amount of money he'd spent decorating her—as if that price would buy her obedience. Instead, his expression shifted as Lexie whirled on her heel, turning back the way she'd come.

"Wait here," she called over her shoulder as she hurried back to her room. She ripped open the top drawer of her dresser and dug out case after case of high-quality gemstones, piling the boxes in front of her vanity mirror. Then she yanked a plastic grocery bag off her closet doorknob, dumped its contents onto her bed, and swept all of Colt's gifts into the sack without a second thought.

When she returned to the living room, Colt, surprisingly, was waiting where he'd been told—though Olivia and her Louisville Slugger might have had something to do with that.

"Here," Lexie said, shoving the bag into his hands. "It's nice to know exactly how much I'm worth to you. Maybe you'll get store credit." She walked to the still-open door and stood beside it, an implicit order for him to leave.

Colt glanced down at the bag in his hands, and Lexie could see his whole body shaking with rage.

"I've spent two years on you, Lexie. *Two years!* And you're just going to throw it away over nothing?"

"Two *and a half* years, actually, and I'm not throwing anything away, Colt. You did that all by yourself."

He took a quick step toward her, his jaw clenched, but when Olivia raised her bat, he seemed to think better of it.

"You were such a waste of time," he spat, as though desperately trying to have the final word. "Don't come crawling to me when your guard dog gets sick of you."

And then he stepped through the door, giving Lexie enough clearance to slam it shut. She turned the bolt and slid the chain home, then leaned back against the wood and sank slowly to the floor as her legs finally gave out.

Outside, Colt cursed loudly, and the door trembled as he took out his anger on it one final time before stomping away. Lexie held Olivia's wide eyes for a breathless moment, listening to his footsteps fade, scarcely able to believe it was really over. Then, she laughed. It was the wildly inappropriate, slightly unhinged laughter born of adrenaline and panic. It was two years of stress leaking out of an overinflated balloon. And it felt good.

Lexie tucked her face against her bent knees and laughed until tears streamed from her eyes, wetting the legs of her soft pajamas. Then, looking up, she caught sight of the bright blue baseball bat in Olivia's hands and the slightly concerned look on her friend's face, and she started laughing all over again.

"GREAT PRACTICE, BLACKHAWKS!" Jake shouted over the chatter of a dozen kids and their parents. "Next practice is on Thursday, and don't forget there's a game right here on Saturday morning at ten o'clock!"

Families scattered, probably trying to reach their cars before the sky opened up. The clouds that had piled on top of each other at the start of practice were growing darker, and the wind was rising. Jake hurried across the field, gathering forgotten soccer cones as he went. He stuffed everything into his bag and threw the strap over his shoulder before jogging toward the parking lot—but he stopped short when he reached the curb. A familiar silver Infiniti was waiting near his truck, and Lexie sat on the tailgate, swinging her legs as she looked up at the sky.

Jake hadn't seen her since Friday night. He hadn't heard from her since Saturday morning. And now he was almost dreading what she might say. She knew how he felt, he was sure of it. He'd watched the puzzle pieces come together in the dark and recognized the moment a switch flipped inside her, like she'd finally seen him for the first time.

The only question was what she would do with that information.

Lexie dropped her gaze from the storm clouds just as the first stray raindrops hit Jake's skin, and when their eyes connected across the nearly empty lot, he felt the voltage from the storm crackle in his stomach. Her legs stopped swinging, and there was a moment when neither of them moved. Then, she hopped down and strode purposefully across the pavement.

Jake couldn't tell if she was angry or just determined.

His tennis shoes were cemented to the sidewalk. He couldn't have moved if he'd tried, and the closer she got, the tighter his rib cage seemed to become. His need to scoop her up and hold her tight tangled with an instinctive urge to run, to put distance between himself and whatever pain might be coming. He couldn't exist in limbo anymore. Either they moved forward together, or he had to walk away.

Her gaze was laser-focused on him as she closed the distance, and he could feel it like hot pinpricks along the collar of his shirt and the edges of his sleeves. When she finally came to a stop in front of him, there was nothing but a roll of thunder to break the silence.

Jake had to remind himself to swallow.

"I broke up with Colt on Sunday," she said finally, and he blinked. That was not the opening he'd been expecting.

"I've spent the last two days telling myself there is a respectful amount of time to wait before I can let myself be happy, like I'm mourning the dead, but I've finally stopped kidding myself," she went on, looking up at him. "I'm not mourning anything. Whatever Colt and I used to be was over a long time ago; I just woke up enough to make it official."

Lightning flashed across the sky, illuminating the green in her eyes, and Jake felt a timid sense of hope poke its head out of hiding and sniff the air.

"If I'm really being honest with myself," she said, "the only person I've wanted for a long time is you."

Jake stopped breathing, picking her words apart in his mind to see if they could possibly mean anything other than what he thought they meant. A dormant sense of self-preservation chose that moment to come alive, opening his mouth and forcing out words he couldn't believe he was saying.

"Lex, I can't just be a change of scenery."

The uncertainty that had spread across her face during his silence began to clear, like clouds rolling back after a storm, and Jake saw the sun break through in her smile. She moved closer, and Jake's fingers tightened around the strap of his sports bag as though reminding himself not to jump ahead. She hadn't answered him yet.

Her hands came up and hovered over his collarbones, and he stood as still as possible, terrified something would spook her. His breath hitched when her palms settled gently against his shirt and began to travel upward. Her fingertips were cool compared to the humid air around them, leaving a trail of goose bumps in their wake as they slid up his neck.

"You're not," she said, her eyes searching his. "You're who I should have seen all along."

Jake moved without thinking, and his bag hit the ground with a thud. All the times he'd kept his distance, all the times he'd stayed quiet, all the times he'd held himself back were suddenly erased as his hand shot out to cradle the back of her head. Lexie made a startled sort of sound when he tugged her forward and kissed her without hesitation, opting instead to make the most of a moment he still wasn't completely convinced was real.

But despite her surprise, she didn't protest. She didn't step back. Instead, she slid her hands the rest of the way into his hair and matched him beat for beat. She was everything Jake had hoped she would be—soft and sweet, molded to fit in all the right places. He'd never had a first kiss that felt so familiar, as if they'd been together long ago and had only just found their way back—a little older, a little wiser, but still made for each other. His whole body sighed in relief.

Unconcerned, Mother Nature chose that moment to open the floodgates, and the lukewarm October rain drenched them in an instant. Jake grabbed Lexie's hand and his gear, and they made a run for his truck. He could hear her laughing behind him, clinging to his hand as they splashed through the puddles that accumulated quickly in the empty parking lot, and a crazed sort of grin took over his face. He tossed his bag into the bed of the pickup and yanked open the driver's side door, urging her in first. She scrambled over the center console and flopped into the passenger's seat as he climbed in behind her.

"Talk about bad timing, huh?" Lexie said, giggling as she shoved a wet lock of hair out of her face. Jake could only grin, and he let himself stare at her without reservation. Even dripping wet, she was gorgeous.

"It was perfect," he said, not even talking about the rain.

Lexie's cheeks turned a pretty shade of pink as she ducked her head, not quite biting back a smile he'd have been able to see from a mile away. Just knowing he'd put it there was deeply satisfying. He twisted in his seat and leaned across the console, reaching for her the way he'd imagined a thousand times. The thunder that shook the windows and the lightning that lit the sky were worlds away as he kissed her again, this time moving carefully, like an explorer on uncharted land.

"Lex, will you go out with me?" he finally asked, barely lifting his lips from hers, and he felt her laugh.

"That's a stupid question," she said, and Jake could hear the smile in her voice. "What do *you* think?"

10

"CAN YOU BELIEVE I've never been out here?" Lexie asked that Saturday as she looked across Valley Lake and the beach-like expanse of grass that sloped from the tree line to the water.

"Seriously? I feel like I spend as much time here as I do at work," Jake said. He unloaded a blanket and a picnic basket from the backseat of his truck, and Lexie watched with a fond smile. He was the only guy she knew who would track down an actual picnic basket for a picnic. Anyone else would have just used a plastic grocery sack.

"What?" he asked, probably catching her odd expression, and Lexie shook her head.

"I'm just wondering where you found that," she said, jutting her chin toward the elaborate wicker container, complete with a red gingham liner that folded down around the edges. Jake carried it easily in one hand and used the other to steer her toward the base of a wide oak tree where the ground seemed level.

"It's my Aunt Christy's, actually. Apparently, it was a wedding present from somebody important," he replied.

"And she's letting you use it?"

"Yeah, but I've been threatened with hard farm labor if it doesn't return in pristine condition."

Lexie chuckled, imagining Jake shoveling out a horse barn or something equally disgusting.

"Did you work on the farm as a kid?" she asked as she helped him spread the old quilt on the grass and smooth it out. She toed off her sandals and settled onto one side of the blanket.

"Of course. We all did," he answered, stretching out beside her. "I've hauled hay, chopped wood, herded livestock, repaired barns and fences, planted crops—the works. It's a family enterprise."

Lexie watched him pull two wrapped sub sandwiches, chips, cut fruit and several kinds of baked goods from the wicker basket, and she bit the inside of her lip when she recognized the university's logo on the wrappers.

"Did you steal this from the cafeteria?" she asked, trying hard not to laugh.

Jake shrugged and gave a sheepish grin. "I have a meal plan, so it's not stealing. It's like . . . taking an advance."

Lexie laughed, then unwrapped her sub and popped open a bowl of strawberries. It was a beautiful day—the kind of October afternoon that could be painted on canvas. The lake reflected wispy white clouds, and dragonflies darted here and there among the reeds lining the shore. Lexie looked around, amazed that she'd spent three and a half years living barely ten miles from this spot and had never taken the time to explore it.

"I take a lot of pictures out here," Jake said, nodding toward a long wooden dock at the edge of the lake. "There's an eagle's nest on the other side, and I've gotten a few good shots of them bringing fish back for the eaglets."

"Do you take a lot of wildlife photos? I've only ever seen you shoot school events."

Jake nodded as he pulled a bottle of Dr. Pepper from the basket. He cracked the seal and passed it to her before opening a second one for himself.

"Wildlife is what I love most, actually. Animals behave in so many different ways, and you never know exactly what you're going to get. Take the eagles, for example. Sometimes I can wait for hours and they do nothing but sit on their nest. Other times, I can be out here for thirty minutes and watch them dive toward the water to hunt and then carry a trout back to their babies and rip it to shreds."

Lexie's eyebrows arched, and she scooted closer to Jake. "Can you show me some?" she asked.

Jake wiped his hands on his jeans before reaching for his phone. He opened a photo album called "Valley Lake" and handed her the device before planting his hand on the blanket behind her. They weren't actually touching, but Lexie could feel him hovering the same way he had during the awards dinner—just close enough to make her squirm. She wondered if he was doing it on purpose, if he knew how all the tiny hairs on the back of her neck were standing straight up.

"This one was after a big rainstorm," he said, reaching around her to enlarge a photo of an adult eagle perched on the edge of a massive nest, water droplets clearly visible on its sleek feathers.

He swiped to another image. "Then this was last June when the trumpet creeper opened up," he said. The photo was stunning—a tiny hummingbird hovering near a crimson blossom, its iridescent wings frozen in time.

Lexie stared at it, mesmerized. She almost expected the bird to move.

"These are amazing!" she said. She flipped through a few more images—a fish breaching the surface of the lake, sending ripples in all directions; a duck stretching its feet toward the misty water as it landed; a tiny frog resting on a leaf. "Why didn't you tell me you were this good?"

Jake shrugged, and Lexie could almost feel the motion against the back of her shirt.

"It's just about patience, really. Half the battle is being willing to wait for the right shot; the other half is knowing how to program your camera."

"Jake," Lexie said, "this isn't just luck. This is real talent! You could put these in magazines."

"Well, that's what I hope to do," he said. "*National Geographic* is the dream, of course, but there are lots of smaller places to start and work my way up. Tennessee Farm Bureau, for example, publishes a magazine a few times a year—lots of wildlife and scenic shots. I could start somewhere like that and get a few years of experience, then transfer to something bigger."

Lexie felt her chest tighten as she shifted to look back at him over her shoulder. He was so sure about his career path, already taking steps to get where he wanted to go. For the first time, she realized that the end of the school year would inevitably take them in different directions. The months suddenly felt too short.

"I've wasted so much time," she said, her voice softer and sadder than she'd expected it to be.

Jake frowned and held her gaze, his eyes studying hers. "What do you mean?"

"I mean we could have been doing this for months." She swept her arm over the blanket and the picnic and the lake. "And it's my fault we didn't."

A spark of something flashed through Jake's eyes, but then he blinked, and it was gone. Instead, he lowered his head slowly and placed a soft kiss against the curve where her neck met her shoulder. He stayed there for a moment, like he was thinking, and Lexie felt her bare skin burn under his touch.

"Maybe we could have dated sooner, but we aren't starting at the beginning," he finally said, shifting until the front of his shoulder was resting against her back.

Lexie frowned in confusion. "What do you mean?" she asked, echoing his words from a moment before.

"I mean this isn't really a first date," he explained. "First dates are awkward. You have to navigate through all the get-to-know-you stuff and decide if the person is worth spending more of your time with or if you'd rather move on to someone else. But we've been doing that for months, and I already know what my choice is. Sure, this might be our first actual date where I can call you my girlfriend, but we're not going backwards.

"I'm not going to worry about graduation until it gets here, and neither should you. Right now is right now, and right now, I want to lie in the shade and eat stolen cafeteria food with the most beautiful girl in the world. And then, I want to take her fishing."

Lexie blinked, feeling heat creep up her neck. She bit the inside of her cheek to keep from breaking into the kind of childish grin that would make her giggle like a teenager.

"I thought you said it wasn't stolen," she quipped, cocking her head back again to see him.

Jake blew out a puff of air. "That's your takeaway?" he asked, though he was smiling.

"I'm dating a strawberry thief," she teased, reaching back to pat the side of his face fondly. "My daddy will be so proud."

Jake chuckled, and Lexie let the sound wash over her, trying to ignore the dull ache that suddenly bloomed behind her rib cage. No, her daddy would not be proud. But that wasn't Jake's fault.

"You said fishing?" she asked, changing the subject. "I don't know how to fish."

"Don't worry, I'll show you," he said, unperturbed. He sat up straighter, his hand coming off the blanket and settling against her waist as he did, and Lexie concentrated on the pressure of his palm against her side. He was right. They weren't starting at the beginning.

Not even close.

⤵

JAKE STIFLED A laugh as Lexie yanked hard on her tangled line, irritation evident on her face.

"I don't know what makes you think I can do this!" she huffed, struggling to retrieve her lure from a bush behind her. He crouched and deftly released the hook from where it had caught on a small branch.

"Because you're an incredibly smart woman who can do anything she puts her mind to," he said.

He watched her reel in the excess fishing line that had unspooled in her agitation, and when Lexie visibly relaxed, Jake felt a surge of satisfaction. She soaked up words of praise like a flower straining for the light, and he was on a personal mission to make sure she heard some every single day.

"You're releasing too early," he explained, coming up behind her. He reached around to close his hand over hers on the fishing pole. He pressed his thumb on the button below the reel and drew his wrist back, taking hers with it. "Flick back over your shoulder like this and then release the line out in front of you," he said, sweeping the pole forward and expertly casting several yards into the lake.

Lexie shook her head and switched the rod to her left hand so she could wind the reel with her right.

"I know what you're doing," she said as Jake settled his arms around her waist and pulled her snug against his chest. He could hear the smile in her voice.

"What am I doing?" he asked.

"You wanted me to need help so you'd have an excuse to snuggle."

He laughed, unsurprised by her observation.

"Busted," he said, though he was actually looking for an excuse to kiss her again. He didn't want her to think that was all he wanted, but he *was* a guy, and there were only so many brain cells he could distract at any given time.

Suddenly, something yanked on Lexie's line as it skimmed through the water.

"Jake!" she said, instantly excited. "Jake, I think I caught something!"

"Well, reel it in!"

"Help me!" she said, fighting against the pull of whatever had taken her bait. The water at the end of her line sloshed violently as the creature fought back.

"You've got it!" Jake encouraged, and he moved away to give her room to maneuver. "Walk backwards and pull him in. Don't let him get the best of you!"

Lexie did as he said, and after a few moments, a large bass breached the surface. Jake whistled and whooped as he snapped a photo on his phone.

"That's my girl!" he hollered, crouching to subdue the bass where it flopped around in the soft grass. Lexie beamed in satisfaction.

"He's big enough to eat!" Jake added, removing the hook from the fish's lip with practiced skill. "Do you want to touch him?" He held the animal out to her, and Lexie shrank back in disgust.

"No, thank you."

"Aww, come on. He won't hurt you," he insisted, but Lexie wanted no part of the creature in his hands. A silly smile spread across Jake's face as an idea took shape in his mind.

"What's that, Mr. Bass?" he said, pretending to listen intently as the fish's mouth opened and closed. "You want to give the pretty lady a kiss? Well, I'm sure that can be arranged." He zeroed in on Lexie as he rose to his feet.

"Jake, don't you dare. Don't even think about it," she warned, her eyes widening as she stepped back. But Jake kept moving toward her, ignoring her shriek when she slipped on a wet patch of grass and stumbled. "Jacob! Stop!" she demanded with a half-laugh.

Jake stilled, processing the use of his full name; nobody but family ever called him Jacob. Strangely, he found he didn't mind when Lexie did. He smothered another smile and tried to keep his expression under control.

"You know what, Mr. Bass? I don't think the pretty lady wants to kiss you," he said, addressing the fish, which only gaped in response. "Well, I don't blame you. I'd feel the same way."

Lexie giggled while Jake returned the bass to the water, talking to it the whole time. He held it just under the surface for a moment to let it catch its breath, then it swished its fins and was gone. He straightened and wiped his hands on his jeans.

"Alright, the big, scary fish went home."

"I never said he was scary. I just think he's gross," Lexie said defensively.

Jake made a tsking noise. "He only wanted to say hello. The least you could have done was tell him you're sorry for putting a hole in his lip."

"He's the one who chomped on the hook! Greedy little monster," Lexie said, her hands on her hips as Jake approached.

He shook his head and made that disapproving noise again. "Well, be that as it may, now you've got a problem."

Lexie raised one eyebrow. "Oh, I do? And what would that be?"

"I charge an outrageous fish-handling fee."

"What?!" Lexie shouted, feigning outrage. "Fees should be disclosed before services are rendered."

Jake shrugged. "It's not my fault you didn't read the contract."

Lexie narrowed her eyes. "Would a dollar cover it?" she asked.

"Nope."

"Five?"

Jake shook his head, stepping into her personal space and looking down at her. He felt every inch of his skin come alive, the way it always did when she was close by.

"What about a kiss?" she asked.

Jake tilted his head from side to side, pretending to think about it.

"I guess that would work," he answered. He started to lean down, but Lexie stopped him with a palm on the front of his shirt.

"But you can't touch me with your fishy hands. Put them behind your back," she ordered, and Jake chuckled in surprise.

"Yes, ma'am." He crossed his arms behind his back and waited. If he couldn't reach for her, then she would have to come to him.

Lexie stepped close enough that he could feel her body heat through the cotton of his T-shirt. She studied him for a moment, her eyes moving over his face as if planning her attack, and Jake closed one hand around his own wrist to remind himself to play by her rules—though she seemed intent on torturing him for as long as possible. Finally, she pushed up on her toes and deliberately skimmed her lips over his with a barely-there touch that pulled an involuntary rumble from his throat. Lexie smiled and did it again before softly settling her mouth against his, her fingers curled in the front of his shirt to keep him close.

Jake inhaled sharply as his mind went foggy, and he forgot to follow instructions. His hands moved of their own accord, reaching until his palms skimmed the top of her jeans.

Lexie broke the kiss without warning. "Uh-uh, I said no fishy hands. Fishy hands are gross," she reminded him, her voice playful. She took a step back, but he followed with a smirk.

"Jake, I said hands to yourself. Jacob!" she shrieked. She pivoted to run, but he snagged one of her belt loops with his fingers and yanked her back, pulling another squeal from her throat. He peppered kisses down the side of her neck, then ended with a loud raspberry when he reached the top of her shoulder.

"Alright, I paid. Now let go of me, you animal," she said, laughing as she squirmed.

"I don't remember you being this bossy before I asked you out," he said.

"Are you regretting that decision?"

"Not yet, but there's still time."

"Shut up!" she said, her voice still full of humor.

Jake spun her around and pulled her closer, unable to contain the smile that took over his face. "Maybe you should make me."

"SO, HOW MANY backpacks have been filled this year?" Lexie asked, holding her voice recorder toward where Principal Hardeman stood with one elbow propped against the hood of an industrial stove.

"We pack nearly two hundred backpacks every Thursday, which means around eight hundred a month," he explained. "At this point in the school year, we've sent home more than two thousand."

"Wow!" Lexie exclaimed. "What does each package contain?"

"Well, it's all nonperishable food that's been donated by local grocery stores, convenience centers and businesses, as well as kids and their parents who choose to bring in food each week. Let me show you," he said. He led the way toward what looked like a classroom door branching off the elementary school's cafeteria.

Lexie was surprised to find the room had been converted into a giant pantry with shelves nearly reaching the ceiling. They were packed with cans and boxes of items like macaroni and cheese, beef jerky, crackers, soup, cereal and almond milk. A huge crate of well-used backpacks was pushed against the far wall.

"We have a team of faculty members and volunteers who come each week and pack the bags with a set list of items for that weekend's meals. The kids who get these don't have reliable access to food outside of school, so we want to be sure they aren't going hungry when they leave here," Mr. Hardeman explained. "We hand the bags out discreetly as they leave on Friday, and they bring the empty packs back on Monday and drop them in the bin as they get off the buses. That way we're bringing as little extra attention to them as possible."

Lexie thanked Mr. Hardeman and turned off her voice recorder as Jake piped up from the doorway.

"Could I get a few shots of you in here?" he asked, addressing their host.

The Cypress Valley alum immediately jumped to accommodate him, obviously thrilled to have his program featured by his alma mater. Lexie hung back as Jake captured images not only of Mr. Hardeman but also of the shelves and food items from various angles. The light in the room wasn't ideal, but she had faith he would work his magic somehow. He always did.

"We make a good team," Jake said later as they made their way out to a black Ford Focus waiting in the parking lot, the gold Cypress Valley State University emblem emblazoned on both sides. Jake twirled the borrowed keys around his index finger before popping the locks and opening her door.

"Didn't we already know that?" she asked as she climbed into her seat.

"Well, yeah, but we've always done the boring things—classroom dedications and awards ceremonies. We've never done this kind of assignment together."

She grinned as she watched him stow his gear in the backseat and then slide behind the wheel. He was right. Travel interviews were normally conducted by full-time staff, but a scheduling conflict had made it necessary to send interns instead. Lexie and Jake had gotten the story by default. Not that they'd had to go very far—Donaldson County Elementary School was only a forty-minute drive from Cypress Valley.

"So, do you want to grab a treat for the way back?" Jake asked, plugging his phone into the car's USB port and cueing up a playlist.

"Ice cream sounds awesome," Lexie replied.

Jake chuckled. "Dairy Queen it is then," he said, turning to look over his shoulder as he backed out of the parking spot. "But no cones in this car, please. Your track record is not good."

Lexie rolled her eyes and reached automatically for his hand where it rested on the gearshift. He caught her fingers between his as he pulled out onto the main road. "And this time, I'm buying," he added, and Lexie felt her heart squeeze a little.

"I wish that first time had been a date," she admitted.

Jake glanced at her quickly before turning his gaze back out the window, where downtown Donaldson flashed past them.

"I'd kind of meant for it to be," he said, not meeting her eye.

"Yeah, I know," she murmured.

"Then why did you say yes?" he asked, his tone somewhat hesitant. They'd never actually talked about this part of their history.

Lexie sighed deeply and squeezed his hand. "Because I wanted it to be."

She could see a smile cross Jake's face, even in profile, as he stopped at a red light.

"How about I take you out for real this weekend?" he asked.

"What do you mean?"

"I mean on an actual get-dressed-up-and-go-somewhere-nice kind of date. Not just lunch by the lake or ice cream in the car."

"I *loved* lunch by the lake!" she protested.

"Well, sure, but I want you to know I can do the fancy stuff, too," he said. There was a self-conscious edge to his voice that made Lexie frown, and she studied his face while he drove. He seemed to be purposefully avoiding her eyes.

"Jacob," she started, "I don't care about 'fancy stuff.' "

"I know, I just . . ." He trailed off, adjusting his grip on the steering wheel. "I just don't want you to be disappointed."

"Jacob Tanner!" Lexie barked, making him whip his head toward her in alarm. "Pull over!"

"What? Why?"

"Pull over!" she insisted, and she could see him scanning the businesses on the right side of the road, looking for a place to turn. When he finally brought the car to a stop outside an empty post office, she shoved the gearshift into park and turned to him with fire in her eyes.

"What is it?" he asked.

"I want to show you something, and I want to have your full attention," Lexie said, her voice firm. She wanted to stop this line of thinking once and for all.

"Okay," he said, his eyes wide, like he'd suddenly found himself in the principal's office at school. His gaze dropped to where Lexie's hand slid into the pocket of her slacks. She closed her fingers around the flattened penny and pulled it out before showing it to him. It was just a tarnished coin he'd probably pulled from the bottom of his pocket. Literally one single cent—now worth even less. He stared at it in confusion, and Lexie waited until recognition dawned on his face before she went on.

"Colt gave me thousands of dollars in jewelry, and he took every bit of it with him when he left because that's all I was worth to him. I was a shiny doll that he used to show off his daddy's money, and when I wouldn't play anymore, he took his expensive toys and went home. He expected me to care, but I didn't. You know why? Because he never gave me a single thing that really mattered.

"But this? This I carry with me every single day. This would break my heart if I lost it. This is more important to me than all the fancy restaurants and five-star hotels and little velvet boxes in the world because it came from you, not because it has any value to anyone else. I would rather wear one of your sweatshirts than any of Colt's diamonds, and I never want you to doubt that."

She finally wound down, having said all she needed to say, and Jake's eyes stayed focused on the little brown oval in her palm. The hush that followed her declaration was calm, and Lexie felt like the air had been cleared in a way she hadn't realized was necessary.

After what seemed like ages, Jake cleared his throat and lifted his eyes to hers.

"Okay," he said, nodding, and Lexie smiled.

"Okay," she repeated. She tucked the penny back into her pocket where it belonged as Jake shifted the car into drive and moved slowly back toward the edge of the highway.

The rest of the trip was quiet, but Lexie didn't mind. It was a thoughtful kind of silence, and she occasionally looked over to find him smiling as the gears in his head continued to turn. She could almost see him processing, working his way through everything she'd said.

And when she arrived at her desk the next morning, she found a ticket to the Hampton Symphony on her keyboard and a well-worn Cypress Valley Redtails sweatshirt on the back of her chair.

11

"WE'RE STILL ON for tomorrow, right?" Lexie asked as she made her way through the empty photography studio late Friday afternoon. She stopped short as she rounded the corner of Jake's partition. His cubicle was empty.

"Apparently I'm talking to myself," she muttered, shaking her head and pulling her phone from her back pocket. Her text conversation with Jake was already open, as it usually was.

LEXIE: Hey. Are we still going to the

A door opened directly in front of her, and she jumped, leaving the rest of her message unwritten. Jake stepped out of the old darkroom—now a storage area for unused equipment—with his eyes on the ground. He looked up and startled, clearly surprised to find her waiting for him.

"Hi!" he said. "I didn't know you were out here."

"You scared me to death!" she said, one hand pressed over her heart.

Jake laughed softly and rubbed his hand across the back of his neck. His eyes darted around, as if checking for witnesses, before he stepped in and pressed a quick kiss to her lips. Dating among the interns wasn't against any office rules, but they didn't want to make it a big deal if they didn't have to.

"So, what can I do for you?" he asked.

But Lexie couldn't answer. Her eyes were glued to the faded wooden door behind him, and heat rushed to her cheeks.

"What?" he asked, his brow furrowing as he glanced over his shoulder, but only Lexie could see the memory playing inside her head.

"N-nothing," she stuttered, trying and failing to contain the blush she could feel traveling down her neck. She pressed her palms against her cheeks, surprised by how hot her skin had gotten.

"Lex?" Jake closed his hands around her wrists and tugged them away from her face. His voice was full of amusement, and his eyes danced in curiosity as they flicked from her expression to the wall behind him. "Why do you look like somebody just read your diary?"

Lexie felt her chest tighten in embarrassment, and she wished he weren't so close to the truth.

"Nothing, it's—it's nothing. It's . . . I just . . . I had a dream once," she stammered, looking everywhere except at him.

"Okay?" Jake arched his brows, clearly waiting for her to go on.

"About . . . that door. And you. You and the d— You know what? It's not important," she babbled, her face still hot enough to cook eggs. She tried to tug her arms away, but Jake held on, looking over his shoulder again. Lexie could almost see him fitting the puzzle pieces together.

Finally, he turned back to her with one eyebrow cocked, his face full of interest. The corner of his mouth tugged up in a half smile, and he stepped to one side and turned them both until they had traded places. Lexie's hip bumped his desk chair as he walked her backwards.

"This dream . . . it wouldn't have gone something like this, would it?" he asked, his eyes still on hers.

Lexie's mouth went dry when her shoulders touched the wood. Jake stepped even closer, pressing her flat against the door until there was barely enough space to breathe. She swallowed, willing herself to answer, but she couldn't seem to form the words.

A loud cough nearby jolted them apart, and Jake backed into his chair, knocking it against his desk with a bang.

"I'm going to pretend I didn't see that," Andy said as he pushed open the door to his office just beyond Jake's cubicle. He moved inside, and Lexie watched through the doorway as he set a steaming mug of coffee on his desk without looking up. She groaned and wiped her hands over her face, then threw a quick glance at Jake from between her fingers. He stood with one hand curled around the back of his neck and the other shoved deep into the pocket of his jeans. He looked as self-conscious as she felt, and he seemed to be breathing harder than usual.

"Are you guys a thing now? Please tell me you're a thing now, because I can't stand to watch him mope anymore," Andy said, not bothering to come out of his office.

Lexie looked at Jake again, but he simply shrugged and gave her a sheepish smile.

"You have the *worst* timing," he said, raising his voice so Andy could hear.

"Actually, I think my timing is pretty good. Any longer and you might have forgotten Chancellor Carmike is coming for publicity shots in, oh, about five minutes," Andy shot back, and Jake's eyes jumped to the assignments calendar tacked to the wall near his shoulder. He huffed out a breath and raked his hand back through his hair.

"Perfect," he mumbled, closing his eyes. Lexie turned to go, but Jake stopped her with a light hand on her wrist. He tugged her closer before taking a step back into the far corner of his workspace. His eyes darted toward Andy's office, as if making sure they were hidden from view. Jake pressed a hard kiss against her mouth, and she could sense his reluctance when he let her go.

"I'll pick you up at five tomorrow," he said.

"Okay," she said as she finally caught her breath. She turned and slipped out of his cubicle without another word. When she reached the hall, she heard the sound of male voices drifting through the door to the stairwell. Chancellor Carmike was among them—on his way up for new pictures.

Andy really did have good timing.

"TRY THE BLACK one again."

"The shirt or the tie?" Jake asked, angling his phone so his sister, Ashlyn, could give her opinion.

"The shirt," she said.

"No, not the black shirt! He doesn't need to look like Zorro," Brooklyn argued. Jake could see her in the background, sitting on Ashlyn's bed back in Copper Hill.

"Okay, guys, can you just make up your minds?" he said,

huffing impatiently as he undid his tie for the third time. The gray striped pattern had been rejected by the girls, who were being as picky about his clothes as they usually were about their own.

"First of all, we're not guys," Ashlyn corrected, holding up one finger as she leaned closer to her camera. "That's why you called us, right? Otherwise, you'd be downstairs modeling for Noah and Conner, and you'd end up wearing a Led Zeppelin T-shirt and Crocs. Secondly, do you want to look like you have some idea of how to dress yourself?"

"I dress myself for church every week, thank you very much," Jake grumbled, furrowing his brow. Maybe he should have done this without them. He would have been finished half an hour ago.

"Are you wearing a sport coat?" Brooklyn asked.

Jake paused. He hadn't thought that far ahead. He was still just trying to choose a shirt.

"You should wear a coat," Ashlyn interjected, nodding quickly. "She might get cold, and you can give it to her."

"Oh, that's so sweet!" Brooklyn gushed. "Jake, we're going to make you the most eligible bachelor alive."

Jake rolled his eyes and tossed the rejected tie onto his bed.

"So, am I changing this shirt or not?" he asked, holding his arms straight out from his sides, waiting for a decision.

The girls looked at each other as though silently conferring.

"You've got a gray jacket, right? Like charcoal?" Ashlyn asked after a moment.

Jake glanced back at his closet, thinking. "Uh, I have black. Like a light black."

Now it was Brooklyn's turn to roll her eyes. "Boys think there are only six colors in the whole world, don't they? Okay, I've got it!" she said, clapping her hands together. "Get the *light black* jacket and those gray slacks you wore at Hannah's wedding."

"Ooh," Ashlyn said, her face lighting up in approval. "I love a man in gray dress pants. Tommy has a pair, and his—"

"Okay!" Jake interrupted, not wanting to hear *anything* about what his sister thought of her boyfriend's pants. "Let's stay focused here. I've got the jacket and the slacks," he said as he pulled both from his closet and held them up. "Now what?"

His sister and cousin looked at each other again, their eyes narrowed.

"White shirt, green tie," they said in unison, and Jake blinked. Had they actually just agreed on something?

"Okay. White shirt, green tie," he repeated, fishing for both in the mess that was currently his bedroom. He didn't actually own that many pieces of dress clothing, but apparently he had just enough options to make his head hurt. Stepping out of the camera frame, he started to unbutton the maroon shirt he was wearing so he could replace it with the new selection.

"Just be careful!" Ashlyn warned. "You're my brother. I don't want to accidentally see anything I can't un-see."

Jake rolled his eyes and ignored her.

"Jake has nothing to be ashamed of in that department, actually," Brooklyn said, not even bothering to lower her voice.

Jake glanced toward where his phone was propped against a pile of textbooks on his desk and bit back a retort. Just because they couldn't see him from this angle didn't mean he wasn't still part of the conversation. He shrugged out of his shirt and reached for the new one.

"How would you know?" Ashlyn asked.

"The last time the boys were all home, they were out in the

yard with their shirts off. I couldn't help noticing," Brooklyn answered matter-of-factly. "Drew has the best abs, for sure, but he does work on the farm every day, so he has an unfair advantage. Jake's are a solid four out of five, though—definitely would recommend."

"You know I can still hear you, right?" Jake shouted from the far side of the room where he was pulling on the pants they'd chosen.

"Yeah. And?"

"And you're my *cousin*!" he said emphatically. He slid a black belt through the loops of his slacks and then tucked in his dress shirt.

"I'm not saying I want to go out with you *myself*," Brooklyn argued. "But I certainly wouldn't feel bad about setting you up with a friend."

"All your friends are seventeen," Jake pointed out, looping his tie around his neck and starting on the knot.

"It's a compliment, Jake! Just take it and run," Brooklyn said, clearly exasperated.

"Where are you taking her again? To a concert?" Ashlyn asked. Jake could hear a loud crinkling noise, like the girls might be opening a bag of chips.

"Yeah, the Hampton Symphony. It's just a small-town sort of thing, but I think she'll like it." He shrugged his sport coat over his shoulders and checked his watch. He only had about twenty minutes before Lexie was expecting him at her apartment. He walked back to his desk and into the camera frame.

"Okay, so this has to be the last one. I'm out of time," he said, backing up until his whole body was in the picture. "Am I presentable?"

The girls peered at him for a moment before breaking into identical grins. Ashlyn reached out and touched something on her phone screen, and Jake heard music start up on her end of the line.

"Seriously? How long have you had that waiting?" he asked, listening as the chorus of ZZ Top's "Sharp Dressed Man" came blaring through his speakers.

"Since the second outfit," Ashlyn admitted. She nodded in approval. "You look good, big brother. Go knock her dead."

"Actually, no, don't knock her dead because we want to meet her!" Brooklyn said, nudging Ashlyn out of the frame. "When do we get to meet her?"

"I don't know. We're not that far yet," Jake said as he tucked his keys and wallet into his pockets and tugged on a pair of black dress boots. "I've gotta go. Thanks for all your help!" He reached out to end the call, but Brooklyn shouted before he could press the button.

"Wait!"

"What?" he huffed, starting to get anxious.

"Let us know what she thinks of your abs."

The girls cackled as Jake felt his face heat, and he hung up without bothering to respond.

◦∾∾◦

HAMPTON'S RIVERWATER PLAYHOUSE wasn't Carnegie Hall by any means, but the warm light and soft music that spilled from its soaring Gothic windows gave the distinct impression of timeless elegance. Jake was pleased to see Lexie's eyes light up in excitement as he helped her down from his truck.

"This is gorgeous!" she exclaimed, tipping her head back to follow the spires toward the darkening sky.

"So are you," he answered, leaning in quickly to kiss her temple.

"Wow, you think you're slick, don't you?" Lexie teased as she let him steer her toward the wide front stairs.

Jake's face split into a self-satisfied grin.

"I have my moments," he admitted, and he loved the way her soft laughter rolled out and wrapped around him like a favorite blanket.

They soon joined a chattering crowd in the spacious lobby, and Jake couldn't help but notice the wide array of concertgoers in attendance—from college students in jeans and sweatshirts to elderly couples dressed to the nines. He and Lexie fell somewhere in the middle, blending in with other young couples who were clearly enjoying a night on the town.

Jake looked down at Lexie, still somewhat in awe of the fact that she was actually there with *him*. She stood surveying the room with her hand nestled casually into the crook of his arm, her head held high and her shoulders back. Several long, golden curls tumbled out of a complicated-looking twist, and a diamond-shaped cutout in the back of her turquoise dress exposed a soft expanse of skin. Jake could imagine putting his hand there and trailing his thumb along the ridges of her spine.

Someone nearby cleared their throat, and Jake was startled to find that he and Lexie had drifted forward with the crowd while he was lost in a daze. An usher in black pants and a playhouse T-shirt stood with his hand held out, palm up, and an amused smile on his face.

"Tickets, sir?" he asked, clearly not for the first time.

Jake felt himself flush as he pulled the papers from his jacket and handed them over. If Lexie had noticed him staring, she didn't show it.

"Right this way, then," the usher said after checking their seat numbers. He led them through a set of doors to the second tier, then gestured along a row near the railing. "Here you are—seats five and six."

"Thank you," Lexie said. The man nodded and turned back the way they'd come. Once he was gone, Lexie turned to Jake, her face full of concern as she laid her hand against his arm. "Are you going to be okay this close to the railing?"

Jake furrowed his brow, confused.

"I mean, I'd hate for your eyes to finish falling out of your head and roll straight down to the first floor," Lexie finished, a teasing smile sneaking across her face.

Jake pursed his lips and shook his head sheepishly. "Very funny," he muttered, inching down the row toward their seats.

"I knew you'd like this dress, but I really thought you were civilized enough not to drool," she quipped, and Jake bit the inside of his cheek to keep from laughing. He didn't need to add fuel to this fire.

When they reached their seats, he sank slowly into the chair, and Lexie reached out to touch the side of his face.

"Thank you for bringing me to this," she said, her voice full of sincerity as a hundred conversations continued around them. She pulled him in for a kiss that he felt was entirely too short and then broke away as the houselights dimmed. An expectant hush fell over the wide room, and Jake draped his arm across the back of Lexie's chair and played with a curl that fell just within reach of his fingers. She glanced at him mischievously, the stage lights reflecting in her eyes. A single spotlight illuminated a speaker who introduced the evening's program as "Classic Rock in Classical Style."

Jake leaned close to Lexie until his mouth hovered near her ear. "It's not Vivaldi, but maybe it'll do," he whispered. He heard her take a sharp breath, and he tried not to feel too triumphant about the goose bumps that popped up along her neck.

"I love it," she assured him, her eyes fixed straight ahead. "Now, behave," she ordered, gently pushing him back a respectable distance.

Jake held in a chuckle as the curtain opened and the local symphony orchestra came into view. He listened respectfully, recognizing some covers and not others, but mostly, he watched Lexie. She sat in rapt attention, following every movement of the musicians below them. When the orchestra began a slow song, Jake reached for her hand.

She didn't look up when his fingertips grazed along the inside of her arm, but he felt her muscles tense beneath her skin. He traced long, lazy trails from her wrist to her elbow, watching her from the corner of his eye. It wasn't until the fourth or fifth pass that she started to squirm.

"That's not behaving," she whispered, and Jake couldn't help but smile. She captured his wrist and held it tightly, but he only raised the back of her hand to his lips and pressed a kiss against her knuckles.

"I can't help it," he whispered back. "It's the dress."

Lexie pursed her lips as though trying not to humor him, but he'd gotten what he wanted. Later, she leaned toward him when the lights came up for intermission, her index finger waving menacingly even though her face was playful.

"I can't take you anywhere, can I?" she asked.

"Apparently not," he quipped, grabbing the threatening finger where it hovered in front of his face. He kissed the tip of it, earning himself another of her beautiful smiles.

Lexie rolled her eyes good-naturedly, taking her hand back.

"I'm going to the restroom. If you get into trouble while I'm gone, you'll just have to wait in the truck," she said.

He scrambled to stand and let her by, brushing his hand across that tempting space on her back as she passed. When he'd lowered himself back into his chair, he felt a soft touch against his shoulder from the row behind him.

"Hang on to her, son," said an older gentleman, the skin around his eyes wrinkled from years of laughter. He glanced at the elegant woman beside him, who looked on indulgently. "You remind me of us so long ago. We're celebrating sixty years this weekend!"

Jake smiled, watching as the man took his wife's hand and brought it slowly to his lips in much the same way Jake had just done.

"Congratulations, sir," he said. "And I'll do my best."

❧

JAKE'S HEADLIGHTS SWEPT across the quiet lot as he parked in front of Lexie's apartment hours later. She pulled the lapels of his jacket closer around herself, still floating on whatever cloud she'd been riding since the concert.

"So, are you not an Aerosmith fan? I noticed you weren't paying much attention during that part," he said, turning toward her as he unfastened his seat belt.

Lexie snorted. "That's because somebody was distracting me," she said.

"Oh? Well, you'll have to tell whoever that was to behave himself next time."

"I *did*! It didn't work."

"It doesn't sound like you tried very hard," Jake teased, and he opened his door and jumped from the cab.

Lexie shrugged out of his jacket and folded it neatly, laying it on the seat beside her while he made his way around the front of the truck. He opened her door with a flourish and held out his hand.

"Can I walk you up?" he asked, steadying her as she climbed to the ground.

The happy glow in Lexie's chest vanished, replaced by uncertainty. She glanced toward her unit's assigned parking spaces. The spot where Olivia's Mustang usually sat was vacant, which meant the apartment was empty.

"Yeah, sure," she answered, though her thoughts weren't as simple as her words. In her experience, relationships were always transactional; men expected certain things in exchange for the time and attention she craved. Jake had always given those things freely, even when he couldn't ask for anything in return.

But now that he could, would he?

And what would she say if he did?

She knew how easy it could be for a single stone to become a rockslide, hurtling out of control until she lost sight of herself in the wreckage. She'd let it happen before, and she didn't want to make the same mistake again. She wanted someone to stay for more than what she could give behind closed doors. She wanted to be special, to be important, to be treasured . . . and as comfortable as she was with Jake, she wasn't ready to give up that much of herself.

Not yet.

Lexie was so lost in thought she didn't realize they'd climbed the stairs and reached her apartment until Jake stopped walking.

"You okay in there?" he asked, his soft eyes searching her face, and Lexie swallowed hard.

"Yeah, I'm just thinking," she said, unsure how to put her concerns into words. She didn't want to disappoint him.

"I can't come in," he said, shifting awkwardly from one foot to the other. "I mean, if that's what you were thinking about."

Her eyes snapped up to his.

"Oh."

"It's not that I don't want to, it's just . . . probably not a good idea," he added, casting his eyes around like he was looking for just the right words.

"Oh," she said again. An odd rush of relief washed over her.

"Everything about tonight was perfect," he said. His hand drifted up to cradle her jaw. The rough pad of his thumb swept across her cheek like she was a fine piece of china—delicate and priceless. It wasn't perfunctory, like a ticket punched before the main event. It wasn't a hoop to jump through on the way to something better. It was everything she wanted, without strings attached, which made it feel like so much more.

Lexie nodded in silent agreement, not quite trusting her voice as he gazed down at her with that look that said she meant the world to him—an expression she still found baffling. He settled his mouth over hers in a goodnight kiss that was soft and sweet, so different from the demanding insistence she'd experienced in front of other doors on other nights.

Lexie snaked her arms around his neck as he trailed kisses along her jaw, and her breath caught in her throat when his lips brushed over a place just below her ear. Jake froze, like it had been an accident, but when he did it again, it was definitely on purpose. She tipped her head to the side, giving him more room to explore, and her eyes drifted closed as his other hand trailed up her spine, pulling her against his chest. She felt herself start to melt, suddenly rethinking her earlier hesitation. Inviting him inside seemed less and less like a risk and more like an inevitability.

But all at once, Jake ripped his lips from her skin with a sharp breath as if he'd been forgetting to breathe at all.

"Yeah, not a good idea," he gasped, dropping his hands and stepping back, though the heat in his eyes was almost painful. "Can we talk tomorrow?"

"Yeah, tomorrow," she said breathlessly, her mind now spinning for a completely different reason. Lexie watched him walk quickly to the staircase and thunder down it before reappearing at the bottom and climbing into his truck. He rolled down his window and waved up to her, like he couldn't stand not to see her one more time, and Lexie felt a smile bloom across her face.

This time, things would be different. She could feel it.

12

LEXIE'S FINGERS PAUSED over her keyboard as she felt Jake approach. She didn't need to look, didn't need to hear him speak to know he was coming even before he moved up behind her. He swept her hair off her shoulder and brushed a kiss just beneath her ear the way he'd learned she liked.

"Hey, are you busy tonight?" he asked, his voice low.

"Tonight? No, I don't think so. Why?"

"How would you feel about pulling an all-nighter to celebrate our first month together?"

She turned her chair to face him, her brow furrowed in confusion. "An all-nighter?"

"Yeah. There's something I'd like to show you."

"In the middle of the night?" she asked incredulously, and Jake only chuckled.

"Are you in or out?"

A fluttery feeling of anticipation took flight in her belly.

"In," she said. The smile on his face grew, and he reached up to brush away a strand of hair that had gotten caught in her lip gloss.

"Perfect. I'll come to your place at eleven. Try to take a nap, if you can," he said, bending to press a quick kiss to her lips. "I'll text more instructions later."

Lexie smiled as excitement filled her from head to toe—though for what, she wasn't sure.

"EXTRA LAYERS?" OLIVIA said skeptically, reading from the text message Lexie had shown her. "What kind of romantic all-nighter requires extra layers?"

Lexie shrugged. "No idea. I've tried to get it out of him, but he's holding this pretty close to the vest." She pulled a pair of faded jeans over her fleece-lined leggings. "The only thing that makes sense is if we'll be outside."

"Outside? It's November!"

"Which is why winter layers would make sense," Lexie argued, choosing a T-shirt to wear underneath a soft, blue sweater. She looked at the clock on her bedside table, which read a quarter to eleven. Only fifteen minutes to go. A familiar flutter started in her gut, but she wasn't sure if it was excitement or nerves. She finished pulling on a sweater and Jake's hoodie, then tucked her leggings and jeans into boots. She felt like the Michelin Man, but at least he couldn't say she hadn't followed instructions.

Finally, a knock echoed through the apartment.

"Ready?" Jake asked when Lexie opened the door. He was obviously bundled well beneath a thick Carhartt jacket, and Lexie narrowed her eyes in suspicion.

"You wouldn't have told me to wear so many layers if you were taking me into the woods to kill me, would you?"

Jake only laughed as he held out his hand. "No woods, I promise."

"That doesn't technically answer my question," Lexie grumbled good-naturedly. She took his hand anyway, and his warmth traveled up her arm and wrapped around her the way it always did. Minutes later, she was standing on her tiptoes beside his truck, trying to peek beneath the blue tarp tied tightly over the bed.

"You don't know how to let yourself be surprised, do you?" Jake teased as he opened her door and helped her climb inside. Lexie looked around as they pulled onto the main road and was surprised to see they were one of the only vehicles moving at that hour. She had thought Friday night in a college town would be busier. She watched the streetlamps flash by her window until they passed the city limits.

"Where are we going?" she asked for the hundredth time as he turned onto a narrow back road.

"You'll see."

He reached across the console and captured her hand in his, threading their fingers together while his headlights swept silently over barns and fields that rolled in all directions. At one point, they crossed over the highway that circled town, and she saw a lone tractor-trailer pass underneath as they continued toward their mysterious destination.

Finally, Jake slowed and pulled onto the shoulder near a break in the hedgerow that was barely visible in the dark. Without a word, he popped open his door and jumped from the cab, leaving Lexie alone in the light-flooded interior. He walked quickly to the front of the truck and unhooked a length of chain from the top of a fence post before pushing open a wide metal gate. Within moments, he was back behind the wheel. He eased the vehicle off the solid roadway into what appeared to be a fallow cornfield. When they cleared the gate, he jumped out again to shut it behind them.

"What are we doing?" Lexie whispered as he climbed inside for the second time and shifted into four-wheel drive. Jake chuckled and peered through the windshield, following what Lexie could now see was a worn path obviously used by other vehicles for one reason or another.

"I know the people who own this land. Danny left the gate unlocked for me," he said, by way of explanation.

The moon was only a sliver in the sky, providing almost no light as the truck bumped slowly along. Lexie looked in all directions, trying to piece together why they could possibly be making this journey in the middle of the night.

"It's so dark. We won't be able to see anything out here."

"Oh, I think we'll see more than you'd imagine," Jake said vaguely, his expression growing more excited the farther they drove. Finally, they topped a small rise, and he turned the truck until they were facing back the way they had come.

"Stay here," he ordered as he turned off the engine. He pulled a small camping lantern from the center console. The noise of his door snapping shut behind him was entirely too loud for the wide, empty space, and Lexie jumped. She twisted in her seat, following him with her eyes as he pulled down the tailgate and started unloading things from beneath the tarp, his face lit eerily from the lantern below. When he saw her watching through the back window, he tossed the tarp itself up onto the cab, which prevented her from spying.

Lexie settled back into her seat, trying to be annoyed with the cloak-and-daggers routine but failing miserably. He'd obviously gone to some trouble to arrange whatever this was, and her excitement was growing. She could hear a lot of rummaging behind her, and at long last, the truck bounced on its suspension as Jake climbed down from the bed. Seconds later, her door popped open with a soft ding.

He smiled and held out his hand. "Close your eyes," he directed. She hesitated, glancing past him into the dark, empty night, and his expression softened even more. "Trust me."

Lexie nodded and closed her eyes, then shifted from her seat, bracing her hands against Jake's shoulders as he guided her down onto the running board.

"Now, hold on."

"To what?" she asked, but her arms tightened instinctively around his neck as he scooped her legs out from under her. "Jacob!" she squealed, pressing her face into his shoulder as he hip-checked her door shut.

"Shh, you trust me, remember?" he reminded her, taking careful steps toward wherever they were going.

Lexie nestled closer, feeling like she was floating through dark space and time. Only the solid feel of Jake's arms kept her grounded to the Earth.

Suddenly, he set her down on something hard.

"Okay, open your eyes."

Lexie did as she was told, opening her eyes and looking in awe at the truck's bed. There was a small sea of blankets and pillows lit by half a dozen camping lanterns, like Jake had built a fairy garden in the middle of the desert. She could see two thermoses and a small basket of snacks tucked into the back corner.

"What's all this for?" she asked in wonder.

"Well, the Leonid meteor shower peaks around 2:00 a.m.," Jake said, and Lexie turned to meet his eyes, catching a flash of uncertainty in them. He shrugged. "I thought we could at least have good seats."

Lexie looked down a slight hill toward what appeared to be a dark hole. She stared until her eyes adjusted to the dimness, finally realizing the hole was in fact a pond filled with tiny points of glittering light. Understanding dawned, and she looked up.

The sky above was alive with thousands—no, *millions*—of stars of all sizes, undiluted by city lights. As she looked in awe, two of them shot across the dark expanse, disappearing as they faded from view. Lexie brought her eyes back down to Jake, who was watching her intently.

"What do you think?" he asked, glancing from the pond to the truck and back to her.

Lexie looked around for another moment or two. She could hardly believe her eyes. No one had ever done anything like this for her before.

"I love it," she said, and Jake exhaled in a relieved rush.

"Yeah?"

"Yeah," she echoed, clearing her throat as a rise of unexpected emotion threatened to cut her off. "Every last bit."

Jake smiled, his dark eyes glinting in the light from the nearest lantern, and he climbed onto the tailgate beside her. They crawled toward the back wall of the cab and settled in among the pillows he'd arranged there. Several more meteors hurtled across the sky, their flaming tails visible behind Lexie's eyelids even after the fire itself was gone.

"So, what are we going to do for the next few hours?" she asked, leaning her head on Jake's shoulder.

"Well, we can talk, make wishes and just . . . be," he finished, trailing off. "Honestly, I didn't plan that part."

Lexie smiled contentedly, tipping her face toward the sky.

"That's the most perfect plan I've ever heard," she said. And she meant every word.

⁂

"WHAT DID YOU wish for?" Lexie asked, watching the blaze of another meteor vanish into the night. They'd turned off the lanterns long ago and were sitting in the dark, but Lexie could make out Jake's profile as he watched the sky.

"I'm still not going to tell you," he insisted.

"Why not?" Lexie whined, poking him in the ribs.

"Because I don't want to, and you can't make me," he said as he squirmed away.

"Oh, really?" She poked him again, just to see, and again, he jumped. Lexie's face twisted into an evil grin.

"Don't even think about it," he growled.

"What? Surely you're not ticklish. Not a big, strong college boy like you," she taunted, but Jake grabbed both her wrists as she reached toward him.

"That is not a good idea."

"Why?" she asked, trying to push past his defenses, but he held her at bay.

"Because like it or not, sweetheart, you are seriously outgunned," he said, and Lexie suddenly found herself flat on her back, her arms pinned above her head as Jake leaned over her.

She wriggled and squirmed, but he held her tight, visibly amused by her efforts.

"If you don't—" she started, but she didn't finish. Instead, she heard something rustling nearby. "Do you hear that?" she asked, twisting her head to one side.

"Oh, you're not getting out of this that easily."

"Shh!" She listened hard, straining to hear through the darkness. Something definitely seemed to be moving. "There's something on the ground," she said, a shiver of fear making its way up her neck.

"Probably just an animal. A bear, or maybe a mountain lion," Jake said, relaxing his grip and letting her slip free.

"A bear or a mountain lion?!" Lexie blurted, jerking back to a sitting position.

Jake shook with silent laughter.

"I'm kidding, Lex. There are no bears or mountain lions out here, I promise." She could hear the humor in his voice as he settled his arm around her waist. "It's probably a raccoon. Or maybe a skunk."

"A skunk? That's hardly any better."

"A skunk isn't better than a bear?" he asked incredulously. "I'll take a skunk over a bear any day."

"But what if it sprays us?" she asked, dropping her voice to a whisper. She relaxed against his side without intending to, taking automatic comfort from his calm.

"Well, if you stay in the truck and don't throw anything at it, it won't have a reason to do that. It'll find whatever it's looking for and move on," he said, his voice low and reasonable against the buzz of adrenaline that had flooded her veins.

"But what if it climbs up here with us?"

This time Jake's laughter rolled out as he dropped his forehead against her temple.

"It won't."

"But what if it does?" she insisted, turning until she could see his face.

"Well, then I guess we'll stink."

Lexie reached up and grabbed a fistful of his hair, tugging just enough to show her annoyance with his blatant disregard for the danger they seemed to be in. The gesture only made Jake laugh harder. He kissed her forehead and then her cheeks, and Lexie could feel him smiling.

"If a skunk climbs up here with us," he started again, his voice more serious, "I will sacrifice myself and give you time to get in the cab."

Lexie smiled, warmth replacing the fear that had filled her.

"What if it's a bear?" she murmured.

"Then you're on your own."

Lexie laughed and tilted her head back against his shoulder until she was looking up at the black sky. She blinked, and the heavens seemed to open up as countless stars arced across the void. The fiery streams crisscrossed each other, creating a web of light where there had only been darkness. In that moment, everything felt right. There was nothing but the two of them, suspended in space, existing all alone beneath a sky full of wishes.

Jake shifted, his arms coming around her from behind as he tucked his face against her neck.

"Lexie?" he asked, breathing her name against her skin.

"Hmm?"

"I love you."

I LOVE YOU.

Lexie stared blankly at her printer as page after page of an advertising case study dropped into the paper tray, but she saw none of it. Instead, she was lost in thought, still picking those simple words apart in every conceivable way, trying to find the hidden meaning. But even after four days, she'd only succeeded in driving herself crazy.

Jake had said, "I love you," and she had said . . . nothing.

Nothing important, anyway. Nothing he'd wanted to hear. Which had been painfully clear by the stilted way they'd watched the sky for another fifteen minutes before loading themselves awkwardly into the truck and heading home. They'd talked about owls, skunks, planets and the phases of the moon—anything she could think of except what was hanging heavy between them.

Jake hadn't mentioned it since.

Lexie, on the other hand, was wracked with guilt. She'd said those words before, and while she'd believed them to be true at the time, they'd turned out to be nothing but wishful thinking. Was it a crime to want to be sure? She was allowed to think about it, wasn't she? And how could he even say it, anyway? They'd only been together for a little over four weeks.

An obnoxious screeching noise sent her thoughts flying in all directions, and she groaned as she stared down at the printer.

"Come on," Lexie muttered, pressing the restart button. She could usually ignore the "refill ink" notice for at least ten more pages, but this time it seemed to be legitimate. She picked up her smoothie and slurped noisily as she watched the printer turn off and back on without change.

Six pages. She only needed to print *six more pages*, and now she'd have to go out and buy ink. She checked her watch. It was ten thirty on a Tuesday night. She only had half an hour before the local office supply store would lock up, but, thankfully, Cypress Valley was a small town with minimal traffic.

Lexie grabbed her keys and headed for the door, not bothering to change out of Jake's hoodie and her soft flannel sweatpants. The hoodie was easily her favorite piece of clothing, anyway. It still smelled like Jake, despite the weeks she'd had it, and she dreaded the day it would finally need to be washed. Maybe she could ask him to wear it for a while afterward, or maybe she could swap it out for another one. That was, if he even wanted her to keep it after Friday's debacle.

She was still obsessing when she pulled into the parking lot of the office supply store. It was the only building still open on this stretch of the highway, and the giant neon letters flickered ominously as she approached. The solitary figure behind the cash register looked up in surprise when the front doors slid open with a whoosh. Lexie gave a quick, apologetic wave.

"I'm sorry! I'll be out in a second!" she called, hating to be *that* person who came in just before closing.

"Don't worry. You're not the last one," the clerk replied, but Lexie was already moving quickly toward the printer ink. She scanned the shelves for the box she needed, finally finding it on the last aisle. But just as her fingers touched the cardboard packaging, a strange sensation ghosted over her—a cold prickle down the back of her neck, familiar yet foreign, all at once. She hugged the ink to her chest and looked cautiously around, but there was no one in sight.

Still, something felt off.

She made her way toward the checkout counter, glancing down every aisle as she passed and checking over her shoulder several times. But she saw nothing and no one out of place.

"Hello," the clerk said as she approached. "Just this, then?"

"Yeah, late study session," Lexie explained, distractedly pulling out her wallet. When the transaction was done, she stood at the counter for a moment longer, trying to figure out why she felt so strange. Looking around one last time, she decided she must simply be imagining things—the stress of her upcoming exam taking its toll.

A rush of night air greeted her as she made her way past the automatic doors. Her Infiniti sat quietly a few spaces away, and the interior lights glowed warmly when she pushed a button on her key fob. There was only one other car in the lot, a dark two-door at the very back, likely belonging to the sweet cashier she'd just met. Lexie shook her head, silently laughing at herself and her runaway imagination. But a moment later, there was a crunch of gravel, and Lexie spun sharply as a strong hand closed over her upper arm, squeezing hard in a too-familiar pattern.

"Well, look who's out after dark."

Lexie's throat closed like a vise, and she willed her heart to slow down. She wanted to say she had no reason to be afraid of Colt, that he held no power over her anymore, but in this lonely parking lot, in front of a nearly deserted supply store, her instincts disagreed.

"Let go," she managed, somehow sounding stronger than she felt.

Colt's eyebrows shot up, and a smirk grew on his lips as he released her. He held both hands up between them in a gesture of surrender and took a step away.

"Hey now, kitten. I just wanted to check on you. You look like you've really let yourself go. Don't tell me your guard dog has gotten tired already."

Lexie knew she should keep walking; there was nothing good that could come from this conversation. But if there was one thing she'd learned in the past two years, it was that turning her back on Colt Derricks was never a good idea.

His eyes lingered on her oversized sweatshirt, and a sneer broke his mask of civility.

"How cute. Obviously, he's figured out you like to feel *special*."

Colt's infuriating smile stoked a fire in Lexie's belly, but her feet still wouldn't move. She didn't have to listen. She didn't have to sit quietly and swallow whatever poison he had ready for her.

But old habits die hard.

"He probably started with pretty dates and presents, right? Little sentimental things? But eventually, when those don't work, he'll bring out the big guns," Colt said, his smile turning feral. "Has he told you he loves you yet?"

Lexie's anger, simmering low in her gut, went cold.

"I. Love. You," he said, emphasizing each word. "Three simple words, but put them in the right order, and they'll get him anything he wants. It always worked for me."

Lexie felt the blood drain from her face, and Colt chuckled, obviously enjoying the show as his words hit home.

"You didn't believe I actually meant them, did you?" he asked, mocking her. "That's the oldest trick in the book! And if your guard dog hasn't tried it yet, trust me, he will. It's only a matter of time," he said, leaning in close. "Let me tell you a little secret, sweetheart. *Nobody* means it, not even your precious pet. Why would he? Girls like you are a dime a dozen. There's nothing that makes you special, and the sooner you understand that, the better."

Don't listen! Lexie's mind screamed, but it was too late. His words bounced around inside her head as he turned away with a triumphant smirk, already knowing he had won. Lexie began to replay every minute of the last month in her mind, letting doubt darken the sunny memories as she watched. The picnic, the concert, the kisses, the keepsakes. The things Jake said, the way he held her.

It wasn't just a game, was it? Just a means to an end? Jake wasn't like Colt. He was better, stronger, more honorable. If he said he loved her, then he meant it. It was *real.*

Wasn't it?

13

" A ND HERE'S TO our cover story—the one we never saw coming," Julie said, raising her plastic cup in Lexie's direction. A chorus of "Hear! Hear!" sounded around the break room as each member of the marketing staff joined the toast.

Lexie blushed, hiding her face behind her plastic punch cup.

Magazine Drop Day was an office-wide event. Everyone took a two-hour lunch, during which the office doors were locked, incoming phone calls were transferred to voicemail, and food was served potluck-style. Everyone ate until they could barely stand, celebrating six months of hard work—the day when the magazine finally landed in mailboxes across the country. Work on the next issue would begin tomorrow; today, they would feast.

Lexie listened as the conversation gradually turned from the magazine to the Redtail's football season and, finally, to the upcoming holiday. She felt little need to join in, especially since her Thanksgiving would include a painfully formal dinner where her father's parents would pick apart every facet of her life and let the entire room know exactly where and how she was falling short of their expectations. Just thinking about it made her queasy.

She risked a glance across the room at Jake where he stood chatting with Andy. They hadn't had much chance to talk since last weekend, what with final exams coming up, and she felt the distance more sharply than she'd like. No matter how her heart tried to erase Colt's words, her brain was stuck on a merry-go-round of what-ifs.

What if she wasn't seeing all the signs? She'd certainly missed them before.

What if her mother had been right, and life was just about accepting what you could get?

What if she'd always be the girl men loved and left and not the one worth keeping?

Jake looked up and caught her eye, offering a hesitant smile. She tried to return it, tried to feel the same excitement she'd had only a few days before, but what came out felt more like a grimace. He started her way at the same moment the phone in her pocket buzzed with an insistent staccato, demanding to be heard. She pulled it out and looked down, and her stomach lurched when her father's name flashed across the screen.

"Everything okay?" Jake asked. He was near enough now that she could hear his voice above the sounds of the party.

Lexie swallowed hard, still staring at the device in her hand.

"Yeah, it's just . . . my dad," she said, forcing the words past the sudden dryness in her throat. She held the phone up as if to show him the evidence. "I'm sorry, I have to take this."

"Sure, of course," Jake said, but Lexie felt his hand graze her arm as she brushed past him. "Lex? You're a rock star, no matter what he says. Okay?"

Lexie felt her chest tighten painfully as she looked over her shoulder and met his earnest gaze. He meant those words; she could tell. And if he meant them . . . if everyone in this room meant them . . . then why did it matter so much what her dad might think? Taking a deep breath, she nodded and continued toward the quieter hallway.

"Hello?" she said, finally raising the phone to her ear.

"Alexis, this is your father," Dr. Garrett Preston said curtly, as if she wouldn't have already known. "I just got off the phone with Anthony Derricks, and he sadly informed me that Colton would not be joining us in Boston for Thanksgiving this year as the two of you are no longer together. I told him he must be mistaken."

There was a heavy pause during which Lexie was obviously expected to confirm his assumption. Instead, she took the opportunity to slip outside into the quad, away from prying ears.

"No, sir. He is correct," she said, waiting for the other shoe to fall. If there was one thing her dad loved more than reminding her she was a waste of space, it was telling everyone else that his daughter would one day be queen of the largest pharmaceutical firm in the southeast. In his eyes, it was her only redeeming quality.

"Do you mean to tell me you managed to screw up the one profitable decision you ever made for yourself?" her father asked, his voice a dangerous rumble, like the beginnings of an earthquake.

"I didn't screw anything up, Dad. Colt wasn't treating me right."

"Wasn't treating you right?" her father echoed. "That boy has professional drive, influence and name recognition. As long as he's giving you the time of day, you should consider yourself blessed! You're just like your mother, expecting the world when all you give is beans and peanuts."

"He was cheating," she pointed out, knowing this would carry no weight with a serial adulterer.

"And whose fault is that? If he had to relieve himself elsewhere it's because you must not have been doing your job! I mean, seriously, Alexis, what else do you have to do?"

Lexie's blood pressure rose, both from anger and embarrassment, as her father went on.

"As if that weren't bad enough, I also received a magazine in the mail today with your name—*my* name—next to a photo of a man in dirty overalls who looks like he probably couldn't make two and two equal four! You think *this* is a more productive use of your time than supporting your husband?" he said, and Lexie could feel each word slice into her heart like shrapnel. "Am I supposed to be proud?" he asked. "Am I supposed to pass it around to the surgical staff? What am I going to tell your grandmother when I see her next week? 'Your only granddaughter has decided making bricks is more worthwhile than finding a way *not* to disgrace her own family.' "

Lexie could feel her hands shaking as her rage grew.

"Colt Derricks is *not* my husband," she pointed out.

"A formality, at best!" her father snapped. "Everything was decided. If you're not bringing Colton to Thanksgiving, there is no reason for you to attend. You contribute nothing to this family, Alexis. Quite frankly, your decisions up to this point are embarrassing. You failed to seek an honorable profession; the very least you can do is marry well. I have done everything I can to make that happen, but once again, you have made a mess of things."

"*I've* made a mess? What about—" she started, but he wasn't listening.

"I expect you to resolve your issues with Colton," he snarled. "Tell him you were mistaken. Tell him you were hysterical. I don't care what he asks for, you make this *right*!"

Lexie froze on the sidewalk where she'd been pacing, and her hatred for this man filled her chest. Fathers were supposed to be heroes, protectors—but hers only cared about selling her to the highest bidder.

"How dare you—"

"The matter is closed, Alexis. We'll speak again when you've come to your senses," her father said. He hung up without waiting for a reply.

Lexie glanced down at her cell phone, her screen now black, and felt her control give way. She raised her arm, intending to hurl the device as far as she could, but someone grabbed her wrist before she could follow through.

"I don't think you want to do that, babe," Jake said, his voice calm as he slid Lexie's phone from her hand and tucked it into his own pocket. He released her as she turned away.

Lexie let out a noise she'd never made before—somehow turning a lifetime of frustration and hurt into an audible sound that tore from her throat and disappeared into the empty air. "Nothing will ever be enough. Nothing!" she raged, hot tears already coursing down her face as she whirled around. He reached for her again, but she shoved him with both hands. "Don't touch me!"

Jake held his hands up, palms out, and took a step forward. "Lex, it's ok," he murmured, as if approaching a wounded animal. When she didn't step back, he closed the gap between them and folded her into his arms.

"He's always . . . It's just . . . I'm not . . ." she babbled, her hot burst of anger fading quickly into grief. She tucked her face against Jake's neck and squeezed her eyes shut, trying to block out the world.

"I'm sorry, baby. I'm so sorry," he said as he held her firmly against his chest.

Lexie felt her adrenaline start to subside. "He told me not to come home," she managed, barely pushing the words past the enormous lump in her throat. "I think, ever."

Jake stood motionless, and Lexie listened to every breath he took, deep and even, one at a time.

"Come to my house for Thanksgiving," he said finally, his voice somewhere over the top of her head.

She opened her eyes and wiped her face with her fingers. "That's sweet, Jacob, but—"

"No buts," he countered, leaning back to look her in the eye. "I love you, and you're coming home with me. And I don't care if you can't say it back right now," he went on, raising his voice when she tried to interrupt. "I didn't tell you because I thought you'd say it, too. I told you because I want you to know I'm not going anywhere."

Lexie felt herself soften, and fresh tears slid down her cheeks, though for an entirely different reason.

"I'm sorry I hit you," she mumbled.

Jake's chuckle vibrated through her bones as he laughed. "Hit me if you need to, Lex. I can take it," he said.

Lexie felt another tear leak from her eyes. She couldn't believe she had ever doubted this man—*this* man, who was so unlike Colt or her father or any other boyfriend she'd ever had. *This* man deserved better than that.

"I can wait until you know how you feel. I'm not in a hurry," he said, toying with the ends of her hair where it fell between her shoulder blades. "But come home with me for Thanksgiving and see what family is supposed to be like."

Lexie wavered for another minute as she thought of all the ways one weekend could possibly go wrong. Holidays with the Prestons were full of criticism and thinly veiled aggression; she had a feeling spending one with the Tanners would be another experience entirely—one she wasn't sure she knew how to navigate.

"I don't want to be a burden," she said, her voice small, but Jake only squeezed her quickly and stepped back, pulling out his cell phone as he did.

"My mom is dying to meet you; she'll be thrilled. Plus, there are so many of us, one more person won't make any difference. Here, I'll prove it," he said, and he guided her toward a nearby park bench as he tapped his screen a few times.

Lexie could hear his call connect as they sat down.

"Hey, baby!" a woman's voice said, and Jake held the phone out in front of them, putting it on speaker.

"Mama, Lexie says she can come for Thanksgiving," he said, meeting Lexie's eyes as he did. They both winced when an ear-splitting shriek cut the air.

"Oh, I'm so excited!" Mrs. Tanner squealed. "When will she get here? Is she allergic to anything? I've already got clean sheets in your old room, so you can have the couch in your father's study. Unless you think she won't want to share a bathroom with Ashlyn? Then we can rearrange a few things and put her downstairs."

Jake raised an eyebrow in question as his mother rambled on, and Lexie took a long breath, willing herself not to cry anymore.

"Sharing a bathroom will be just fine, Mrs. Tanner," she cut in, leaning closer to Jake's phone so his mother would be sure to hear. There was a sudden pause on the other end of the line.

"Is that you, Lexie? Oh, I'm so glad to hear your voice. Please call me Kathleen. There are too many Mrs. Tanners around here; it gets very confusing."

Jake bumped his knee against Lexie's, beaming.

"If you're sure it's not any trouble, I would love to come next week," she said, feeling her chest fill with gratitude.

"It's no trouble at all, dear!" his mother responded. "Now, you just tell me what you like to eat best, and I'll be sure to have a whole plate of it waiting for you."

"I'll have her make a list," Jake interrupted. "Right now, we have to get back to work."

"Oh, alright," his mother said, sounding disappointed. "But Lexie, you come as soon as you can and be ready to stay the whole week. I'll get out all Jake's old photos, and we can have a hen party."

Lexie laughed and said goodbye before Jake hung up, feeling lighter than she had in days. Maybe in years.

"Well, now I *have* to go," she said as they stood. "Pictures of baby Jake? Who could pass that up?"

Jake groaned good-naturedly. "I knew there would be a downside," he said, and Lexie cackled, her father's words slowly losing their sting.

"No takebacks!" she said, wagging her finger.

"Never," he said, and Lexie felt him tug on her hand.

She went willingly into his arms, tipping her face up to meet his as he settled into a kiss that warmed her all the way to her toes. His arms went around her waist, pulling her close, and Lexie suddenly realized nowhere had ever felt more like home.

LEAVES OF EVERY color dusted the narrow back roads and flew past Lexie's window as her tires bumped through the little town called Copper Hill. "Town" was probably a generous term for it—it was more a collection of farms and a four-way stop in the middle of nowhere, but it had a deep-southern charm that Lexie found soothing.

Finally, she turned into a long driveway that snaked across an open field and disappeared into a grove of towering oak trees still clinging to the last of their autumn brilliance. When Jake's childhood home came into view, she felt another wave of nerves wash over her. What if this was a mistake? What if his family took one look at her and knew she didn't belong?

She pulled slowly into the wide clearing at the front of the house, then parked along a fence row where three other vehicles, including Jake's truck, already sat. The wide porch and yard were empty, but Lexie could hear the sound of a hammer coming from a barn not far away. There were flower beds around the base of every tree and along the sides of the house, just waiting for spring. An old tire swing hung from a low limb, and a set of wind chimes tinkled merrily from the eaves of the porch. She was still standing next to her car, taking it all in, when the front door opened and a woman who could only be Jake's mother stepped outside, followed closely by a flap-eared dog.

"You must be Lexie!" the woman gushed, a blinding smile already lighting up her face. She trotted down the wooden porch steps and immediately wrapped Lexie in a hug. "Jacob has been waiting by the window like a puppy for the last hour, but of course you would pull in the second he finally goes to the bathroom."

"Thank you so much for having me, Mrs. Tanner," Lexie said, trying to stand up straight as her hostess studied her with warm eyes. The dog sniffed her shoes intently before licking the hem of her jeans.

"Now, now," Jake's mother chided. "What did I say about calling me Mrs. Tanner? My name is Kathleen, and I want you to use it." Her eyes twinkled with mischief. "But that's the advantage of meeting a big family—if you forget who's who, just ask for Mrs. Tanner, and someone will come running."

Lexie smiled, and Jake's mother led her gently toward the house, talking all the while.

"If you've forgotten anything, just let us know. We girls stick together in a place like this," she said, but if she kept talking, Lexie didn't hear. Instead, her eyes were glued to Jake as he appeared on the porch, crossing it with long, restless strides. The front door banged shut behind him.

"I'll let him get your bags and show you around," Kathleen said, releasing Lexie's arm with a knowing smile. Then she turned to her son. "You're both expected for dinner in a few hours. Don't get lost," she told him, patting his arm as she passed.

He nodded obediently, waiting with his hands in his pockets until his mother had disappeared into the house. As soon as the coast was clear, he grabbed Lexie's hand without a word and made a beeline for the nearest corner of the farmhouse.

Lexie laughed, jogging along behind him as he rounded the edge of the house with single-minded determination. He didn't stop moving until they'd disappeared into the tree line.

"Jacob, where are we—"

But she'd barely said the words before his hands came up against her face, warm despite the outdoor chill. Jake sealed his mouth over hers, stealing her breath and all coherent thought at the same time, and Lexie tightened her fingers in the front of his sweater, holding him close. When he pulled back, it was only far enough to rest his forehead against hers.

"Hi," he said, grinning sheepishly.

"Hi." Lexie rolled her lips together to keep from laughing.

"I missed you," Jake added.

"Yeah, I got that," she said, letting a chuckle escape. "You know you saw me yesterday, right? Not three months ago?"

"That's basically the same thing."

Lexie brushed his bangs off his forehead, basking in his full attention. She didn't think she'd ever get used to it. Jake leaned in again and planted soft kisses on her cheeks and along her jaw, making Lexie melt just a little more each time.

"My cousins are getting together tonight since we're all actually in town," he said between kisses. "We don't have to go, but if you're up for it, I think you'd have fun."

Lexie bit her lip, thinking about meeting so many Tanners all at once. She knew Jake meant it when he said they didn't have to go, but she could also tell he was hoping she'd say yes.

"I want to go if you want to go," she said, pulling back to look him in the eye. "Just, maybe don't leave me alone with all of them?"

Jake laughed. "Don't worry. I won't."

THEY PULLED UP to a sprawling ranch house later that night and parked beside a dozen other vehicles left near the fence without rhyme or reason, like discarded Jenga pieces. Jake killed the truck's engine and jumped out, hurrying around to open her door before she had a chance. He helped her down and stole another kiss as she landed.

"Can't help myself," he said, and Lexie laughed. "Alright, so this is my Uncle Rob and Aunt Christy's house, but they're having dinner with my grandparents, so you probably won't meet them tonight," he explained, taking her hand and leading her across the grass. They went up another set of wide porch stairs, and when the front door opened easily, Lexie was surprised to hear nothing but silence. She glanced at Jake, but he was unconcerned. He led her through an empty living area and down the hall. A low rumble grew louder as they reached the last door, and Jake paused with his hand on the knob.

"I should probably warn you, it gets pretty chaotic when we're all together. So, if at any point you want to go home, just let me know. Also, there's a point system. It's completely arbitrary, and the loser has to kiss a duck."

Lexie snorted in surprise. "Kiss a—"

"Duck, yes. It's harder than it sounds," he said with a grin. "But don't worry, visitors never lose. Well . . . almost never."

He gave Lexie's hand a squeeze and opened the door with a flourish, releasing a hurricane of noise that drenched them from head to toe. Jake led her down a narrow flight of stairs, and Lexie gradually became aware of distinctions within the maelstrom of sound—specifically, a furious clacking noise and someone screaming "Eat, you yellow devil! Eat!"

As they reached the bottom of the staircase, the partial wall ended to reveal a massive basement filled with at least a dozen people in various states of competition. There was a dart board on one wall, a pool table near the corner and a bookcase crammed with board games of every conceivable type. Two guys and two girls were huddled on the floor near the stairs, engrossed in the fiercest game of Hungry Hungry Hippos Lexie had ever seen.

"Take that, gorilla brain!" the youngest of the four players said, throwing his hands into the air triumphantly as his exhausted hippo devoured the final marble. "Sixty-eight points for me!"

"What?" his opponents shrieked together.

"Thirty, at most," the young woman across from him amended. "Deductions for excessive trash talk."

The group around her agreed, and Lexie watched a young man in a Tennessee Vols sweatshirt approach the whiteboard on the far wall and add thirty points to a column labeled "Sawyer." Scanning the rest of the board, Lexie noticed Jake's name a few columns from the left and—to her surprise—her own in the one beside it. She already had 284 points to her credit.

"Probably a newbie bonus," Jake explained, leaning close to her ear, and Lexie smiled at how he'd known exactly what she was thinking. Suddenly, a familiar-looking girl appeared as if from nowhere and wrapped Lexie in a crushing hug.

"I'm so glad you're here!" she exclaimed, visibly vibrating with energy. "I'm Brooklyn, Jake's favorite girl cousin"—Lexie heard Jake snort beside her—"and I can't believe you're real! He's been going on about you for so long I wasn't sure you existed, but here you are! Okay, have you met everyone yet?"

She was talking so fast Lexie scarcely had time to shake her head before Brooklyn raised her voice and bellowed, "Hey, you guys! This is Lexie, Jake's lucky lady. Everybody say hello!"

A chorus of welcome echoed back, but Brooklyn was already talking again, pointing to each person in turn.

"This is Sawyer, Jonah, Hannah and her husband Oliver, then over there we have Morgan, James, Drew"—the Volunteers fan scowled—"and I'm sure you've met Ashlyn by now . . ."

The list was exhaustive, fifteen people in all, including cousins and a few friends, and Lexie's head spun with the challenge to keep them all straight, a task made especially difficult by the way they kept moving around.

"And you may have noticed that you're on the board already," Brooklyn said, gesturing to the whiteboard across from them. "We started you off with five hundred points for being brave enough to attend as a guest, but then the group decided coming with Jake shows poor judgment overall, so deductions were made."

"That's a big deduction!" Jake protested from Lexie's side, but Brooklyn ignored him.

"Come with me, and we'll get you started!" she insisted, all but dragging Lexie across the room.

Brooklyn was so full of enthusiasm, and everyone she met was so glad to see her, that Lexie forgot to be nervous. Before she knew it, she'd won 305 points in Jenga and lost 200 more for tanking a game of darts, though she did win back 592 points for accidentally landing one of said darts in Sawyer's Mountain Dew. Jake had gained 619 points for sinking four balls on his first break in a game of pool but then lost 112 of them for the victory dance that followed.

Fifteen minutes into a heart-stopping game of Operation, Lexie scanned the room to find Jake sitting at a card table studying a Monopoly board. As if able to feel her gaze, he looked up and met her eyes over the heads of several cousins stretched precariously across a Twister mat. He winked, and that simple acknowledgement filled her with a warm sort of confidence—both grounding and exhilarating at the same time.

He went back to the game as his turn began, and Lexie watched him for a moment longer before dragging her attention back to the poor patient on the table. She'd already lost too many points for surgical ineptitude—a fact that would have dismayed her father—though a quick calculation said she was still well out of duck-kissing territory.

"So, what is it about Jake that brings you all the way to this madhouse?" Hannah asked later while she and Lexie held down a set of beanbag chairs near the kitchenette.

Lexie watched Jake collect another pile of pastel-colored dollar bills from Drew.

"Everything," she said, surprised by her own frankness. Hannah gave an understanding nod and followed Lexie's gaze.

"He's a good one, for sure," Hannah agreed, taking a sip of her drink. "You know you're the only girl he's ever introduced to us? Even when we were all in school and he was dating someone we knew, he never brought her to cousin night. I think—"

"That's cheating!" Drew yelled suddenly, causing pandemonium at the Monopoly table. Tiny playing pieces went flying as he upended the board, and Jake dove to the ground after his substantial pile of paper money. There was a mad scramble by the others to retrieve what he couldn't reach. A heated argument broke out between Drew and another of the boys, whose name Lexie couldn't remember, and Brooklyn and Oliver stepped in.

When things had calmed down, Brooklyn took out her phone. "Alright! This seems like a good time for a quick tally of the standings so far," Brooklyn said.

Everyone followed suit, tallying their own gains and losses, and the final numbers were confirmed and written below their names. Oliver was on top of the heap with 2,472 points, followed by Sawyer and then Ashlyn. Jake ranked sixth with 1,621, and Lexie claimed a respectable eighth place with 1,394. James was sitting sadly at the bottom of the pile.

As the current totals were announced, Jake wandered toward Lexie and flopped down onto her beanbag, bouncing her a bit as he landed.

"Having fun yet?" he asked, reaching to tuck a strand of hair behind her ear.

"Yeah, I am," she answered as she looked around the room with a smile. She didn't quite have the words to explain how a room full of strangers already felt more like family than her own. Jake must have read some of it in her eyes, because his expression softened and he slipped his hand behind her head, pulling her close. He placed soft kisses first on her forehead and then on one cheek, but he made it no farther before he was caught.

"Minus five hundred for PDA!" Drew shouted, pointing in Jake's direction.

"What?!" Jake popped his head up and scowled.

"Another two hundred for protesting!" someone else called, and Jake watched open-mouthed as he slipped firmly into eleventh place.

An hour later, he'd fallen three more spots after heavy deductions for aggressive dice rolling, excessive mockery and aiming a dart at Drew's backside.

"I'm being sabotaged," he announced after surveying the new rankings. "*Aggressive dice rolling*? Seriously?!" He glared around the room, and Lexie was delighted to see more than one of his cousins openly smirking. A lightbulb flicked on in Jake's eyes.

"You want me to have to embarrass myself, don't you?" he demanded, and the laughter that filled the room brought joy to Lexie's heart. Jake raked one hand through his hair and looked from the tally on the whiteboard to her with amused resignation.

"Well, I should probably go out with a bang," he said, shrugging innocently. He crossed the room to where Lexie was leaning against the pool table, caught her by the back of her neck and kissed her so thoroughly there were catcalls from the cheap seats. When he let go, Lexie could do no more than tent her hands over her face and wait for her runaway grin to subside.

Hannah laughed and rubbed one of Lexie's shoulders in friendly solidarity, while Ashlyn pretended to gag into her drink. Jake, however, gave a cocky grin and backed away, fully owning the –12,478 points that Brooklyn scrawled beneath his name.

"Well, that's that then," Oliver said, coming up behind his wife. "Jake's got to kiss a duck. Might as well get started."

The whole group bundled into their coats and scarves and drifted into the backyard, where a small pond gleamed beneath a full moon. Cracking his neck and tucking his jeans into his boots, Jake headed resolutely for the water's edge while Lexie and the rest of his family made themselves comfortable along the split-rail fence. When he finally cornered a duck and held it aloft in a swirl of feathers, she cheered along with the rest of them.

And later, when he chased her around his truck and smeared mud from his clothes onto hers, she felt a palpable shift in her chest—as if all her jumbled pieces were finally falling into place.

14

T HE RUMBLE OF a pickup truck woke Lexie much earlier than she'd intended the next morning. She looked around the unfamiliar room in the cold, gray light before dawn, trying to place where she was. Everything came flooding back when her eyes landed on a collection of gold-colored soccer trophies on the tall dresser.

She was in Jake's childhood bedroom, surrounded by the first eighteen years of his life. She sat up, reached for the bedside lamp and flipped it on. In its warm glow, she could see stacks of thin comic books on the shelves, racks of sports awards on the cream-colored walls and an emblem for the Mason County Raiders embroidered onto the black-and-gold bedspread tucked around her waist.

A door snapped shut somewhere downstairs, and she pushed herself up onto her knees to peer through the gauzy white curtains behind the double bed. A dirty gray flatbed truck idled in the open driveway, and Lexie was surprised to see both Jake and his dad step off the porch beneath her window. Jake was bundled in what seemed to be his muddy clothes from the night before, a dark knit hat pulled low over his forehead and a shining silver thermos clutched in his gloved hands. His breath appeared in white clouds as he spoke to two other young men riding on the truck bed. She recognized them both as cousins, but she couldn't remember which ones.

Jake's father, who had insisted she call him Logan, paused near the passenger's side door of the truck, talking to his wife. One of his hands rested comfortably on her hip as the other accepted the thermos she handed him. He bent and kissed her, then leaned against her hand as she brushed it through the hair that poked from beneath his cap. The tenderness of the gesture made Lexie's throat clench, and she swallowed hard.

Logan Tanner was a quiet man, tending to listen far more than he spoke, and it hadn't taken Lexie long at all to see where Jake had learned how to treat a woman. His father seemed to stay connected to his wife in one way or another—an arm across her chair, a hand on her back, a knee touching hers as they sat on the couch. He served her in small, silent ways, and she visibly basked in his affection. Jake was that way, too, always quietly anticipating what Lexie might need and hurrying to provide it before she could ask. She could feel his heart in everything he did, which was both thrilling and unnerving at the same time. If this was love in action, it was unlike anything she'd ever seen before.

Logan opened the front door of the truck and disappeared into the cab as Jake climbed onto the flatbed beside his cousins, his long legs hanging off the tailgate. As the truck slowly bumped forward, Lexie saw him raise his eyes toward the window where she watched. She didn't know if he could see her, but she waved anyway. A slow smile spread over his face, and he raised one hand in return as the pickup trundled away. As he disappeared from sight, Lexie felt an odd sort of tugging beneath her breastbone, almost like a rubber band being stretched but not broken. She rubbed the heel of her hand against her sternum, trying to massage away the unfamiliar feeling.

Too awake to drift off again, she got up and padded quietly around the room, looking at photos of Jake surrounded by friends and cousins over the years. He'd obviously been well-liked, not that she could ever imagine otherwise. She pulled Jake's hoodie on over her pajama shirt and swapped her flannel pants for jeans before cracking open the door to the hallway. Her stomach grumbled as she listened for signs of life in the rest of the house. The hallway carpet was soft, muffling her footsteps, but she hit a squeaky step about halfway down the staircase. She froze as the noise split the silence, listening hard, and then smiled when she thought of Jake moving through this same house. He would undoubtedly know to skip that step.

The house Lexie had grown up in was cold and sterile, less a place to live and more a place to store the things that made her father feel important, including his wife and daughter. There were no squeaky stairs in that house, though if the walls could talk, they'd tell of scars that ran decades deep.

After reaching the first floor, Lexie made her way quietly into the kitchen, where she was surprised to find Kathleen sitting at the table, a steaming mug of coffee and an open Bible in front of her.

"Oh! I'm sorry!" Lexie said, taking a quick step backward, but Jake's mom only smiled and beckoned Lexie into the room.

"Come in, come in!" Kathleen said, closing her book. "I was finishing up anyway. I'm sorry if we woke you. I guess Ashlyn is so used to sleeping through the truck that I didn't even think about it."

"Where were they going so early?" Lexie asked, sinking into a chair across from where Jake's mom was settled. A large picture window along the back wall showed the sun starting to peek above the edges of a bare field, its light slowly touching the frost that covered the ground.

"Oh, there are always animals to feed—cows, mostly, but sheep and goats, too. Fences to check, waterers to fill. Just the everyday life of a working farm." She smiled warmly and gestured toward the stove. "I was just about to start breakfast. Would you like some hot chocolate? And how do you feel about pancakes and eggs?"

"That sounds delicious! Can I help?" Lexie asked, but Kathleen clucked her tongue as she stood.

"Oh, don't worry, I'll put you to work later. But right now"—Kathleen went to the nearby baker's rack and grabbed something off the top shelf—"this is for you." She grinned as she set a thick photo album on the gleaming wooden tabletop in front of Lexie and then turned back to the counter.

Lexie was delighted to see a tiny, red-faced baby staring up at her from the cover, where the gold script read "Jacob Ryan Tanner, born April 18, 1990." She opened the book and poured over photo after photo, watching Jake grow older with each turn of the page. The child who started out as a squalling infant transformed into a chubby-cheeked toddler and finally a lanky little boy, complete with a farmer's tan. Lexie ran her fingers over a snapshot of young Jake standing on the bottom rail of a split-rail fence, waving as his father's harvester went by. He was wearing a tiny pair of Wranglers, his bare chest and feet bronzed by the sun.

"How old was he here?" Lexie asked, looking up at Jake's mother.

Kathleen brought her a cup of hot chocolate and set it down as she peered over Lexie's shoulder.

"About four, I think," Kathleen said. She went to the pantry and pulled out a bag of flour and a small container of vanilla extract. "He was a typical country boy. He loved to ride on the tractors and chase the animals and always came home covered in mud from who-knows-where. But he's a hard worker, always has been. If there were jobs to be done, he was out doing them—even though staying on the farm wasn't ultimately his calling."

Lexie's eyes moved to the opposite page, where she saw a photo of Jake sitting cross-legged on a barn floor, bottle-feeding a tiny goat that lay curled between his knees.

"He's always had a soft heart, too," Kathleen continued, measuring ingredients into a massive silver bowl. "If any of the animals were hurt, he was the first to notice. If someone fell in the creek, he was the first one in after them. He hated to see anyone be left out or mistreated, and he's still that way. It's part of what makes him such a good man."

Lexie felt her chest warm. Jake certainly was a good man, and she could see how he'd become that way.

Kathleen came up behind her, a metal whisk clicking against the mixing bowl as she prepared the pancake batter. She paused and reached one finger down to point out a photo of Jake taken from behind. "And then, of course, there's all the times I caught him peeing in my flower bed. Boys that age will go absolutely anywhere," she explained wryly. Lexie felt a blush rush across her face, and Jake's mother laughed outright. "He would hate for me to tell you that, but it's the truth. If you ever have any sons, you'll find out," she added as she made her way back to the stove.

"Yes, you will," said a voice from the hall. A wheezy laugh announced Grandma Ruby's arrival moments before she shuffled through the kitchen doorway. "I raised four of them, and I know."

Lexie grinned as the tiny woman worked her way across the kitchen, grabbing a small glass from a low cabinet as she went. There was already a bottle of apple juice waiting on the counter—Kathleen's part in a dance they obviously did on a regular basis. Grandma Ruby poured herself a drink and shakily pulled out the chair next to Lexie, then sank into it as if she'd traveled a great distance.

"I say just let them go in the yard. The house stays cleaner that way," the older lady advised. "I'll never forget the time he tried to 'water' all my orchids, though he missed most of them. His aim was terrible."

Lexie nearly choked on her hot chocolate.

Grandma Ruby, however, took a tranquil sip of her juice before going on. "There's a reason we used to call him 'Squirt,'" she said.

"Squirt?!" Lexie blurted in disbelief, and Jake's mother and great-grandmother laughed heartily.

"Don't worry, dear. I'm sure he's gotten better," Grandma Ruby added.

Lexie couldn't help but laugh with them, though she knew Jake would be mortified. She stopped when she heard the front door open.

"What's so funny?" a voice called from the entryway, and seconds later, Jake and his father came into the room, rubbing their hands together and tugging off their hats.

"Goodness! I didn't hear the truck," Kathleen said, wiping her eyes with the back of her wrist.

"We walked back," Jake's dad supplied, and he brushed a kiss across his wife's cheek. "Rob was going to check on Paul's place since they're out of town, so he dropped us off at the road."

Kathleen nodded in understanding, then turned back to the eggs she was cracking into a large measuring cup. Without being asked, her husband lifted a cast iron skillet from the rack above her head and set it gently on the counter. Kathleen touched his arm as he started back toward the hall—a silent "thank you" in a language all their own.

"Nobody told me what's so funny," Jake added, pulling Lexie's attention away from his parents as he crossed the room toward her.

"I'm just hearing stories about baby Jake," she said, lifting her drink to her lips. "And finding out why they called you Squirt."

Jake blanched, a pained look crossing his face. "Really?!" he blurted, turning to his mother.

"I didn't do it," Kathleen said, holding her hands up in surrender, but the amused expression on her face said she wasn't sorry at all.

"Relax, Jacob. It's not like I told her about the time you stripped naked and paraded through ladies' Bible class like the King of Persia," Grandma Ruby said, and Lexie doubled over, resting her forehead on the table. Tears streamed from her eyes as her shoulders shook, and she was only vaguely aware of an argument taking place above her head.

"Grandma Ruby!" Jake shouted. "Do you have to?"

"Don't tempt me, boy," the older woman said, her voice full of fond affection.

Lexie was still gasping for breath when she sat up, wiping her wet cheeks with the palms of her hands. Her stomach ached, and her face felt like it might split open from the force of her smile, but it was a good feeling—even if it did come at Jake's expense.

"How old was he?" she managed to ask.

"Oh, about seven, I think," Grandma Ruby answered.

Lexie burst into another fit of giggles, and Jake groaned, his face locked in a grimace.

"I love that you're all getting along," he grumbled, kneading his fingers into Lexie's shoulders.

"Hush, or she'll think of something worse," Kathleen warned, plating the first stack of golden pancakes. "Now, go wash up. Breakfast will be ready shortly."

Jake gave Lexie's shoulders another squeeze before bending down close to her ear.

"Please don't hold this against me," he begged in a loud stage whisper.

Lexie chuckled and shooed him out of the room so Grandma Ruby could keep talking.

❦

"TOMMY'S SISTER TOLD me he came home with a jewelry store bag the other day—a really small one," Ashlyn told Grandma Ruby.

"Tommy's sister ought to keep her mouth shut," the older woman said, leaning down to inspect the assortment of treats that sat cooling on the kitchen counter. All the women had been baking since the breakfast dishes had been cleared, and the house was now filled with the scent of everything from cookies and brownies to fruit tarts, pies and creme cakes.

"I think he might ask me to marry him!" Ashlyn went on. "Wouldn't a Christmas proposal be romantic?"

"Ashlyn, honey, take off your running shoes and give the boy a chance to catch you," Grandma Ruby said, shuffling to the table. Jake's mother, who sat mending a pair of her husband's pants, chuckled softly.

"Oh, Grandma Ruby," Jake's sister sighed.

"Don't 'Grandma Ruby' me, young lady! This is not my first trip around the sun," the older woman said, sinking into a chair beside her great-granddaughter. The family matriarch glanced up and caught Lexie's eye, shooting her a wink. "Come sit down, Lexie. This is good for you to hear, too."

Lexie wiped her hands on her borrowed apron, leaving white flour smudges on the patterned fabric. Then she drifted across the kitchen to join the conversation—not that she'd have much to contribute.

"You see, girls, most people seem to think falling in love is like being struck by lightning," Grandma Ruby continued. "But I've lived a long time, and one thing I know for sure is the love that lasts is less like a rainstorm and more like snowfall. It builds quietly, and by the time you look up, it has changed the landscape of your life, and you realize you'll never see the world quite the same way again.

"Real love isn't luck or magic or fate. It's a choice. One you make every day, rain or shine, to give your best to the person you've chosen. Love shows up. It trusts and hopes and is patient. And most importantly," she said, looking pointedly at Ashlyn, "it is not on a schedule."

"But Tommy—"

"Might be the one, and he might not," the older woman interrupted. "But don't push him or yourself to make a decision you can't undo just because you think it's time."

The distant sound of men shouting broke through the large picture window, and all four women looked up in time to see Jake and Drew burst out of the barn and into the weak sunlight, both gesturing wildly. Drew shoved Jake hard and stormed away, pulling a sigh from his great-grandmother's throat.

"I'm coming for that one next," she said, her gnarled index finger following Drew as he stormed across the backyard, kicking several empty flowerpots out of his way. "I'm going to teach him to control his temper if it's the last thing I do."

"You can't fix them all, Ruby," Kathleen said, rising to her feet.

"Maybe not, but I can try," Grandma Ruby muttered, still watching her great-grandson. "He and Jake used to be thick as thieves. I wish I knew exactly what happened to them."

Ashlyn started offering her guesses, but Lexie wasn't listening. She was thinking about snow.

❧

"I MISSED YOU today," Jake said as he lay back against one end of the couch in his father's study. He shifted sideways, and Lexie settled into the gap between his body and the couch, feeling herself relax as his arm came down around her. He'd showered after coming in from the barn, and she took a deep breath of his clean pine scent, which always made her feel safe and wanted. He'd already pulled off his thick green pullover, and his white T-shirt was warm under her cheek. "Do you feel like I just threw you to the wolves?" he asked, and Lexie shook her head.

"I've actually had a lot of fun," she admitted. "Your family is *nothing* like mine. Do your parents ever fight at all?"

Jake chuckled slightly, his arm tightening around her back. "Sure! Just not in front of anybody."

"I think you could add up all the cookies I've made in my entire life, and I still beat that total today. Exactly how many people are coming to dinner tomorrow?" she asked.

Jake paused, thinking.

"I'm not sure, to be honest. Grandma Ruby and Grandpa Jacob had four sons, and then they all had kids. There are a few relatives here and there who have passed away, but most of their descendants are still alive. They'll come in from all over," he said. "Grandma Ruby wants to have everyone together at least once a year until she dies. There are so many of us that we'll have to eat in the barn; we spent most of today cleaning it."

Lexie nodded, feeling the fabric of his shirt move as she did.

"I get that. I mean, my grandmother likes to have everyone all together, too, but that's more so she can tell us what we're doing wrong with our lives than anything else."

"I'm sorry," Jake said quietly, and Lexie knew he really meant it.

"It is what it is," she replied. Truthfully, she'd tried to be sad about her family situation. She'd really tried to miss them. But it was awfully hard to wish you were sitting in a cold, stuffy house having your sins read aloud when the Tanner family was bustling around you with open arms.

"You fit here," Jake added after a pause. "I'm not going to lie, coming in at lunch to find you baking may be the greatest thing I've ever seen."

Lexie laughed, and a matching rumble moved through Jake's chest.

"Jacob Tanner, are you telling me a woman's place is in the kitchen?" she teased, lifting her head to watch his face.

"No! Not at all," he protested. "I'm just saying any time you want to make cookies with my mom, I can get on board with that." There was a mischievous glint in his eyes, and Lexie rolled hers good-naturedly. He turned and pressed a kiss to her forehead as she snuggled back against him.

"It was actually more about how happy you looked, and the fact that you were here when I came in," he admitted. "It felt like you'd always been here. Like you might always be here."

A silence fell between them, and Lexie was acutely aware of the way the knuckles of his right hand trailed lazily along her arm where it lay draped across his stomach.

"I made the meringue, too, you know," she said, mostly just to fill the silence.

"*You* made the meringue? Grandma Ruby's dark chocolate cherry mile-high meringue?" Jake asked, his voice filled with surprise.

"Yeah, I guess so. She gave me the recipe card, anyway."

"Grandma Ruby *gave you* her recipe card?" he asked incredulously.

"Yes . . . Why?" Lexie narrowed her eyes. It had been a complicated recipe, but it seemed odd for Jake to be so interested.

"That pie is like a family heirloom. *Nobody* makes it except Grandma Ruby," he explained, running his fingers through her hair.

"Why would she let me do it, then?" Lexie asked.

Jake shrugged. "I guess she really likes you. Although I can't imagine why," he said dryly, and Lexie smacked his shoulder.

"Be nice to me, or I might start calling you Squirt," she warned, and Jake let out a resigned sigh.

"You have learned too many things today," he complained, but his smile said he didn't really mind.

Lexie chuckled and raised herself on one arm so she was looking down at him. His hand dropped from her hair to her waist as she traced the dark stubble on his jaw.

"I learned you aren't close to Drew anymore," she said, sobering. "Why is that?"

Jake didn't answer immediately, and his eyes darted around her face as if he were looking for the right words.

"Honestly? I'm not sure."

Lexie furrowed her brow in confusion, and he went on.

"Drew and I were basically twins growing up. We're only two months apart, so we did everything together for years. But something changed around the time we started high school."

Jake's voice was sad, and Lexie longed to smooth away the crease that deepened between his eyes.

"I really think it started with a girl, actually," he added.

"A girl?"

"Yeah. Savannah, the one I told you about with the answering machine?"

Lexie nodded, remembering the story.

"We'd all been friends for ages, and I wanted to ask her to be my girlfriend, but I sort of thought Drew might have a crush on her. When I asked him about it, he said he didn't . . . but everything was different after that," Jake explained. "Even after Savannah and I broke up, Drew was always upset with me about something. He'd get mad when good things happened, like when

I made the soccer team or got good grades; he acted like I didn't deserve it. And then when I moved to Cypress Valley, it just got worse."

Lexie ran her hand through his hair, wishing she could somehow make this a better story.

"What was the problem today?"

"Today?"

"Yeah. We saw you arguing after lunch."

"Oh," Jake sighed and leaned absentmindedly against her hand. "What is it always about? How he's here every day, slaving away in the hot sun to keep this place running, while I'm kicked back on a Barcalounger in my cushy bachelor pad," he said, his voice dripping with sarcasm. "He acts like I just abandoned him here in purgatory, like I shouldn't have had any other dreams. But he *likes* working the farm. He's proud of it; he's good at it. This is what he *wants* to do!

"And I'm proud of it, too! I'm proud to come from a century of farmers, but it's not in me to spend the rest of my life driving the combine and checking the cows. I mean, I would, if I had to," he amended quickly. "If there were nobody else to continue the farm, I would do it; I'm not just going to let a hundred years of hard work die with me. But that's why I'm so grateful that he *is* here and that he *wants* to be a farmer. He and Sawyer and James . . . they'll inherit this land and keep it running. They'll be the next generation of Tanners here, and I'm proud of them for it. But he makes me feel like I decided I was too good for them."

Lexie watched guilt war with aggravation as both danced across his face. All the muscles in his torso were tense where she leaned against him, and his jaw rolled back and forth as he stared at a point somewhere past her shoulder.

"Jacob?" she asked, trying to regain his attention.

"Hmm?" he grunted, his eyes coming back to hers.

"If I've learned anything at all in the last few months, it's that we can't let other people make our choices for us," she said softly. She watched his eyes as he seemed to drink her in. "You're allowed to have dreams. You're allowed to be talented, and you can't let anyone hold you back from that. If Drew wants to be here, then thank him for it, but don't let him make you feel like his choices were better than yours just because they were different."

Lexie cut off suddenly as the words *I love you* darted through her mind. She could taste them on her tongue, feel the shape of them in her mouth, but the idea of saying them out loud—of *meaning them* the way she thought she might—made her pause.

Jake's gaze stayed locked on her face for a long moment, like he was memorizing every detail of what he saw, before he threaded his hand into her hair and tugged her down to him. Lexie closed her eyes and let him kiss her like it might be the last time, and like it was the first time, and like they'd never stopped at all. She felt his grip tighten against the back of her neck as she shifted above him, hoping to make him understand all the things she didn't know how to say.

"Jacob? Can you open this peanut butter for me? I've tried everything," his mother called from down the hall, her voice breaking them apart with a gasp.

"She has radar," Jake mumbled, his eyes still closed.

Lexie was surprised to realize she was barely touching the couch. She started to ease away from him, but Jake stopped her with a hand against her back.

"I didn't say I wanted you to move," he whispered against her ear, and Lexie felt the world shift beneath her when he rolled, flipping her onto her back as he stood up.

"Jacob? Where are you?" Kathleen called again, and he chuck-led softly.

"Just a second, Mama!" he called before leaning down and pressing another hard kiss against Lexie's mouth. "You're a dangerous woman," he muttered. Fire flashed in his eyes as he pulled away, watching her with an expression she rarely saw from him. He took a deep breath, rolled his shoulders and disappeared into the hall.

Lexie speared her fingers through her hair, raking it away from her face as she tried to breathe normally. What had she almost said? Where had it come from?

But even as she asked herself, she knew.

Real love had grown quietly, while she wasn't looking, and she was pretty sure nothing would ever be the same again.

15

"RUN, JACOB!" LEXIE screamed, her hands cupped around her mouth as she stood on the edge of an empty pasture and watched most of the Tanner men and a few of the neighbors play what was supposed to be touch football, though the younger cousins were doing a fair bit of roughhousing anyway. Lexie winced when Jake went down hard.

"That was a rough one," Ashlyn said, taking a sip from her copper-colored thermos. "At least his team is winning, though. Tommy's is down by three touchdowns," she added, nodding toward the far side of the field where her boyfriend and his teammates stood discussing their next play.

"What do they get if they win?" Lexie asked as she settled into a camp chair beside Gomer the dog and scratched behind his ears.

"Well, there used to be a trophy," Brooklyn answered, leaning over the arm of her chair, "but somebody either broke it or lost it a few years back, we aren't sure which. Either way, it vanished. Now, they just get bragging rights."

Lexie propped her sneakers on top of the drink cooler and made herself comfortable. The football game was a Thanksgiving tradition for the Tanners, and while everyone had been given the option to play, Ashlyn had convinced Lexie to sit with the girls instead. Hannah and her twin sister, Morgan, the two oldest of Jake's cousins, completed their spectators' circle.

"Who are you cheering for, Bee?" Hannah asked, her voice lilting up suspiciously.

Lexie watched Brooklyn turn a dark shade of pink as Ashlyn laughed and prodded her cousin with her foot.

"Shut up," the youngest girl grumbled, sinking deeper into her purple sweatshirt and using the hood to hide her face.

Lexie leaned forward, eager to be part of the secret. "Which one?" she asked, scanning the makeshift football field for any unfamiliar faces.

"That one," Hannah said, pointing to a tall young man wearing a Mason County Raiders football jersey. "Tommy's brother, Jon. They're biology lab partners, and Bee's got it *bad*."

"Oh, he's cute," Lexie said, watching as Brooklyn's color changed again.

"I do not 'have it bad,' " the girl grumbled, but Lexie could tell it was a half-hearted protest.

"Oh, so there's no particular reason you disappeared into my bathroom the second he got here and came out with fresh curls and a full face of makeup?" Ashlyn asked with a smirk. "Just think, Bee! We could be cousins *and* sisters-in-law!"

"Ugh, never mind. The last thing I need is to be related to you *twice*," Brooklyn retorted. She groaned and rolled her eyes while the other women laughed. Their affection for each other was almost a tangible force, and Lexie was overwhelmingly glad to be part of it.

"Speaking of people who've got it bad," Hannah said, her gaze darting to Lexie with obvious meaning. "If I were putting money on which of us is head over heels, I'd pick Jake."

Lexie felt her cheeks heat up as she looked across the field. When her gaze came back to the girls, every single one of them was staring at her with questions in their eyes.

"Spill!" Brooklyn said, grinning. "I want to hear all about this concert he took you to. Did he tell you we helped him get dressed? He was so nervous! It was adorable."

Lexie felt her face split into a wide grin as she remembered Jake's obvious anxiety when he'd come to her door.

"Do you want the concert story or the meteor shower story?"

"The *what*?!" the girls screeched, all leaning in closer. They listened in rapt attention and made appropriately impressed noises as Lexie shared the details—all the good ones, at least. When she reached the end, there was silence while the four cousins exchanged a loaded glance.

"Okay, who wants to break the news?" Hannah asked, looking around the group with a satisfied smile.

Lexie frowned. "What news?"

Morgan grinned. "You are so far gone," she said, her eyes sparkling with mischief. "Go ahead and have the tea towels monogrammed, because you'll be one of us before you know it."

Lexie sat for a moment, considering the possibility, but a tremendous shout went up from the field before she could respond. The game appeared to be over, and both teams were advancing toward the cooler at an alarming rate.

"Your feet are in the way," Jake told Lexie as the girls were overrun. But instead of simply moving her legs, he swooped down and grabbed her around the waist before hauling her over his shoulder. Her eyes went wide as the other girls laughed.

"Jacob Ryan, put me down!" she demanded, struggling to push herself upright.

"Ooh, she middle-named you," somebody shouted, which only made Jake hike her up higher on his shoulder.

"Guess I'd better go before I get in trouble then," he said.

"What? No!" Lexie shrieked, laughing despite her embarrassment, but Jake kept walking toward the house.

"What did I tell you? Totally gone," she heard Morgan say, catching Lexie's eye with a wink. Lexie could only wave back helplessly.

"You are incorrigible," she told him, twisting so she could at least see where they were going. Jake only grunted, but Lexie could hear his amusement anyway. He finally put her down on the far side of a small garden shed among some old windowpanes, a rusted car fender and a peeling wooden door that might have come from someone's closet.

"I want to know what all the cackling was about," he said as he backed her up against the shed's metal siding.

"What cackling?" Lexie asked, playing dumb.

"At your hen party," he said. "There was pointing and laughing, and I want to know why."

"Oh, I'm sorry, that's confidential information," Lexie answered.

Jake made a displeased sort of noise, though it was clear the act was hard to maintain.

"Were you talking about me?"

Lexie scoffed and rolled her eyes in mock derision. "No, actually. Believe it or not, you're not the only cute guy at this party," she teased, pursing her lips against a smile.

"Oh! Wrong answer," he said. His fingers brushed against a sensitive spot below her ribcage.

"Jacob, stop that!" she shouted, laughing, but when she tried to squirm away, he went for the other side as well.

"Take it back, woman!" he demanded, obviously holding back a laugh of his own as he started prodding all the ticklish places he could reach.

He'd shed his sweatshirt during the game, and his navy T-shirt was streaked with mud and grass, some of which Lexie was sure would transfer to her sweater. She giggled as she tried to fend him off, but stilled when he pinned her wrists above her head, holding her easily in place.

"Take it back," he murmured, his face now only millimeters from hers.

Lexie could count the shades of brown in his eyes, and she watched them all grow darker as the air between them shifted, turning into something more heated than before. The words she still hadn't said bubbled just below the surface, and she tried to catch her breath enough to let them out. But the moment didn't last.

"Jacob!" somebody sang, sounding downright gleeful. "Jacob, you're up to something!" The footsteps came closer, crunching through the old garden nearby, and Jake straightened.

"Jonah," he mouthed. He let go of Lexie's hands and stepped back seconds before his cousin appeared around the corner of the shed.

"Whatcha doin'?" Jonah drawled, a Cheshire-Cat grin plastered across his face. He was a few years younger than Jake, though he had the same lean frame. The family resemblance was unmistakable.

"None of your business. What do you need?" Jake said, with only a hint of irritation in his voice.

"Oh, nothing in particular," Jonah replied with a grin. "Just saw you wander off with this poor girl over your shoulder like a caveman and wanted to be sure you weren't holding her against her will." His eyes darted over to Lexie with a smirk. "Do you need to be rescued, Miss Lexie? Maybe let a real man take care of you for a change?"

As unfortunate as the interruption was, Lexie couldn't help but laugh. Jonah had been a good sport when she'd beaten him in Jenga the other night, and she'd quickly developed a soft spot for his particular brand of cocky humor. She thought about his offer for a second and decided to turn Jake's own game against him.

"I might, actually. Maybe you can teach this one a thing or two," she said with an exaggerated grimace, and Jake's head whipped in her direction. The younger boy howled in laughter as Jake shook his head slowly, an impish warning in his eyes. But Jonah grabbed Lexie's hand and pulled her away, all the while talking animatedly about a tackle where he'd sent Jake rolling.

Lexie glanced over her shoulder and saw Jake still standing beside the shed, his hands in his pockets and a smile on his face as he watched her leave. She'd catch up with him again later. For now, he could simmer in a stew of his own making.

❧❧❧

"TAKE THIS PLATTER, Lexie. Hannah, those cake pans are ready to go. Oliver, carry a few more chairs out, would you, dear?"

Kathleen Tanner was in full command mode by eleven thirty, giving orders as people scurried between the barn and the house.

The women checked and rechecked every dish, loading the long folding tables in the barn with enough food for a mid-sized army, while the men joined the fray wherever they could.

By noon, all was ready.

The inside of the barn had been scrubbed to a shine the day before. The concrete floors were covered in a fresh layer of clean straw, and the walls and doorways were decorated with leftover corn stalks and small pumpkins taken straight from the fields. Half a dozen standing propane heaters created pockets of warmth to ward off the chill that drifted in whenever the large doors were opened. It was a job that would have taken one person three weeks, but, thankfully, there were about a hundred Tanners—every one of whom had welcomed Lexie like she was one of their own.

She'd stopped trying to keep track of their names about an hour before, simply wishing everyone a happy Thanksgiving as their paths crossed hers. Having lost Jake in the mayhem, she was glad to find Hannah and Morgan chatting with a few other relatives close to the buffet line.

"Where did all these people come from?" she asked, latching onto Hannah's arm.

Jake's cousin laughed and patted Lexie's hand with affection. "We're a lot, I know, but don't worry. Nobody here will eat you," she said.

"Except maybe Jake," Morgan added, leaning in close so only Lexie would hear. "He looked like he was pretty hungry earlier."

Lexie laughed and felt heat flood her face, which only prompted snickers from her new friends.

After the blessing was said and the food officially served, she joined the line behind them and started to fill her plate, still keeping an eye out for Jake. She hadn't been able to talk to him since she'd left him in the garden earlier.

"Well, it's nice to finally meet the great Lexie Preston," a deep voice behind her said, and Lexie turned, expecting to find an uncle or maybe a grandfather. Instead, she came face-to-face with Drew. He looked down at her with a smile that didn't quite reach his eyes. "We haven't had a chance to chat."

"Sorry, I've been trying to get to know everyone," Lexie said, trying to brush off how nervous he suddenly made her. Just because he and Jake weren't close didn't mean Drew was a threat.

"Oh, believe me, I know how hard it can be to keep up with the prodigal son," he said, his voice more casual than his words. "I just wanted to check in . . . see if you're living up to the hype."

"The what?" Lexie asked, frowning as she scooped up a helping of chicken salad.

"The hype, the fame, the glory," Drew said. He dipped a spoon into the green beans. "I mean, Jake's only been going on about you for the last three years. That's a lot of pressure for one person."

Lexie shook her head, catching his mistake. "Jake and I have only known each other since August, so maybe three months, but definitely not three *years*."

"Oh!" Drew said, a look of almost-genuine surprise taking over his face. "I guess he hasn't told you that part. Although, I can't really blame him; it's a stupid story, really."

Lexie's hand paused over another spoon, this time for the mashed potatoes.

"Sorry, but I don't know what you're talking about," she said, glancing toward where Hannah was making her way along the line in front of her. There wasn't any good way to disengage from this conversation without being incredibly rude.

"I'm talking about how everyone's favorite hero has been starry-eyed over you since freshman year," Drew said as he stepped around her to reach the glazed carrots. "Something about a beautiful girl across a crowded room and how angels sang and the Earth turned backwards and whatever else. And now, surprise, surprise, he's finally got you. Must be a nice view from that golden pedestal you're standing on—a long fall, too."

Lexie's mind turned his words over, replaying them faster and faster until they sounded like the squeal of cartoon chipmunks.

"That's really not possible. He didn't even know me until this year," she said, moving toward the dessert table, but Drew kept pace with her as she went. "I mean, I think we might have had a class together or something, but . . ."

"Oh, trust me, sweetheart," he said, suddenly reminding her so much of Colt that a chill went down her spine, "he didn't have to know you to name your six children and pick out your minivan. I think he's decided on a Dodge, one of the blue ones with sliding doors—better for all the soccer games you'll be going to. He'll be *so* disappointed if they aren't all varsity players. Only the best for Jake Tanner, you know."

Lexie opened her mouth to respond, but no words came out. Drew reached past her and grabbed a chocolate chip cookie from the plate near her hand.

"I heard you made the meringue, by the way. I hope it's good," he said before turning and making his way toward an open seat next to Ashlyn and Tommy. Setting his plate down, he caught her eye with a smirk and raised his disposable cup in a silent toast similar to the ones she'd gotten from Colt in the past. The ones that always meant he had her right where he wanted her.

The roar of too many conversations suddenly wasn't enough to drown out the voices that plagued Lexie in moments of weakness.

"What could you possibly have to offer him?"

"There's nothing that makes you special."

"He'll be so disappointed."

She was frozen, surrounded by the kind of family she didn't know how to have—a family that had accepted her readily and without question. A family that hadn't yet discovered what a disappointment she really was.

"There you are," came a voice over her shoulder, and the warmth of Jake's hand at the small of her back temporarily slowed her spiral. "Have you found a place yet? I saw a few open chairs by Jonah, but considering how easily he stole my girl earlier, I'm going to say no," he said, laughing to himself. "What about with Hannah?"

Jake must have looked down then, because he paused.

"Lex, are you okay?" he asked. He dipped his head to put himself in her line of sight, and her eyes slipped back into focus on his face.

She forced a smile, deliberately keeping her breathing even, and nodded. "I'm fine," she replied, hoping he wouldn't press any deeper.

Jake furrowed his brow and scanned her face again before guiding her to a table where Hannah and Oliver seemed to be saving them seats. He set his plate down before taking Lexie's from her hands.

"Are you sure you're okay?" he murmured. He wrapped one arm around her shoulders and turned her into his chest like a hug. "I know this is a lot. We can eat in the house if you want."

Eating in the house would not help. It would not change all the ways she would inevitably fail him.

"I'm fine, really," she said again, pushing the words past a hard lump in her throat. After a moment, Jake relented, though she could tell he wasn't convinced. Lexie sat down and started to eat, putting one forkful in her mouth at a time purely to keep from joining the conversation that sprang to life around her. If she could just keep her mouth full, maybe nothing damaging would come out of it. Maybe these people wouldn't know exactly what a train wreck they were dealing with.

The voices in her mind got louder, chanting a litany of adjectives like stock market ticker tape.

Mediocre. Selfish. Ungrateful. Incompetent. Embarrassing. Exhausting . . .

She'd thought it was different this time; she'd thought it was real. But if Drew was right, then it was only a dream—a dream Jake had cooked up years ago and was only playing out the way he'd imagined. He could only see the girl he'd made her out to be—and reality would never measure up. It never did.

"Must be a nice view from that golden pedestal you're standing on—a long fall, too."

Jake kept his left arm across the back of her chair, his hand a steady pressure on the edge of her shoulder. Lexie caught a few odd glances from Hannah and her husband, and then from Brooklyn, who sat down later.

They're starting to realize, she thought, her panic growing. *They're starting to see that something is wrong with me. That I don't belong here. That I won't fit.*

Lexie felt like the water around her was rising, lapping at her face and pulling at her clothes. In a minute, she'd be submerged, drowning, unnoticed and forgotten in a sea of people. Her chest was too tight, and the flood made it hard to breathe.

Any minute now, she thought. *Any minute now, they'll see.*

"Lexie, you did an amazing job on this pie!" Hannah said, giving her an uncertain smile as she lifted a forkful of the dark chocolate to her mouth. "I still can't believe Grandma Ruby let you make it."

"That pie is like a family heirloom. Nobody makes it except Grandma Ruby."

"Have the tea towels monogrammed, because you'll be one of us before you know it."

"Only the best for Jake Tanner."

"I need some air," Lexie mumbled, pushing unsteadily to her feet. She saw the glances that went around the table, passed from cousin to cousin like a telegram.

Something is wrong with this girl . . .

"I'll come with you," Jake said, his voice somehow very far away, but Lexie shook her head.

"No, please. Stay. Eat," she managed, then she shoved past him in the direction she had come. The door was near the end of the food line. It had to be. Without it, she was trapped.

She could feel the tide of conversation turning toward her. The eyes that followed her out the door, the whispers that snagged her skin. She knew they were all discussing her now, asking themselves how they'd been so blind, how Jake could have been deceived so completely.

Poor Jake. Poor, poor Jake.

She passed his parents sitting near the exit, and Kathleen reached a hand up as she barreled by, but Lexie ignored it. Her own mother had told her what a disappointment she was more times than she could count. She didn't need to hear it from his mother, too.

Pushing through the doors, she sucked cool air into her lungs and then hurried toward the house. Just a few more steps—across the yard, onto the porch, through the front door. Within moments, she stood in the empty, quiet living room clutching the back of the sectional couch, desperately looking for something, anything, to ground herself.

What do you feel? What do you smell? What do you hear?

The couch's worn leather was cool beneath her hands, and a rough place on one of the seams caught her skin as she rubbed her palms over it. The lingering scent of smoked turkey drifted from the kitchen, as did the hum of the refrigerator. The ice maker clattered as it dumped another load into the tray. A television had been left on somewhere down the hall, and the artificial sound of a laugh track grated on Lexie's ears.

But it wasn't enough.

Five things you can see, she reminded herself, looking around. There was a multicolored quilt hanging on the back of Logan Tanner's armchair, the star pattern swirled with silver thread. A half-empty glass of clear soda sat abandoned on the end table, the bubbles still rising quietly to the surface. A magazine, its cover displaying a piece of green farm equipment, was partially tucked into the crease between two of the couch cushions. The gauzy curtains on the front windows shifted slightly over an air vent in the floor, and one of the picture frames on the wall was slightly off-center.

Lexie's gaze caught on the photographs, all Jake's work, each showing a different part of life on the farm—a black-and-white print of a barn in the fog, a newborn calf wobbling on brand-new legs, the pink tint of sunrise beyond a hay-strewn field.

"National Geographic is the dream, of course . . ."

He had so much potential. He had plans, dreams, passions . . . and she was drifting. She didn't know what she wanted from her life or how to go about getting it.

"You're allowed to be talented, and you can't let anyone hold you back from that."

Lexie turned so fast she stumbled, knocking a vase of dried flowers to the floor. She was already up the stairs, cramming discarded clothing into her weekend bag, before she realized the vase had broken.

16

J AKE WATCHED LEXIE make her way to the barn door and sidestep his mother before vanishing from sight. He furrowed his brow, trying to see the missing piece of the puzzle. Surely she wasn't mad about how he'd carried her off earlier. She hadn't seemed upset about it at the time, but maybe he'd gone too far. Maybe she didn't like that he'd done it in front of so many people.

He was still piecing his thoughts together when he noticed both Hannah and Brooklyn staring at him with wide, expectant eyes.

"What?" he asked, his gaze bouncing between them.

"Aren't you going after her?" Brooklyn asked as she gestured toward the door where Lexie had disappeared.

Jake looked in the direction she'd pointed, debating. "Maybe she just needs a minute," he said.

"Get up, you idiot!" Hannah practically shouted. "Something's wrong!"

The frantic tone of her voice spurred Jake to action. He scrambled out of his chair but had only moved a few feet before he was intercepted.

"Jacob! It's good to see you. How is college going? Senior year, right?" asked an elderly man. Jake recognized him as one of his grandfather's brothers.

"Yes, sir. It's going well," Jake said distractedly. He kept glancing toward the door, but his great-uncle started talking about his own days at Cypress Valley and how much the little town had grown.

"Uncle Jamison!" Hannah's too-bright voice chirped from Jake's right. "It's fantastic to see you! How are all the grandkids?" Her smile was comically wide, and she bumped Jake with her hip, a silent command for him to run while he still could.

Jake took the opening and began to move more quickly toward the door. He avoided two more aunts and a handful of second cousins before making it outside, but Lexie was nowhere to be found. He made his way to the house and opened the front door cautiously. Hurried footsteps sounded above his head, and he followed them until he found Lexie in his old bedroom, frantically shoving a curling iron and a makeup bag into her duffel.

"Lex? What are you doing?" he asked, alarmed. She jumped at the sound of his voice.

"I'm—I'm sorry, Jacob," she stammered, shoving another T-shirt into the bulging bag. "I can't do this. I can't be here. I just . . . I can't. I can't do it."

"Can't do what?" he asked as he watched her dart toward the dresser and pull a phone charger from the wall. She really was leaving.

"This, Jacob. All of this."

"All of *what*?" he asked again, finally moving into the room.

Lexie whirled around and threw both arms wide, as if trying to encompass everything at once.

"*This*! The happy, loving family. The baking and the family games and the prayers before meals. It's too much! Nobody actually lives like this. It's like being a guest on *The Brady Bunch*!"

Jake pulled back, stunned. "Lexie," he said. "Everyone loves you."

"That's because they don't know me, and neither do you! I thought maybe you did, that all of this was real, but you've just got your head in the clouds."

Jake's chest tightened painfully, and he resisted the urge to rub it with his hand.

"What are you talking about? I *do* know you, Lex!"

"No, you don't!" she said, her voice shrill. "You know an imaginary version of me, some perfect fantasy girl you fell in love with on the spot. That doesn't happen, Jacob! Life isn't a fairy tale!"

Jake's thoughts whirled in a blinding vortex of color and sound, replaying all the ways he'd tried to show her how he felt, all the things he'd done to make sure this moment wouldn't happen. All the things that had obviously meant nothing.

"Do you not trust me at all?" he heard himself ask, though it wasn't what he'd planned to say.

"It's not about trust. It's about reality," she said, her voice thick as she wrestled with the zipper on her bag. "You're so blinded by daydreams that you can't see what's actually in front of you."

"You think I don't see you?" he asked, his volume rising. His mouth had officially gone rogue. "I have told you, over and over, how much I want to be with you. Do you think I've just been making that up?"

"I think you honestly believe it, but that doesn't mean it's true," Lexie said, finally yanking the zipper closed and throwing the strap over one shoulder. The tears that had gathered in her eyes slid down her cheeks, but for the first time, Jake didn't move to wipe them away. For the first time, he was angry with her.

"So, I'm nuts, is that it?" he demanded as she pushed roughly past him and headed for the stairs. Jake followed hot on her heels. "You want to know about the shooting stars, what I wished for that night? I wished for you! Every single time. Not for some imaginary dream girl. For *you*! You are everything I've ever wanted, Lex. I don't know how many other ways I can say that!"

She charged down the stairs, and he followed a step behind.

"You wanted somebody to fight for you? Well, here I am!" he shouted, his hands in the air. "All I do, every day, is fight for you, but that's still not good enough? Just tell me what you want!"

"I don't know what I want!" she shot back, crashing through the front door and onto the porch.

"So, what, you're just going to leave? Now, in the middle of Thanksgiving dinner, with my entire family standing by to watch?" he asked, his feet pounding down the porch stairs and onto the gravel driveway. "What am I supposed to tell my parents?"

"I don't know, Jacob! Tell them whatever you want," she said as she strode toward her car which, unfortunately for Jake, bordered the open driveway. She'd be able to turn, whereas his truck was blocked in three cars deep. It would be hours before he could follow.

Jake felt frustration surge through him as she yanked her car door open and tossed her bag onto the passenger's seat.

"Lexie, I love you! Why can't you see that?" he demanded, grabbing her arm and snatching her away from the open car door.

Lexie flinched, and the fear that flashed across her face took Jake by surprise. His grip loosened automatically.

"Don't do this," she said, finally meeting his eyes. "This was never going to work—you and me. We should have left things the way they were."

Jake felt the blood drain from his face. He looked at her without breathing, hoping to see some sign, a single flicker, that she didn't mean what she'd said, but he found nothing. He released her without realizing he'd done it. Lexie turned away quickly and slid into the driver's seat of her Infiniti before quickly starting the car. She reached for the door, and he narrowly avoided being caught as she slammed it shut.

The crunch of her tires on the gravel was too loud in Jake's ears as she maneuvered until she had a straight shot down the driveway. He watched her car pull away until it disappeared beyond the trees, and the tugging behind his sternum became painfully tight, stretching until it was hard to breathe. It hurt so badly he almost wished it would break.

"Well, looks like you don't get everything you want after all."

A low drawl from across the driveway brought Jake back to the yard, the house, the barn, the people who would soon come out of it.

Specifically, to the one who already had.

"What did you do?" he growled, turning on his cousin with all the anger he had left.

Drew shrugged, his face already covered in storm clouds. "I just told her the truth—that you've got high expectations, and she's got a lot to live up to. Though, I'll be honest, she freaked out more than I expected. That girl's got issues."

There was an odd moment where time seemed to hover. The steady rhythm of Jake's own heartbeat was white noise in his ears, drowning out the singing of the birds and the creak of the old tire swing. He didn't register the slip of loose gravel beneath his boots, and he barely noticed the soft fabric of Drew's shirt collar in his hand. But he *did* feel the rattle in his bones when his fist connected with his cousin's jaw, bringing the world around him sharply back into focus.

"Why do you hate me?" Jake shouted as Drew staggered backwards. His cousin looked up, eyes ablaze, and rushed forward with all the force of an angry bull. Both boys crashed to the ground in a heap.

"You're the chosen one!" Drew grunted, taking aim. Jake felt the gravel beneath him rip into his skin at the same time his head whipped to one side, pain exploding where Drew's fist made contact near his temple.

"The golden boy!" Drew hissed, drawing back for another hit.

Drew was bigger and stronger the way only years of constant physical labor could make him, but Jake had pure adrenaline on his side. Years of pent-up frustration surged into his hands as he drove both fists into his cousin's gut, knocking the air from his lungs. He shoved hard, forcing Drew to the ground and rolling on top of him before slamming into his cousin's face for a second time.

Several pairs of hands suddenly closed around his shoulders, dragging him backwards as he aimed again.

"Get off him, Jacob!" a deep voice yelled, but Jake was past the point of obedience. He lashed out blindly, flailing as he was hauled to his feet. Uncle Rob and Oliver grabbed Drew around the waist as he tried to scramble forward, obviously hoping to even the score.

"You get everything you want. Why wouldn't I hate you?" Drew shouted as he strained against the hands that held him.

Logan Tanner stepped in front of his son. "Take a walk!" he commanded, shoving Jake toward the house.

Sawyer looped a supportive arm around Jake's shoulders, but Jake flung him off, stalking toward the old garden shed. When he got there, he looked wildly around, his eyes landing on the bare spot against the siding where he'd stood with Lexie only hours before. He could almost see the indentation of her shoes in the grass, hear her voice in the air.

"This was never going to work—you and me. We should have left things the way they were."

"I've got to tell you, that gut check was impressive," his younger cousin said from somewhere behind him, though he sounded much farther away. "I don't know how he didn't see it coming. *I* saw it coming, and I was halfway across the yard."

"I'm going in," Jake snapped, ignoring his cousin completely as he turned on his heel and stalked toward the back porch.

"You want me to get Lexie? Where is she?"

"Gone," Jake muttered. "Long gone."

HE WAS GLAD it was raining. The steel-gray clouds reflected his mood as they dumped sheets of water on the barren fields, washing the leaves from the trees and effectively flipping the world from autumn to winter in a single stroke.

Jake had been awake most of the night, alternatively pacing and staring at the ceiling in his father's office. He could have slept in his own room, of course, but everything in there smelled like her. It was enough to drive him crazy.

He'd been over their argument a million times, trying to catch every word in his hands so he could turn them over and examine them from all sides, but somehow his memory always caught on Lexie packing to leave, moving like the house was on fire and she only needed to save herself. Everything after that felt blurred, like one continuous rush of motion, though bits and pieces came back to him, dancing like fireflies in the dark.

"I can't do this. I can't be here . . . Life isn't a fairy tale."

He rolled his neck, wincing with every movement. He had a huge scrape across one shoulder blade where the driveway gravel had torn his favorite sweater, and he ached from his neck to his knees. The knuckles of his right hand were a nasty violet color to match the bruise near his left temple, which had spread overnight to give him the worst black eye he'd ever had. Drew, however, would have two, and that fact gave Jake a childish sense of satisfaction.

The clock hit six, and just as he'd expected, there was a knock on the door that was neither polite nor quiet, despite the early hour.

"Can you see straight?" his father asked gruffly, striding into the room without waiting to be invited.

Jake answered with a grunt that his dad obviously took to mean yes.

"Good, get dressed. There are cows to feed."

His dad stalked out, leaving the door open behind him. To say his father was unhappy with his behavior would be an understatement, but Jake was having a hard time caring as much as he usually did.

He didn't even bother with clean clothes; he'd be soaked to the bone by the time he got back anyway. Instead, he pulled on an old pair of jeans and the shirt he'd played football in the day before. He reached for a red hoodie draped over a chair near the bookshelf and recoiled when he realized it was the one he'd given Lexie. She must have left it behind.

Jake stared at it for a long moment, letting memories play like a film without sound: Lexie curled up under his arm, Lexie laughing in the bed of his truck, Lexie combing her fingers through her hair after a long day. Lexie, in all her moods and all her shapes.

"I would rather wear one of your sweatshirts than any of Colt's diamonds."

She'd said that, but it obviously wasn't true. Nothing he'd given her was enough.

He snatched the sweatshirt off the chair and stuffed it deep into his duffel. The motion was familiar; he'd done almost the same thing yesterday. But yesterday, the bag had been Lexie's, and that package had been carefully wrapped. He wondered if she'd found it yet. And, with a stabbing pain in his chest, he wondered if it would matter.

Probably not.

He zipped the bag closed and turned on his heel, trying to forget.

"Now, Logan, this is not the first time Andrew and Jacob have fought."

Grandma Ruby's voice drifted down the hallway as Jake approached the kitchen.

"No, but it's the first time they've done it as grown men in front of all their living relatives," his father snapped.

"Andrew has had it coming for ages, and you know it," she went on. "Now, should they have gone at it in the driveway while the whole family was watching, probably not."

"They didn't have to watch," Jake muttered, pausing outside the kitchen door to grab a coat from the hall closet.

Grandma Ruby chuckled, even as Jake's father glared at her from across the room.

"Look, son," he started. "I don't know what's gotten into you boys over the last few years, but it's a shame you can't figure out how to get past it."

His chair scraped the ground as he pushed it back, and then he headed for the front door without giving Jake a chance to answer. "We're driving ourselves, for obvious reasons. You have two minutes to be in the car, or I'm making you walk," his father added, disappearing through the kitchen doorway.

Jake heard the screen door snap shut and the engine of his dad's work truck roar to life a moment later. Sighing, he went to the coffee pot and filled his thermos to the brim. As he tightened the cap, he caught sight of his reflection in the microwave door. His face wasn't as swollen as it had been earlier, but that didn't mean it was pretty.

"If something Andrew did is why Lexie ran scared, then he deserved every bit of what he got and more," Grandma Ruby said, nodding her head with a decisive jerk.

Jake turned around, surprised. Lexie's abrupt departure had been somewhat overshadowed by the mayhem that followed. He'd told his parents something had come up and that she'd needed to get back to campus, and they hadn't pressed the issue. Even hearing her name made his chest ache.

"You think she was scared? I think she was glad to get out of here," he muttered, snatching his coffee off the counter and hurrying toward the door.

The last thing he wanted to do was walk to the cattle barn in the rain.

17

ONE DAY PASSED, and then another, and before Jake knew it, final exams were over. He checked his phone on his last day of work before winter break, finding nothing from Lexie, as usual. It had been two weeks—fourteen days—since he'd stood in the driveway of his parents' house and begged her not to go. Two weeks since she'd left him behind like an old teddy bear damp from the rain. Two weeks of silence that weighed heavy on his soul.

In a moment of weakness, he forgot to watch where his feet were taking him, forgot to avoid the paths where he was likely to find her, and looked up to find himself standing in front of her empty desk, her computer already shut down and her materials stacked neatly away. There was a dust-free rectangle in the back corner where a picture frame had once rested, the photo of them now tucked away who-knew-where.

"Julie?" he asked, the word coming out before he could stop it.

"Yes, Jake?" Lexie's boss replied from her office nearby.

"Where's Lexie?"

"Oh, she took off after her last exam—said she's going to the mountains with some girlfriends," Julie said.

Jake turned toward Julie's office and saw her look up with a funny look on her face.

"You didn't know?" she asked, a crease forming between her eyes.

"No, I didn't know," Jake mumbled, looking down at Lexie's empty chair. He didn't know anything these days. He'd been waiting in suspended animation, hoping to hear from her, but her life had been moving forward. She'd been planning trips, leaving town, enjoying herself . . . all while he was curled in a ball like a bear in hibernation, conserving his energy and waiting for the ice to thaw.

In the end, there was nothing left for him to say. No words he hadn't already used, no grand gestures he hadn't already made. Lexie had washed their slate clean, clearing him away as easily as wiping frost from a windowpane, not even bothering to say goodbye.

And that hurt worst of all.

⁓

"I STILL CAN'T believe it cost over a hundred dollars just to park my car at the airport. We could have stayed another night in Jackson Hole for that amount!" Olivia complained, shouldering open the door of their apartment and dropping her bags on the floor with a thud.

Lexie wandered in behind her, stepping over her friend's mountain of luggage and rolling her own suitcase down the hall.

"You've said that about a thousand times since we got on I-40."

"Well, it's still true!" Olivia said, throwing her hands in the air. "Although, I've had my fill of dirty taxis. Can you believe Robin wanted to go home with that driver who picked us up from the ski lodge? The police would have found her in somebody's freezer." She shuddered dramatically, and Lexie rolled her eyes.

"It was a great trip. Let's focus on that part," she said.

"Was it, though?" Olivia continued as she followed Lexie toward her bedroom. "Because you're still in the same funk you've been in for weeks now."

Lexie hauled her heavy bag up onto her bed and unzipped the top. "I'll be fine, Liv. I am fine. Just leave it alone."

"You keep saying that, but I don't think I believe you."

Lexie ignored her friend, instead opting to start the process of unpacking. She began sorting through the clothing in her suitcase, putting still-clean clothes on the bed and dropping what needed to be washed on the floor near her feet.

"Just call him, Lex," Olivia finally said, breaking the heavy silence. "If it's this bad, just call him. It's been almost three weeks; you've punished yourself enough."

"It's not that easy," Lexie muttered as she looked up. But Olivia had already drifted back down the hall, leaving Lexie alone with her thoughts.

She'd thought walking away from Jake would be like walking away from every other broken relationship she'd ever had. She'd thought it would sting for a few days before fading into a dull ache that gradually dissipated as she lost herself in other things. But burying herself in final exams hadn't helped. Flying across the country and spending four days in the Rocky Mountains hadn't helped. Even forcing herself to flirt with strangers hadn't helped.

Nothing would erase the memory of Jake's warmth leaving her skin as he'd let go that last time or the blank look on his face as she'd driven away. She'd done her best to make him see that she wasn't what he wanted, that she wouldn't fit into his life the way he needed her to, and, apparently, it had worked. He'd stood there and let her go, and she hadn't heard from him since.

It was the silence that really got to her—the gap that now felt unbridgeable. She'd picked up her phone so many times to share a story or send a photo from her trip only to remember that she'd thrown their friendship out with the bathwater. Just like always, she had ruined everything.

But she'd kept him from wasting his life on her, and that was what really mattered.

Her hand closed over the sleeve of a faded red sweatshirt near the bottom of her large suitcase, and her chest tightened. She pulled it out with care, and her heart fell as Olivia's high school crest came into view. This wasn't what she'd thought it was. Of course it wasn't. Jake's hoodie was still buried in her smaller weekend bag, the one she'd stuffed into her closet the moment she'd returned from Tanner Farm. She'd only removed the bare necessities, choosing to leave the rest of that memory tucked away where she wouldn't have to look at it.

Just one second . . . her mind taunted, urging her toward her closet. *Just one look. Just see if it still smells like him. Just check, then you can put it back . . .*

Lexie eased her closet door open and rummaged behind her hamper for the crumpled duffel, pulling it out by the straps. She sat cross-legged on the carpet of her bedroom floor and slowly removed several soft sweaters and a pair of old jeans. But instead of finding what she was looking for, her fingers brushed against something hard along the bottom of the bag.

It was a box. A flat, white box, maybe eight inches square

and tied with a wide, green ribbon. The front was plain except for two words in a familiar scrawl.

For you.

Lexie's fingers hovered over the gift, and she paused for a moment, frozen in both fear and anticipation. Whatever this was, it was from *before*. She took a long breath and let the satin ribbon slide between her fingers. Finally, she tugged it free, lifted the box's lid and pulled out a white photo album with the letter L etched into the cover in curling script. She opened it with shaking hands and took a sharp breath, looking down at what had to be the worst picture ever taken of her.

She recognized it immediately. It was one Jake had snapped while testing his camera before an interview. Her eyes were crossed, and her neck was bent at an odd angle, her tongue sticking out to one side as she did her best to distract him.

Lexie cocked her head, confused. Why had he kept such a terrible photo? She turned the page, and on the back of the image she found Jake's handwriting.

You are hilarious.

Lexie swallowed past the lump in her throat as she traced the letters with her eyes. She could hear him beside her, laughing as he had that day, his face full of affection. He was still just her friend back then; he had always been her friend. Even when she'd felt most alone, Jake had always been there.

Her eyes jumped to the second photo, which showed her holding up a local newspaper and pointing to an article that held her byline. She was beaming.

You are talented, the back said.

She flipped through page after page, finding pictures of herself working at her desk, catching her first fish, and twirling through the autumn sunshine. In some, she was smiling; in others, she was deep in thought. In another, she was clearly angry, though now she couldn't remember why. One captured her dismay after an acorn had fallen directly into her smoothie. Another showed her looking straight up, probably into the bell tower.

They all had something written on the back.

You are incredible.

You are brilliant.

You are beautiful.

You are more than enough.

The words swam in front of her as her vision blurred, tears running freely down her cheeks. She turned to the last image, which held none of Jake's usual finesse. It wasn't professionally focused or balanced. It wasn't even well lit. Instead, it was dark with the harsh glow of a television in the background. The iconic car from the *Ghostbusters* movie sat frozen on screen as Jake looked up into his cell phone camera, an ironic smile on his face. Barely visible was Lexie, her head nestled against the crook of his neck where she'd fallen asleep.

She turned the page with trembling hands and found a longer entry printed on the back.

Lex, I always thought the girl of my dreams would love Ghostbusters marathons as much as I do. But guess what? You're not that girl.

You're even better.

Love, Jacob

Lexie's hand flew to her mouth to stifle a sob as she remembered the words she'd thrown in his face on that last day.

"*. . . they don't know me, and neither do you. . . . You know an imaginary version of me. . . . you've just got your head in the clouds . . .*"

She couldn't believe how wrong she'd been. Jake *knew* her. He *saw* her—all of her—the way nobody else ever had. And he loved her anyway.

Lexie took a shuddering breath and wiped the tears from her cheeks with the palms of her hands, suddenly filled with a singular sense of purpose. She'd always hoped to find someone who would fight for her, but maybe love was about more than that. Maybe it was about finding someone who was worth fighting *for* in the first place.

She rose to her feet and hurried toward her desk, where she ripped a blank sheet of paper from the printer tray. Then, she uncapped a pen and began to write.

⁓

"SO, WHY ARE you here again? I usually get the house to myself over breaks," Noah said as he came in from work.

Jake didn't look up from where he lay sprawled on the stained couch, one leg hung over an armrest and the other trailing toward the floor. He rolled his jaw irritably, flipping the television from a sitcom rerun to an NFL game where the linemen were facing off in a flurry.

"Because I got sick of being at home and having everybody hover over me. If I have to listen to Grandma Ruby talk about snow and choices and patience for one more second, I'm going to explode," he snapped, changing the channel again.

"Okay, still in the angst phase. Got it," Noah muttered. He shrugged out of his thick jacket and tossed it over the back of a kitchen chair. "So, have you thought about dinner at all? Want to order a pizza?"

Jake grunted noncommittally, still staring at the television.

"Fine, then I'm putting everything on it, and you don't get to complain," Noah said as he kicked his shoes into a corner near the back door.

They hit the floor with a loud thud, and Jake winced.

"Actually, what does Lexie like on her pizza?" Noah asked, looking out the window.

"What?" Jake lifted his head off the cushion where he'd parked it hours before.

"What does Lexie like on her pizza?" Noah repeated slowly, and he stared at Jake as though waiting for his words to register.

"Why?"

"Because she just pulled in, and she might be hungry."

"What?!" Jake surged to his feet, his head whipping toward the front window where, sure enough, he could see Lexie Preston climbing from her car, bundled from head to toe. The mild winter weather had finally taken a turn, and the shoulders of her coat were already dusted with tiny snowflakes that drifted down from the slate-gray sky. She looked hesitantly toward the house as if she were deciding whether or not to knock.

"Good luck with that," Noah said as he headed for the safety of his bedroom, but Jake barely acknowledged him. Instead, he stood rooted to the floor, watching as Lexie picked her way carefully over the gravel driveway and up the broken sidewalk.

She'd only been to his place a handful of times, and then only to pick him up outside. He looked around frantically, scanning the dilapidated interior with a groan. There were still faded orange paint splatters on some of the walls and cabinets from Noah's paintball assault months ago, and dirty dishes were piled high in the sink. Actually, he couldn't remember the last time they'd been washed.

He scrubbed his palm over the week-old beard he'd been neglecting in favor of self-pity. Nothing he could do about that now, but at least he'd showered that morning. That was something.

A knock sounded at the door, and his eyes jumped to the plain wood that separated him from the girl who still had the power to rip him to pieces. He didn't tell his legs to move, but something propelled him forward anyway, and before he knew it, he was looking down into the green eyes that had haunted both his waking and sleeping hours for weeks now. He'd spent so much time thinking of a thousand things he wanted to say when he finally saw her again, and yet, now that the moment had come, his throat was too tight to speak.

"Hi," Lexie said softly, her eyes wide, as if surprised he'd actually come to the door. She scanned his face, and her eyes dropped to his socked feet and then traveled back up, like she was making sure all his details were as she remembered them.

"I found the pictures. Finally. I never unpacked after . . . So, I just . . . anyway," she babbled, her gaze falling as she raised one gloved hand to push a lock of hair out of her face. She tried and failed to tuck it beneath the edge of her knit cap, and Jake felt his fingers twitch at his sides as if they wanted to do it for her. Her cheeks, already flushed from the cold, turned redder still.

"I know it's not gift wrapped or anything, but I wrote you a story," she explained, lifting her other hand to show him a sheet of paper that looked like it had been folded and refolded countless times. "It's not much, I know, but . . . here it goes."

She cleared her throat nervously, and her eyes darted from the paper to his face as she started to read.

"Once upon a time, a king and queen were given a magic music box. Inside, the queen found a tiny ballerina, plated with gold and polished to a shine. 'What a lovely gift!' she exclaimed, but when she turned the key, she was met only with silence. 'Oh, dear! The dancer is broken. She is good for nothing; take her away!' she ordered, and the box was set upon a shelf.

"Years passed, and whenever someone opened the box, the dancer would stretch her golden limbs to the sky and wait. But the music never came. 'She can't dance,' the people said. 'What good is a ballerina who can't dance?' And they shut her away, closing her into the darkness again and again. The dancer's beautiful face began to change, until finally, she looked as unhappy as she felt inside.

"Then, one day, a boy opened the box and gazed down on the golden girl inside. He turned her key and, as she'd expected, nothing happened. But instead of casting her aside, he began to sing. At first, the ballerina stayed motionless, her frozen feet locked in place. But then, something incredible happened, and for the first time, the tiny girl began to dance."

Jake forgot about the cold, listening in rapt attention as Lexie described a girl who blossomed, learning to dip and spin as she was meant to do, and who waited each day for the boy to appear.

"He was patient and kind, and even though the girl was a little bit broken, he didn't seem to care," Lexie read, her voice cracking on the last words, but she cleared her throat and kept going. "Over time, he became her friend, and then he became more, and then one day, she realized he was everything she'd ever wished for and that she loved him more than she'd ever thought she could love anyone."

A tear rolled down Lexie's face, and this time, Jake felt himself drift forward and wipe it away. Still, Lexie kept reading.

"There were so many things the girl wanted to tell him, but she didn't know how. She wanted to tell him he was her favorite part of every day, that he was worth fighting for, and that he was always, *always* more than enough. But as it was, he was a real boy, and she was only a pretty trinket in a box—a plaything without a voice. So, one night, she pushed open the lid of her box and looked up into the sky beyond her shelf. She found a falling star, and she wished, harder than she'd ever wished before, and in the morning, when the boy returned, the little golden girl was gone."

Lexie stopped, looking up at Jake again, and he reminded himself to blink.

"Where did she go?" he asked, his voice rougher than he'd expected, and a hesitant smile spread across Lexie's face.

"She'd wished to be human, and she was right there, waiting for him to find her. Because falling in love might be an accident, but living in love is a choice, and she chose to be with him, if he would have her," Lexie whispered, her eyes full of something Jake had waited a long time to see.

He slid his hand around the nape of her neck and rested his forehead against hers in a motion that felt as natural as breathing. Again, his words wouldn't come, but this time for an entirely different reason.

"You are worth fighting for, Jacob," Lexie said in a soft voice meant only for him. "I'm sorry it took me so long, but I'm choosing you, if you'll ha—"

But Jake didn't let her finish. Instead, he stopped her words with his mouth, pulling her close and letting her fill the hole in his heart—a hole where only she would fit. He took his time, exploring all the landmarks he knew by heart. It may have been a long time coming, but he'd been right; Lexie had been his all along. Finally, he pulled back and framed her face in his hands.

"I love you," she breathed.

Jake's grin spread like wildfire, threatening to burn the whole house down around them.

"Say that again," he urged.

Lexie pushed up on her toes and pressed another soft kiss to his lips.

"I love you, Jacob Tanner. More than I ever thought I could."

Epilogue

(Four and a half months later)

"WHY WON'T YOU tell me where we're going?" Jake smiled as he raised Lexie's hand to his lips and brushed a kiss across her knuckles.

"You still don't know how to be surprised, do you?" he asked, taking his eyes off the road long enough to catch the way she pursed her lips in an attempt to hold back a laugh. Jake shook his head fondly and turned to watch the road again as they headed north, Cypress Valley's last residential neighborhoods fading away behind them.

"You said we were going to dinner." She waved her hand toward the cornfields passing by outside. "*This* doesn't look like dinner."

Jake chuckled but kept his eyes on the road, watching closely for their turn. "Just trust me, Lex. Have I ever disappointed you?"

He glanced over just long enough to see her soften, her shoulders relaxing against the seat as she looked out her window.

"No," she admitted quietly.

"Okay, then," Jake teased, squeezing her hand where it now rested beneath his on the gearshift. He casually ran his thumb along the backs of her fingers, feeling his stomach flip when he got to her ring finger. This might be the last time he'd ever hold her hand when it was bare.

He sure hoped so.

The box in his pocket felt like it weighed twelve tons, even though it was smaller than a Post-it note. He didn't need to pull it out to see the six small diamonds that formed a sparkling flower atop a gold band. He'd been looking at that ring all his life.

"Choose well," Grandma Ruby had said, placing it gently into his palm. *"May it bring you all the happiness I've ever had, and more."*

That had been in February. Three days later, she'd gone to be with Grandpa Jacob for all eternity, home again at last.

The mild April evening was fading into that golden hour when everything was bathed in rich, warm light. The sun glinted off each road sign as they passed, and Jacob felt his nerves grow as they approached their destination. He pulled his hand away and set it on the steering wheel before turning left onto a plain, two-lane road that was almost indistinguishable from any other country lane.

Almost.

Jake drove until he could see three giant grain bins peeking from above the tree line and then eased his truck onto the gravel shoulder in the precise spot he'd scouted out the day before. A line of cattle had congregated along the fencerow as if they'd been specifically invited, and Jake smiled.

"I need to get out and check something. I think we might have a flat," he said, glancing over to see if Lexie was putting the pieces together—but she was still looking around in confusion.

"You what?" she asked, her brows raised, and Jake almost laughed out loud. She'd never been one to pick up on clues when they were right in front of her.

"I think we might have a flat tire," he repeated, watching her face for any sign of understanding. But she was still lost. "I'll only be a second. Stay here."

He reached for his door, popped the handle and climbed down from the cab as she started to protest. A grin spread over his face when he shut the door, cutting her off midsentence. Now that his girl was finally finding her voice, she didn't like to be ignored.

Jake rounded the back of the truck quickly, feeling his boots slide on the uneven gravel. He counted silently in his head.

Five . . . four . . . three . . . two . . .

"Jacob Tanner, don't you walk away from me!" Lexie shouted as she opened her door. She climbed down as fast as she could, and Jake was glad she'd decided to wear the turquoise dress he loved so much. "And don't tell me to stay in the truck!" she added, her voice laced with irritation.

"How are you going to help?" he asked, trying to keep his face under control. "Do you know how to change a flat?"

"Yes, actually, I do! You taught me, remember?" she demanded, her hands planted firmly on her hips with the kind of sass he saw a lot of these days. And he loved every second of it.

Jake let his grin go full throttle. "Yes, I did," he said. "Right here, actually."

"Right wh—" Lexie started, but her exasperation died on her lips as she finally stopped to take in their surroundings. She looked down the road first in one direction, then the other, and her eyes went wide as they skimmed over the granary and the fencerow where several cows lowed in greeting. "Right *here*?" she asked, blinking rapidly.

"Right here," Jake echoed, stepping forward to take her hands in his. It was only then he realized how badly he was shaking. His face sobered completely as he took a deep breath, praying he'd get his next words exactly right.

"Lexie, the last time I stood on the side of this road, I came just to change a tire, but I left knowing I was completely and totally in love with you," he said. "I want to spend the rest of my life coming to your rescue, even though I know you're strong enough to save yourself. I want to be the one you run to and the one you cry on and even the one you fight with. I want to have all the ups and downs and in-betweens with you for as many years as God will give us.

"I promise to fight for you and choose you over and over again. I promise to come home to you every night and spend every waking minute trying to be the man you deserve. I want to be your forever, because I already know you're mine," he finished, finally reaching for his jacket pocket. Sinking to his knees—since he figured two were better than one—he opened the box and offered her his name, his heart and the rest of his life.

"Lexie Preston, will you marry me?"

LEXIE FELT JAKE'S fingers tighten around hers as he waited for an answer. She had pictured this moment a hundred times over the years—sometimes with nerves she mistook for excitement, but usually with outright dread. The idea of spending the rest of her life with any of the men she'd dated before had always filled her with terror, and even now, she waited for the paralyzing fear to wash over her.

But this time, it didn't.

This time, she felt a familiar pull in her chest as the golden flecks in Jake's eyes turned into the constellations that always led her home.

She looked at the ring he held out and recognized it as the one she'd admired on his great-grandmother's finger several times. The one that had been missing the night she'd stood beside him and helped him say goodbye to such a remarkable woman. The one that would make her a Tanner for good.

"It's not my engagement ring," Grandma Ruby had explained when she'd seen Lexie looking. *"It was a gift from my Jacob on our fiftieth wedding anniversary. There's half a century of love already built in."*

Half a century.

Lexie had never been able to picture more than a month at a time with Colt. But now, looking down at Jake where he waited on his knees, she could see every one of those fifty years stretching out before them—happy ones, sad ones and all the in-between ones—and all she felt was overwhelming peace.

"Yes," she said at last, sure of her choice in a way that filled her with joy. "Yes, I will."

Jake seemed to sag under the weight of his exhale, finally letting out the breath he'd apparently been holding.

"Yes?"

"Yes," Lexie repeated, her voice thick as she helped pull him to his feet. He carefully took the ring from its box and slipped it on her finger before wrapping her in a hug that nearly lifted her out of her shoes.

"Even if I make you watch *Ghostbusters* every year for the rest of your life?" he asked, his question muffled against her hair.

Lexie laughed wetly as happy tears finally gathered and fell. "Yes, Jacob. Even then."

Want a peek at Jake and Lexie's wedding plans? Sign up for new release announcements and download a free bonus chapter! (Plus, give Drew a chance to redeem himself.) download.erinchesnutbooks.com/jakebonus

Please consider leaving a review on Amazon, Goodreads or wherever you bought this book. Jake has to kiss a duck for every star, so be generous. The Tanner cousins will thank you.

And if you haven't read the free prequel—"At First Sight"— you can find it, as well as a Facebook discussion group and other goodies, at linktr.ee/erinchesnutbooks

Don't miss the rest of the Cypress Valley Sweethearts!
Olivia will meet her match
(whether she wants to or not!)
in book two.

AUTHOR'S NOTE AND ACKNOWLEDGEMENTS

ACCORDING TO family legend, my great-grandfather saw my great-grandmother for the first time and told his friends, "That's my girl." Five generations later, that statement helped inspire Jake and the rest of the Tanner family. I hope you've enjoyed this first part of their story!

There's no way I could mention all the people who have helped me get to this point in my life, but here are a few of them. First of all, my husband Matthew. Thank you for the endless hours spent listening to me brainstorm, rant, ramble, mutter, mumble, cry and otherwise think out loud since I decided to take this writing thing seriously. (Oh, who are we kidding, I've been doing that since we met! I'm glad you embrace my crazy.) Jake Tanner is your sweet, southern-boy side that I fell in love with years ago, and I am blessed to build a life with you. (I'm sorry I didn't work in those things you wanted. Maybe next time.)

Next, my children. I would write three times faster if you didn't constantly need to be fed, washed or entertained, but life would be a lot less colorful without you. Your laughter feeds my soul, and I wish you'd both stop growing up so fast. You give me more book material than you'll ever know.

Then, my parents, grandparents and in-laws who have done nothing but encourage me, and my great-grandmothers—Vera and Ruby—who together inspired Grandma Ruby Tanner. Maybe someday I'll tell your stories, too. I miss you both.

Then, of course, my incredible editors!! Courtney and Sara at Mild Mannered Editors… you guys took my work to the next level, and I am forever grateful for all your tiny comment bubbles— even the ones you left "just to say don't change a thing." Special thanks to Tasha Newcomb, whose early feedback helped turn Jake, Lexie and Colt into believable people, and another million thank yous to all my awesome beta readers: Julie Hodges, Emily Grissom, Erica McCollum, Kallie McCullough, Julie Austalosh, Nicole Lamb, Nicole Gunter, Allison Ary, Lindsay Chester, Logan Workman, Norma Coalter and of course my parents and in-laws. To my ARC team, you guys are amazing! And last, but definitely not least, to the talented people at Alt 19 Creative for bringing Jake and Lexie to life on my cover.

And finally, to you, reader. Thank you for taking a chance on a new author and a new series. I hope you'll join me for the rest of the Cypress Valley Sweethearts and get to know Noah, Olivia, Conner, Ashlyn, Hannah, Brooklyn, Drew and all the others. (Yes, you'll like Drew. I promise.)

Happy reading!
Erin

ABOUT THE AUTHOR

ERIN CHESNUT writes sweet contemporary romance novels from her home in West Tennessee, where she lives with her husband and two children. She spends her days reading, writing and homeschooling. As a former journalist and public relations writer, she has had non-fiction work published in numerous state magazines and regional publications, and she placed third in the Writer's Digest 86th Annual International Writing Competition's magazine feature article category. She'll accept third place beneath a New York Times journalist any day! She can be found in her hammock whenever possible, probably with a bag of gummy worms and a book. Disturb her at your own risk.

BOOK CLUB DISCUSSION QUESTIONS

1. Jake believes in love—or at least "like"—at first sight. Do you? Why or why not?

2. How do Jake and Lexie's family lives and childhood experiences shape the way they approach relationships as young adults?

3. Jake shows Lexie how he feels through wordless actions—the same way his father shows affection for his mother. How much of the way we treat people is learned and how much is instinctive?

4. Drew gives Jake grief for having left the family business. Is this fair?

5. Grandma Ruby says love is less like a lightning strike and more like silent snowfall. How would you describe it?

6. Lexie finds the kind of family in the Tanners that she never experienced growing up. How important is found family?

7. Olivia sees several warning signs during Lexie's relationship with Colt but is reluctant to jump to conclusions. What warning signs did you notice?

Visit thehotline.org/identify-abuse/ to learn more about spotting a potentially abusive relationship and how you might be able to help a friend or loved one in need. In the United States, the national domestic violence hotline is ready to assist you or a loved one 24/7. Just call 1-800-799-7233 or text START to 88788.